FIC OFARR
O'Farrell, John.
The best a man can get :
novel of fatherhood and its
R0018674164

SIMI VALLEY LIBRARY

P9-DXE-352

The Best a Man Can Get

The Best a Man Can Get

A Novel of Fatherhood and Its Discontents

John O'Farrell

Broadway Books

New York

BROADWAY

THE BEST A MAN CAN GET Copyright © 2000 by John O'Farrell. All rights reserved. Printed in the United States of America. No part of this book may be reproduced or transmitted in any form or by any means, electronic or mechanical, including photocopying, recording, or by any information storage and retrieval system, without written permission from the publisher. For information, address Broadway Books, a division of Random House, Inc., 1540 Broadway, New York, NY 10036.

Broadway Books titles may be purchased for business or promotional use or for special sales. For information, please write to: Special Markets Department, Random House, Inc., 1540 Broadway, New York, NY 10036.

BROADWAY BOOKS and its logo, a letter B bisected on the diagonal, are trademarks of Broadway Books, a division of Random House, Inc.

Visit our website at www.broadwaybooks.com

Library of Congress Cataloging-in-Publication Data

O'Farrell, John.
The best a man can get / John O'Farrell.
p.   cm.
1. Fathers—Fiction. 2. London (England)—Fiction. I. Title.
PR6065.F34 B47 2001
823'.914—dc21
00-066736

First Edition in the United States of America

Designed by Paul Randall Mize

ISBN 0-7679-0713-2

01 02 03 04 05 10 9 8 7 6 5 4 3 2 1

To Jackie, with love

R0018624164

ACKNOWLEDGMENTS

With thanks to Georgia Garrett, Bill Scott-Kerr, Mark Burton, Simon Davidson and Charlie Dawson.

The Best a Man Can Get

1

The Best a Man Can Get

I FOUND IT HARD working really long hours when I was my own boss. The boss kept giving me the afternoon off. Sometimes he gave me the morning off as well. Sometimes he'd say, "Look, you've worked pretty hard today, why don't you take a well-earned rest tomorrow." If I overslept he never rang me to ask where I was; if I was late to my desk he always happened to turn up at exactly the same time; whatever excuse I came up with, he always believed it. Being my own boss was great. Being my own employee was a disaster, but I never thought about that side of the equation.

On this particular day I was woken by the sound of children. I knew from experience that this meant it was either just before nine o'clock in the morning, when children started arriving at the school over the road, or around quarter past eleven—mid-morning playtime. I rolled over to look at the clock and the little numbers on my radio alarm informed me that it was 1:24. Lunchtime. I had slept for fourteen solid hours, an all-time record.

I called it my radio alarm, though in reality it served only as a large and cumbersome clock. I had given up using the radio-alarm function long before, after I'd kept waking up with early morning erections to the news that famine was spreading in the Sudan or that Princess Anne had just had her wisdom teeth out. It's amazing how quickly an erection can disappear. Anyway, alarm clocks are for people who have something more important to do than sleeping, and this was a concept that I struggled to grasp. Some days I would wake up, decide that it wasn't worth getting dressed and then just stay in bed until, well, bedtime. But it wasn't apathetic, what's-the-point-of-getting-up lying in bed, it was positive, quality-of-life lying in bed. I had resolved that leisure time should involve genuine leisure. If it had been up to me there would have been nothing at the Balham Leisure Centre except rows of beds with all the Sunday papers scattered at the bottom of the duvet.

My bedroom had evolved so that the need to get out of bed was kept to an absolute minimum. Instead of a bedside table there was a fridge, inside which milk, bread and butter were kept. On top of the fridge was a kettle, which fought for space with a tray of mugs, a box of tea bags, a selection of breakfast cereals, a toaster and an overloaded plug adapter. I clicked on the kettle and popped some bread in the toaster. I reached across for that day's newspaper and was slightly surprised as a set of keys slid off the top and clinked onto the floor. Then I remembered that I hadn't slept for fourteen solid hours after all; there had been a vague but annoying conversation very early that morning. As far as I could remember, it had gone something like this:

" 'Scuse me, mate?"

"Uh?" I replied from under the duvet.

"Excuse me, mate. It's me. Paper boy," said the cracking voice of the nervous-sounding teenager.

"What do you want?"

"My mum says I'm not allowed to deliver the paper to the end of your bed anymore."

"Why not?" I groaned, without emerging.

"She says it's weird. I had to stop her ringing Child Line."

"What time is it?"

"Seven o'clock. I told her you paid me an extra couple of quid a week to bring it up here and everything, but she said it's weird and that I'm only allowed to push it through the letter box, like I do for everyone else. I'll leave your front door keys here."

If anything had been said after that I didn't remember it. That must have been the moment when I went back to sleep. The clink of the keys brought it back like some half-remembered dream. And as I flicked through the stories of war, violent crime and environmental disaster, I felt a growing sense of depression. Today was the last day I would ever have my newspaper delivered to the end of my bed.

Lightly browned toast popped up and the bubbling kettle clicked itself off. The butter and milk were kept on the top shelf of the fridge so they could be reached without leaving the bed. When I'd first bought the fridge and placed it in my room I had sunk to my knees in mortified disbelief. The fridge door opened the wrong way—I couldn't reach the handle from the bed. I tried putting the fridge upside down, but it looked a bit stupid. I tried putting it on the other side of the bed, but then I had to move my keyboard and mixing desk and all the other bits of musical equipment that were packed into my bedroom-cum-recording studio. After several hours spent dragging furniture into different positions around the room, I finally found a location for the bed that would comfortably allow me to take things from the fridge, make breakfast, reach my phone and watch telly without having to do anything as strenuous as standing up. If Boots had marketed a do-it-yourself catheter kit, I would have been the first customer.

The only thing more self-indulgent than breakfast in bed is having breakfast in bed at lunchtime. There's a decadence to it that makes lightly buttered toast taste like the food of the gods. I sipped my tea and, with one of several remote controls, switched on the telly just in time to see the beginning of one of my favorite films, Billy Wilder's *The Apartment*. I'll just watch the first few minutes, I thought to myself as I fluffed up the pillows. Just the bit where he's working in that huge insurance office with hundreds of other people doing exactly the same monotonous job. Forty minutes later my mobile phone jolted me out of my hypnotized trance. I switched the television to mute and removed the mobile from its charger.

"Hello, Michael, it's Hugo Harrison here—from DD and G. I'm just ringing in case you'd forgotten that you said you'd probably be able to get your piece of music to us by the end of today."

"Forgotten? Are you joking? I've been working on it all week. I'm in the studio right now."

"Do you think you'll be able to deliver it when you said?"

"Hugo, have I ever missed a deadline? I'm just doing a remix, so you'll probably get it around four or five o'clock."

"Right." Hugo sounded disappointed. "There's no chance that we might get it before then, because we're sort of hanging around waiting to do the dub."

"Well, I'll try. To be honest, I was going to go out and get a bite of lunch, but I'll work through if you need it urgently."

"Thanks, Michael. Bloody brilliant. Speak to you later, then."

And I turned off my mobile, lay back in bed and then watched *The Apartment* all the way through.

What I hadn't told Hugo from DD&G was that I had in fact completed my composition four days earlier, but when someone pays you a thousand pounds for a piece of work, you can't give it to them two days after they commission it. They have to feel they're getting their money's worth. They might have imagined that they wanted it as soon as possible, but I knew that they'd appreciate and enjoy it far more if they thought it had taken me all week.

The slogan the agency were going to put over my composition was "The saloon car that thinks it's a sports car." So I did a ploddy easy-listening intro which switched into a screeching electric-guitar sound. Saloon car, sports car. Easy-listening for the humdrum lives of all those thirty-something saloon-car drivers and electric guitar for the racy, exciting lives that they are starting to realize have gone forever. Hugo had thought this was a great idea when I'd put it to him, so much so that fairly quickly he was talking about it as if it was his own.

Generally speaking I did every commission straightaway, and would then phone the client at regular intervals and say things like, "Look, I've got something I'm really pleased with, but it's only thirteen seconds long. Does it really have to be exactly fifteen seconds?" And they'd say, "Well, if you're really pleased with it, maybe we should have a listen. But is there no way you can make it fifteen? Like, just slow it down a bit or something?"

"Just slow it down a bit! What are you talking about?"

"I don't know. I'm not a composer."

And then I'd pretend to find a solution and the client would hang up feeling reassured that I was still working on it and pleased that they had helped me get that much closer to completion. And all the time a fifteen-second jingle was already on a DAT in my studio. Whenever I had sent ad agencies work straightaway, they were always initially enthusiastic, but then came back to me a few days later saying they wanted it changed. I had learned that it was far better to give it to them at the last minute, when they had no choice but to decide that it was great.

I had persuaded myself that actually I probably did roughly the same amount of work as many men my age, namely around two or three hours a day. But I was determined that I wouldn't waste the rest of my life *pretending* to be working, flicking my computer screen from Solitaire to a spreadsheet, or suddenly changing the tone of personal phone calls when the managing director walked into the office. From what I could gather from my contemporaries, there were a lot of jobs where you arrived in the morning, chatted for an hour or two, did some really useful work between about eleven and lunchtime, came back in the afternoon, sent a stupid e-mail message to Gary in accounts before spending the rest of the afternoon in apparent total concentration while downloading a picture of a naked transsexual from http://www.titsandcocks.com.

The film was interrupted by adverts and I couldn't help but take a professional interest in the music they employed. The jingle for the Gillette commercial claimed that the new twin-blade swivel head with lubrastrip was "the best a man can get." I thought that this was a pretty bold claim for a disposable plastic razor. A new Ferrari maybe or a night in bed with Pamela Anderson might arguably have the edge for most men, but not according to this singer, no, give him a good shave any day of the week. Then *The Apartment* came back on and I thought, No, this is the best a man can get: just being tucked up warm and cozy, watching a great film with tea and toast and nothing at all to worry about.

When people asked me what I did I generally mumbled that I was "in advertising." I used to say that I was a composer or a musician, but I found this prompted a level of fascination that wasn't fulfilled when they discovered this meant I'd written the music for the Mr. Gearbox ad on Capital Radio. I was a freelance jingle writer—although other people in the business were too pretentious to call them jingles—working at the bottom end of the freelance jingle-writing market. If the man who composed "Gillette! The best a man can get!" was the advertising equivalent of Paul McCartney, that made me the drummer for the band that came fifth in last year's Song for Europe.

People always presume there's lots of money in advertising, but I was beginning to sense that I was never going to make a fortune writing twenty-second radio jingles, even if I took it upon myself to start working an eight-hour day.

There had been a time in my life when I'd really believed I was going to be a millionaire rock star. When I'd left music college I had returned to my home town and formed a group that played in pubs and at university summer balls. Call me immodest, but I think I can honestly say there was a point in the late Eighties when we were the biggest band in Godalming. Then it all fell apart when our drummer left the group because of "musical differences." We were musical, he wasn't. Despite being the crappiest drummer I'd ever heard, he had been the most important member of the band because he had been the one with the van. I found you couldn't fit many amplifiers on a moped. After that high point I had carried on recording songs and trying to form bands, but now all I had to show for those years was a box of demo tapes and one precious copy of my flexi-disc single.

I got out of bed and played this track again as I got dressed. I was still proud of it, and had never quite forgiven John Peel's producer for saying they didn't play flexi-discs. The journey to my place of work involved walking from one side of my bedroom to the other. Before I started I generally preferred to convert the room from bedroom to studio, which involved transforming my bed back into a sofa and removing any socks or underpants that I had left on top of my keyboard. As well as my Roland XP-60, the recording studio side of my room contained a computer, an eighteen-channel mixing desk, a sampler, a reverb unit, a midi-box, several redundant sound modules, amplifiers and tape decks and, behind it all, seven and a half miles of intertwined electrical cable. If you knew nothing at all about music I suppose all this gear might look quite impressive, but the reality was far more chaotic. The more equipment I acquired, the longer I had to search every time a mystery buzz made it impossible to do any work. Generally I relied upon the keyboard, with its built-in sound module and my multitalented sampler, which would gamely have a stab at the noise produced by most musical instruments. Although there appeared to be a lot of state-of-the-art technology on display, the stuff was either several years out of date or would be by the time I'd worked out how to use it. Because I'd never got round to reading the manuals I was like the owner of a Ferrari who only drove around in first gear.

I lumbered into the bathroom and stared in the mirror. During the night the gray strands on the side of my head had fought their way to the front and a whole swathe of hair above my ears had acquired a silvery sheen. Those of the wiry gray variety were thicker and stronger than the wispy dark hairs they were gradually replacing. The grays were still in a minority, but I knew that, like the squirrels of the same depressing color, once a few had got a foothold eventually all the indigenous hair would be pushed to the brink of extinction, with maybe a couple of breeding colonies remaining on either eyebrow and perhaps a few shy black hairs that would occasionally be spotted peeking out of my nostrils. On the side of my nose a large yellow-headed spot had ripened and was deftly milked with the dexterity that came from nearly twenty years' practice. In my teens I think I'd presumed there would be a golden period in my life after my spots cleared up and before my hair started to turn gray. Now I realized that was hopelessly naive of me; in my early thirties I was already past my physical peak. The summer seems to have only just begun when you realize the nights are already drawing in.

At around four o'clock I finally strolled into the living room, where Jim had spent the last couple of years researching his Ph.D. Today this involved playing Tomb Raider with Simon. They both managed to mumble hello to me, though since neither of them managed to look up from the screen I could just as easily have been the creature from the black lagoon wandering in to put the kettle on. Jim and Simon

looked like the "Before" and "After" drawings in the Charles
Atlas body-building adverts. Jim was tall and muscular with the
healthy complexion of a boy who'd been skiing every winter
since he was five years old, and by contrast, Simon was skinny,
pallid and awkward. If they made Tomb Raider any more
realistic, Lara Croft would turn around and say out of the TV
screen, "Stop staring at my tits like that, you little creep," and
blast him off the sofa. He had a promising career serving pints
of lager in plastic glasses to students of the university from
which he had graduated some years ago. He had got the job
on the day he'd left and was hoping to earn enough money to
one day pay off the debts he had accumulated on the other
side of the bar.

At that moment the front door slammed and Paul returned home, dumping a pile of tatty exercise books on the
kitchen table with a martyred sigh that was far too obviously intended to elicit concerned inquiries about his day and conse-
quently received none.

"Dear oh dear," said Paul, but we all still refused to bite. He
put a carton of milk back in the fridge and took a couple of old
tea bags out of the sink, tutting quietly to himself. His sighs not
only announced his irritation that everyone else didn't tidy up
as they went along, but also his annoyance that it should be left
to him to clear up when he had already done a full day's teach-
ing. It was as if he was implying that Simon's evening job or
Jim's Ph.D. or my composing at my keyboard were somehow
less-demanding work. The fact that this was true was entirely
beside the point.

The four of us had shared this place for a couple of years
now. None of them had known me when I had first taken the
room, and in some ways that was how I preferred to keep
things. The flat boasted views across the splendor that is
Balham High Road, and was conveniently located above a
shop, where we could pop down and buy halal meat at any

time of the day or night. But it was not the tatty run-down flat that you would expect four men sharing to wallow in; there was a strict cleaning rota, in which we took turns to leave all the clearing up for Paul.

Paul put what was left of a slab of butter into the butter dish and then folded the foil neatly before throwing it in the bin. Since talking to the entire room failed to get him any attention, he attempted to address someone directly.

"Michael, how was your day?"

"It's been a fucking disaster," I said.

"Oh no, what happened?" he replied, sounding genuinely concerned.

"Bloody paper boy woke me up at seven o'clock to tell me he's not going to deliver the paper to the end of my bed anymore. He said his mother thinks it's weird. I distinctly remember saying to him when we first agreed on the arrangement that it would probably be wise not to mention it to his parents."

There was a pause.

"No. *I* told his mother," confessed Paul with the defiant air of a man who had been preparing himself for this confrontation.

"You! What on earth did you do that for?"

"Well, for a start I am not particularly wild about you handing out the front door keys of our flat to a thirteen-year-old delinquent."

"He's not a delinquent."

"Yes, he is a delinquent, and do you know how I know that? Because I teach him. Troy is in my class. And the day before yesterday, at seven A.M., I walked out of the bathroom stark bollock naked to see Troy standing there on the landing staring at me."

At that moment Jim laughed so much he had to spit his tea back into the mug. "What did you say?"

"Well, I said, 'Hello, Troy.' "

"What did he say?"

"He said, 'Hello, Mr. Hitchcock.' He looked a little confused, to tell the truth. In fact, it was pretty bad luck on his part as well; he'd been trying to avoid me for a few days because he owed me an essay on the character of Piggy in *Lord of the Flies*. I think for a moment he thought I'd broken into this house at seven in the morning with no clothes on just to ask him for his essay."

I was still irritated. "So you bumped into him on the landing. So what? Doesn't mean you have to tell his mother."

"I am his teacher. It doesn't look too good, does it? BOY VISITS NAKED TEACHER'S FLAT BEFORE LESSONS. Besides, I do not appreciate having to tell my class that the correct pronunciation of my name is Mr. Hitchcock, not Mr. Titchy-cock."

Jim's tea had now been spat out so many times it was undrinkable.

"And so, at last night's parents' evening," Paul continued, "I told his mother that her son had a key to my flat and that the previous morning he had seen me naked."

"That probably wasn't the best way to put it."

"Well, with the benefit of hindsight I realize I might have phrased it differently. She went mad and started hitting me with her shoe. Had to be pulled off by the deputy head."

Paul looked hurt to be the unwitting subject of such general amusement.

"Don't take it personally, Paul," I said, "we're not laughing at *you*."

"I am," said Jim.

"Yeah, I am as well actually," added Simon.

Paul settled down to do his marking, and his pupils got far lower marks than they would have done if we had been nicer to him. He was clearly one of those teachers who are unable to keep control in the classroom. There was just something about him that marked him out as the injured wildebeest limping on the edge of the herd. He always tried to play this down, even when one of the pupils sold his car.

I don't know why they felt they needed to go to such lengths to wind him up when he seemed to get infuriated by the littlest things. He once told us that from now on he would only be removing his own hairs from the gunge that was blocking the plughole, since no one else ever seemed to do it, and so we found him crouched in an empty bath trying to separate the red hairs from all the others. It wasn't that Paul was petty, it was just that he got annoyed when anyone squeezed the toothpaste from the wrong end of the tube. In fact, all sorts of things about us aggravated him.

We sat around the kitchen table for a bit longer and then Jim announced that he was going to make a brew. Paul always declined Jim's offer of tea because the way Jim made tea was the essence of what Paul found so irritating about him.

Jim's tea-making routine was a triumph of daydreaming inefficiency. First he would take the mugs from the cupboard and arrange them on a tray. Then he would stop near the sink and look a little lost for a while as he tried to remember what it was that he had been meaning to do. Then it would come back to him: get the milk out of the fridge. After the milk had been poured into each cup he would get the tea bags and put them into the teapot. And then, when he had done all that, when he had got everything ready and realized he'd got out one mug too many and so put it back in the cupboard, and then put the sugar bowl on the tray and decided that there was nothing else he had to do, *then he would put the kettle on.*

For Paul, this sequence alone made Jim virtually impossible to live with. And he didn't just put the kettle on last, he also filled it right to the top so it took far longer than necessary for three cups of tea. And while it was taking an eternity to boil he would just stand there waiting, occasionally moving the mugs about on the tray. And all the while he would be completely unaware that Paul was about to explode with frustration at the impracticality of this order of doing things. Try as he might, Paul could not let Jim do things his way. I knew that within sixty seconds he would ask Jim why he didn't put the kettle on first.

"Jim, why don't you put the kettle on first?" he asked three seconds later.

"Hmmm?"

"I was just saying, it would be a bit quicker if you put the kettle on first. You know, before you put out the mugs and everything."

Jim gave an indifferent shrug. "Well, it wouldn't boil any quicker, would it."

He was as slow to see Paul's logic as he was at making tea.

"No, but it would boil *sooner*, because you would've put it on earlier, and then you could do the tea bags and milk and everything *while* it was boiling." He had to stop himself screaming the last four words in Jim's face. Jim was bemused by his flatmate's concern.

"They're not in a hurry to go out or anything, are they? You're not in a hurry to go out, are you, Simon?"

Simon looked up from the paper. "Me? No."

"No one's in a hurry, so what does it matter?"

I could see Paul's frustration rising; his face went bright red, which at least had the consolation of making his little ginger beard less prominent. "It's just a really inefficient way to make a cup of tea."

"But you're not even having a cup."

"No, I'm not, because it's so annoying that you always do it wrong." And with that he stomped out of the room. Jim looked completely perplexed.

"Have I been putting sugar in Paul's tea when he doesn't take it or something?"

Simon mumbled that he didn't think so and Jim shrugged

and stood by the sink for a while and after five minutes realized that he hadn't pressed the 'on' button on the side of the kettle.

When the tea was made, the remaining three of us drank it in contemplative silence. Simon was reading the "Dear Deirdre" column in the *Sun,* in which Deirdre tackled the sexual problems of members of the general public, which I was convinced had been made up by journalists in the next-door office.

" 'My brother-in-law is my lover,' " he read out. " 'Dear Deirdre, I am an attractive blonde and people say I have a good figure. The other night, when my husband was away, his brother came round and one thing led to another and we ended up in bed . . .' " He broke off from reading out the letter. "They always say that: one thing led to another. How exactly does one thing lead to another, because that must be the bit that I'm getting wrong. I understand the brother coming round, and I understand that they were in bed together. But how did they get from the first stage to the last?"

"It's easy, Simon," said Jim.

"Well, what? How do you do it?"

"You meet a girl."

"Yes."

"She comes back for coffee."

"Yes, but then what?"

"Well, one thing leads to another."

After my second cup of tea I felt I'd finally run out of valid excuses for keeping the advertising agency waiting any longer, and so I collected the tape from my room and headed toward Balham tube station. Thirty minutes later I was walking down Berwick Street, where a couple of French students with a disposable camera nearly got run over trying to re-create the cover of *What's the Story Morning Glory?* I loved coming to Soho; it felt exciting and happening, and for a brief moment I liked to pretend I was part of it all. There were people here who earned a thousand pounds a day just for doing one voiceover for an advert, and then they'd blow it all by buying a prawn and avocado on focaccia with a café latte to go.

I glanced across the road and caught sight of Hugo from DD&G, staring at a shop window. That's peculiar, I thought. Why is Hugo staring into the window of a wholesale Asian jewelry shop? Then he glanced up and down the road quickly and disappeared into a tatty open doorway under the glow of a dangerously wired red light. I was shocked. I approached the open doorway and looked in. The words "New model. Very freindly. First floor" were scrawled onto a piece of card that was stuck by the entrance with thick brown masking tape. I looked up the rickety uncarpeted stairs and wondered what lay beyond. Maybe Hugo was just going in to offer to improve their advertising, to suggest a professional copywriter who could produce a snappier slogan and spell "friendly" correctly. It seemed unlikely. I was part repulsed, part fascinated and strangely disappointed in Hugo, as if he had let me down personally.

I continued up Berwick Street and finally entered the reception of the grand offices of DD&G, where a certificate boasted that they were runners-up for Best Investment and Banking Commercial at last year's Radio Advertising Awards. Apparently, Hugo had just popped out to get his wife a birthday card, so the tape was left with the beautiful waif of a receptionist, who sat in the window framed by lavish arrangements of fresh flowers.

My work for the week was done. It was time to head for North London. In the rush hour I squeezed my way onto the tube with all the people who had spent the day at work. Hundreds of sweaty office workers pressing their bodies together and yet managing to give the impression that they were not the slightest bit aware that there was anyone else in the carriage. Arms bending into impossible angles to read paperbacks bent over at the spine. Necks craning to read someone else's newspaper. Christians re-reading the Bible as if they didn't know it all by now.

Suddenly a seat became available and I moved toward it as quickly as is possible without revealing that I was doing anything as undignified as hurrying. As I sat down I breathed out a satisfied sigh, but any relaxation soon flipped over into anxiety. A woman was standing right in front of me, and from under her dress protruded *The Bulge of Uncertainty*. Was she six months pregnant or was she just a bit, well . . . fat? It was just impossible to say. I looked her up and down. Why can't she give me a sign? I thought. Why couldn't she be carrying a Mothercare bag or wearing one of those naff sweatshirts that say, "Yes I am!" I looked again. The dress hung loosely everywhere else; it was just on her rounded stomach that the material was stretched and taut. Which was worse, I wondered, denying a seat to a pregnant woman or offering a seat to a woman who wasn't pregnant but just looked as if she was. Maybe this is why men used to give up their seats to *all* women, to escape this embarrassing dilemma. No one else seemed concerned, but I felt I had to do the decent thing.

"Sorry. Would you like to sit down?" I said, getting up.

"Why would I want to sit down?" she said aggressively.

Shit, I thought. "Erm . . . Well, you just looked a bit tired . . . um, and I'm getting off at the next stop anyway," I lied.

On this understanding she took my seat, and I was forced to leave the carriage to maintain the deceit. I fought my way through the throng on the platform and rushed to get back on the train a couple of carriages further up. The not-pregnant woman had given me a very odd look, but it wasn't as strange as the one she gave me when we both went through the barriers at Kentish Town station fifteen minutes later.

As I emerged back into the open air, my mobile phone signaled that I had a message. It was Hugo. He said he was sorry he'd missed me but that he had been in and out all afternoon, which was more detail than I needed. He was pleased with my piece of music and told me that I'd come up with something "pretty bloody special." Although I generally found Hugo very insincere and of poor judgment I was prepared to make an exception in this case. I never felt confident that the snippets of music I wrote were any good. Whenever a decent tune came into my head I couldn't believe that I hadn't just subconsciously stolen it from somewhere, so any form of praise was eagerly gobbled up. Sadly, the track was only for a pitch and the agency would probably never use Hugo's production company, so no one would ever hear it. I had known this when I'd taken the job, but I knew I could do it quickly, it paid the bills and it meant I could afford to spend a couple of stress-free days in the cocoon I had created for myself.

I turned into Bartholomew Close. Tall, monolithic gray wheelie bins lined the street, like Easter Island statues waiting impassively for strangers. I walked up to number 17 and put the key in the lock. As I opened the front door I was hit by the chaos and noise.

"Daddy!" exclaimed my two-year-old daughter Millie with delight as she ran up the hallway and hugged my leg. There was a tape of children's nursery rhymes playing on the stereo and Alfie, my baby boy, was jiggling his limbs delightedly in his mother's arms.

"You're earlier than I expected," said Catherine with a smile.

I tiptoed over some wooden bricks that were scattered on the carpet, gave her a kiss and then took Alfie from her.

"Yeah, and guess what? I've finished the job and won't have to work at all this weekend."

"Fantastic," she said. "Then it's a double celebration. Because guess who wee'd in her potty today?"

"Did you, Millie?"

Millie nodded with extraordinary pride, which was only surpassed by that of her mother.

"And you didn't get any on the floor, did you, Millie? Which is better than your daddy usually manages and he's thirty-two."

I gave Catherine an affectionate poke in the ribs. "Look, it's not my fault the toilet seat always falls down."

"No, it's that idiot who fitted it," she concurred, referring to the evening when it had taken me three hours to fit a new wooden toilet seat incorrectly.

Millie had obviously enjoyed the praise that had been heaped upon her, so she quickly found another way to get some more attention. "I done cat drawing," she said, presenting me with a scrap of paper, which I took from her and studied carefully. Frankly, Millie's drawing was rubbish. To represent our cat, she had taken the blue crayon and scribbled it up and down on a piece of paper.

"Ooh, Millie, that's a super picture. You are a clever girl." One day she would turn round and say, "Don't patronize me, Father, we both know the picture is crap," but for the time being she seemed to buy it. I loved coming home when I hadn't seen them all for a couple of days; they were always so delighted to see me. It was the return of the prodigal father.

Catherine grabbed the chance to start clearing up the kitchen as I played with the kids for a while. I played hide and seek with Millie, which was made easier by the fact that she hid in the same spot behind the curtains three times in a row. Then I made Alfie giggle by throwing him up in the air until Catherine came back into the room to see why he'd suddenly started crying.

"I don't know," I said, trying not to look up at the metal chandelier swinging back and forth above her head. She took the crying baby back, and at that moment I thought she looked a little tired, so I said I'd take over tidying up. I slipped upstairs, gathering scattered toys as I went. I ran a big foamy bath, turned off the light and lit a couple of candles. Then I placed the portable CD player in the bathroom and put on Beethoven's *Pastoral Symphony*.

"Catherine, can you just come upstairs a minute," I shouted. She came up and surveyed the instant sanctuary that I had created.

"I'll take over the kids and load the dishwasher and everything. You get in there and I'll bring you a glass of wine, and you're not allowed out till the end of the final movement, 'Shepherds Song; Beneficent Feelings After the Storm.' "

She leaned against me. "Oh, Michael. What have I done to deserve this?"

"Well, you've been looking after the kids on your own for a couple of days and you must need a bit of space."

"Yes, but you've been working hard, too. Don't you need a rest?"

"I don't work as hard as you," I said sincerely. After a few halfhearted guilty protestations she clicked on the heated towel rail and turned up the volume loud enough to drown out the indignant shouts of "Mummy!" that had already started to emanate from the kitchen.

"Michael," she said as she kissed me on the cheek, "thanks for being the best husband in the world."

I smiled a half smile. When your wife says something like that, it doesn't seem like the right moment to put her straight.

2

Live Life to the Max

WE'VE ALL DONE IT. We've all kept little secrets from our partners. We've all avoided telling them an awkward detail or subtly skirted over something we'd rather they didn't know. We've all rented a secret room on the other side of the city where we could hide half the week to get away from all that boring, exhausting baby stuff. Oh, that last one is just me apparently.

Different marriages work in different ways. Adolf Hitler and Eva Braun got married, spent one day in a bomb shelter and then committed suicide together. Fine; if that's what they found worked best for them, who are we to pass judgment? Every couple have their own way of doing things—bizarre rituals, idiosyncratic little routines that keep them together. Often these evolve and grow until they completely disappear off the scale of rational behavior. Catherine's parents, for example, go out into the garden together each evening and find woodlice, which are then ritually crushed in a pestle and mortar before the remains are sprinkled on the roses. They think this is perfectly normal. "I've got another one, Kenneth." "Hang on, dear, you've got a centipede in there as well, we don't want to crush *you* now, do we, little fellah."

Once Catherine and I went on holiday with another couple, and on the last night we heard them nonchalantly chatting about us through the wall. They were saying they could never be married to anyone as peculiar as Catherine or me. They thought that our relationship was completely weird. Then we heard her muffled voice saying, "Are you coming to bed or what, because this clingfilm's making my tits sweat." And then we think he said, "All right. Hang on, the zip's stuck on my wetsuit." Every marriage is bizarre if you look under the surface.

There are, of course, plenty of relationships that do not develop tailored survival strategies and these are the ones that don't last. My parents split up when I was five and I remember thinking, Can't you just pretend to be married? Having experienced the grim and twisted diplomacy of Mum and Dad's divorce, I was determined that my children's parents would stay together. It was because I thought our marriage was so important that I kept *resting* it. The strain that small children brought into our lives suddenly seemed to create such tension and petty hostility between us that I was terrified of the damage becoming irreparable. Admittedly, I had developed a personal solution to a joint problem without ever talking it through with Catherine. But I didn't feel I could confess to wanting time away from my children. It's not something that men who are running for president boast about in their election broadcasts. "You know, sometimes I like to walk alone on the beach because it reminds me of the wonder of God's work and how little time we have in this world to make it a better place. But most of all, it gives me the chance to get away from my bloody kids for a while." I loved Catherine and I loved Millie and Alfie, but sometimes I felt as if they were driving me mad. Wasn't it better to get away rather than let the pressure just build and build until the whole marriage exploded and the kids had no dad for seven days of the week like I'd had?

So I didn't feel guilty about it. I'm sure I still would have run her a big foamy bath, even if I'd genuinely been working as hard as she imagined I did. I took her the wine bottle and a copy of *Hello!*, which I worried that she was no longer reading ironically. I poured us both a glass and she pulled me down for a loving kiss on the lips, which I engaged in a little awkwardly.

"What are the kids doing?"

"Millie's watching the *Postman Pat* video; the one in which he goes on a shooting spree through Greendale. And Alfie is strapped in his chair watching Millie."

"Oh well, as long as the telly's on. We wouldn't want to leave them unsupervised."

"You'll never guess what I saw today: Hugo Harrison disappearing into a prostitute's doorway."

"Really? Where were you?"

"Well I was just coming down the stairs obviously, doing up my trousers."

"He's married, isn't he? Remember we met his wife? I wonder if he's going to tell her?"

"Of course he's not going to tell her! 'Did you have a nice day at the office, dear?' 'Very nice, thank you. I popped out to visit a whore in the afternoon.' 'That's nice, dear. Supper's nearly ready.' "

"Poor woman. Imagine if she found out."

"I was a bit irritated to be honest. I wanted to know what he thought of the bit of music I'd brought for him and he'd disappeared to have it off with a prostitute."

"So did you find out if he liked it?"

"Well, you don't like to ask, do you."

"Your bit of music."

"Oh yeah, he called me on the mobile. He said it was great."

"I don't know how you do it. Was it another four o'clock in the morning job?"

"No, not as late as that."

"I can't see why you don't just work normal hours and tell them they'll have to wait a bit longer."

"Because they'd get someone else to do it and then we'd

have no money and I'd have to look after the children while you worked as a prostitute for the likes of Hugo Harrison."

"It doesn't bear thinking about—*you* looking after the children."

We laughed and I kissed her again. I loved it when she hadn't seen me for a couple of days; those were our most perfect times together.

Catherine had smooth pale skin, a pointy little nose and big brown eyes with which I was struggling to keep eye contact as she shifted her body in the steaming bath. She would always contradict me if I told her she was beautiful because she had this ridiculous notion that her fingers were too short. Sometimes I would catch her with her jumper sleeves right over the ends of her hands, and I knew she was doing this because she thought everyone was looking at her and thinking, Look at that woman; she'd look lovely if she didn't have such awful short fingers. Her hair was long and dark, and though it wasn't particularly elaborately styled, for some reason she would travel fifteen miles for a haircut because the man who had always done it had moved shops and she didn't want to risk letting anyone else have a go. I was just glad he hadn't emigrated to Paraguay because we would have struggled to raise the air fare every eight weeks.

What I wanted to do right now was jump into the bath with her and attempt foamy, clumsy sex, but I didn't suggest it because I didn't want to spoil the moment by precipitating rejection. More importantly, I knew there were no condoms in the house and there was no way I was risking a third baby. It wasn't as if I was the perfect father to the first two.

The first time we had ever made love we followed it by sharing a foamy tub like this one. On our first date she said she knew a lovely place for a drink and drove me all the way to a luxurious hotel she had booked in Brighton. On the way down a policeman pulled her over for speeding. She wound down her window as he slowly strode across and then he said to her, "Are you aware that you were doing fifty-three miles an hour in a forty-mile-an-hour zone?" And with a superior sneer he waited to see how she was going to try and explain herself.

"Pardonnez-moi; je ne parle pas l'anglais donc je ne comprends pas ce que vous dites . . ."

He looked completely thrown. And considering she'd failed French A level, she almost convinced me. The policeman then decided that the English language might be more comprehensible if it was spoken more loudly and with a number of glaring grammatical errors.

"You break speed limit. You too fast. Driving license?"

But she just responded with a confused Gallic shrug, saying, *"Pardonnez-moi, mais je ne comprends rien, monsieur."*

The bewildered officer looked at me and said, "Do you speak English?" and I felt forced to say, "Er—non!" in an appalling French accent. I lacked the chutzpah to chat away to the policeman like Catherine; my French was far more limited than hers and I didn't think he would be particularly impressed by my observation that "on the bridge at Avignon, they dance there, they dance there." She jumped in before I risked giving myself away, but this time she found a few words of English. "Mais Gary Lineker—eez very good!"

The officer visibly softened, and with a little bit of patriotic pride restored he felt able to send us on our way with an over-enunciated warning to "Drive—more—slowly."

"D'accord," she said, and he didn't even notice anything unusual when she added *"Auf Wiedersehen"* as she drove away. We had to pull into a side road a hundred yards later because we were both laughing so much she was in danger of crashing the car.

We had first met when she appeared in an advert for which I had arranged the music. She had just graduated with a drama degree from Manchester University and this commercial was her first professional acting part. She was cast as one of five dancing yogurt pots. She played fruits of the forest flavor and she was easily the best. It still galls me that orange and passion fruit flavor went on to star in *EastEnders*. After that Catherine got a few walk-on parts in minor soaps and appeared in a health and safety video in which she informed viewers that they should not walk into glass doors but should open them first. I got very excited when she told me she had landed the part of Sarah McIsaac in a major TV drama called *The Strange Case of Sarah McIsaac*. She showed me the script. Page one went like this: a woman is sitting at her desk, working late in a London office. A man walks in and says, "Are you Sarah McIsaac?" She says, "Yes," and then he takes out a gun and shoots her dead. Still, it was the title role and that was definitely a step up.

Then she got a good-size part in a West End play—in the west end of Essex that is—and I drove out to watch her in the glamorous setting of the Kenneth More Theatre, Ilford, every night. At first she said it was very supportive of me, but after a while I think she found it a little distracting to have me sitting in the front row, mouthing all her words as she said them. She was on the stage on her own for quite a lot of the play and was completely mesmerizing, though I didn't like the way all the other men in the audience just stared at her all the time.

But she saved her best performances for when she was winding people up. She could burst into tears if the bus conductor wouldn't let her on the bus without the right change and she was prepared to faint into a chair if the doctor's receptionist tried to prevent her from seeing the doctor. Once, when the bloke in the video shop wouldn't let us take out two films on the one card, she suddenly seemed to recognize him.

"Oh my God, you're Darren Freeman, aren't you?"

"Er, yeah?" he said, looking amazed.

"Do you remember me from school?"

"Er, oh erm, vaguely?"

"God, you were always interested in films and stuff; it's funny that you're working here. Blimey, Darren Freeman. Do you remember that stupid geography teacher? What was he called?"

And then they chatted nostalgically for ten minutes and it turned out that Darren had married Julie Hails, who Catherine said she'd always liked, and he gave us two films on one ticket and, as he handed them over, I noticed he was wearing a badge that said, "My name is Darren Freeman, how may I help you?"

We shared a casual attitude toward deception. When she asked me to marry her I gave her a cautionary sideways look to see if she was just having me on. I had this vision of myself as a ninety-year-old man at my wife's funeral, with her suddenly sitting up in the coffin going, "Ha! Ha! Had you fooled!" So to an outsider my double life might seem like some sort of shocking betrayal, but I liked to think it was just part of the fun we had with one another; another round in our ongoing game of one-upmanship. Her deceptions always made me laugh. The only trouble with the scam I was pulling was that I wasn't sure what the punchline was going to be.

My double life had started to evolve soon after Millie had been born. For years our relationship had been perfect and happy and I never would have imagined that anything could have made me want to run away. But then she fell in love with some-one else. Perhaps that was what I had been afraid of. Maybe that was why I had tried to put her off having kids for so long.

I never said I didn't want them, I just said I didn't want them *yet*. Of course I was going to have children *eventually*, just like I was going to die eventually, but I didn't spend a great deal of time planning that, either. Catherine, however, always talked about our future children as if they were imminent. She didn't want a two-door car because it would be such a struggle getting the baby seat in and out of the back. What bloody baby seat is this? I'd felt like asking. Baby clothes would be pointed out in shop windows, and she would insist on calling our spare room "the nursery." "You mean my recording studio," I would assert every time. Some of her hints were even less subtle. "It would be nice to have a summer baby, wouldn't it?" she said exactly nine months before the summer. Friends with small babies would be invited around on a Sunday and I would have to pretend to be interested as the mother and father casually chatted about Baby's bowel movements.

I don't know why parents think this is an acceptable way to carry on; it is not a subject we stray onto when we politely inquire about the health of fellow adults.

"Hello, Michael, how are you?"

"I'm fine, thanks. I did quite a big poo this morning, but soon after I did another smaller one that wasn't quite so firm, which is unlike me because I normally only have one poo a day."

Babies' bodily functions are discussed at length because that's all there is to them. They feed, they puke, they crap, they sleep, they cry and it starts again. And though there is nothing more you can say about the activities of a newborn, their parents still talk about nothing else. If by some miracle our visitors from the Planet Baby did happen to wander from the fascinating topic of the infant digestive system, the conversation only switched to the equally unsavory subject of the mother's bodily functions. At this point, some of the fathers at least had the good grace to look embarrassed and awkward, while Catherine and the new mum chatted at great length about breast pumps and episiotomies. Those dads were not beyond saving. The fathers I really couldn't tolerate were those who had clearly been turned into gibbering idiots by the trauma of it all. These self-deluding infants' entertainers would maniacally roll around on my carpet, blowing raspberries at their babies and shouting made-up words in the forlorn attempt to engender the slightest response from their new offspring. "Ooooooohhh-bla-bla-bla-bla-bla bum-bum," they'd squeal. "Oh, she loves this," the mother would say with an approving smile, and you could tell the baby loved it because it blinked—possibly—just the once.

After a while the mother would punish me for my obvious indifference by saying, "Would you like to hold the baby, Michael?"

"Oh, that would be lovely," I'd dutifully reply and I would take hold of the baby with all the relaxed composure of the Minister for Northern Ireland being handed a mystery parcel during a walkabout of West Belfast. All the while, both mother and father hovered right next to me, keeping their hands under his head, back and legs, just to show how much confidence they had in my ability not to drop an eight-pound baby for the twelve seconds that I held it.

These new parents reminded me of born-again Christians. They had a smugness and a superior air that suggested my life was somehow incomplete because I hadn't heard the Good News about babies. I would only be a whole person once I had joined their throng of happy clappy parents who went to the church hall every week to sing "Three Little Men in a Flying Saucer." They all thought I'd be converted sooner or later. Eventually my soul would be saved and I would take babies into my life. This was Catherine's plan, hence the newborn charm offensive. If she was trying to persuade me that I might like to have a baby then you would have thought that exposing me to a lot of babies was the worst possible tack. But in the end she wore me down. What could I do; the thing that would bring the greatest happiness to the woman I loved was in my gift and I couldn't keep denying her forever.

I finally agreed that we should start trying for children on one of those let's-be-really-in-love days. These are times of total intimacy and mutual adoration, when all you want to do is agree with everything your partner says. To actually cut across and contradict her by saying, "No, actually I think 'Hotel California' is a dreadful song," would completely ruin the atmosphere, so you nod and smile and say, "Mmmm, yeah, that's one of my favorites, too." It was in one of these moments that I acceded to the idea of being a parent. I agreed to a lifetime of fatherhood so as not to spoil a nice afternoon.

I could never understand those men who complained that it took them and their partners years to conceive. Month after month of constant eager sex! Catherine got pregnant in the first month we started trying. "You're so clever," she said to me with a hug, and I was supposed to be proud that we had managed it so quickly. But inside I was thinking, Damn! Is that it, then? Can't we keep doing it every night anyway, just to be sure. She wee'd onto a little stick and we watched it change color. The instructions said that if it went *light* pink she was not pregnant, but if it went *dark* pink she was pregnant. It went pink. Sort of halfway between light and dark pink, a sort of pinky-pink with just a hint of pink. She went to the doctor's, because that's the only way to be really sure you are pregnant, and the best start an expectant mother can get is to sit for an hour and a half in a hot, stuffy waiting room, inhaling the germs of as many infectious diseases as possible.

Before the baby arrived I was actually more consumed by it all than she was. I read every pregnancy manual I could lay my hands on, researched the best car seats and monitored Catherine's weight gain, which I logged on a wall chart in the kitchen. I was rather hurt when she took it down before a dinner party; I thought it showed just how supportive and interested I was being. This birth was my new project, my new enterprise, an exam that could be passed if I did enough revision. I learned the expectant parents' script off by heart.

"What are you hoping for, a boy or a girl?"

"I don't mind, as long as it's healthy."

Correct answer.

"What sort of birth are you going for?"

"As natural as possible, but we're not completely ruling out intervention if it's necessary."

Correct answer.

Maybe I thought mastery of the subject matter might endow me with some sort of control, but as the pregnancy progressed I began to see the warning signs. Women have babies, not men; there is no getting round that fact. "It's not our show, chaps," said one of the fathers-to-be at the antenatal classes. And as much as I dutifully went along to all these gatherings, being supportive and nodding and listening along with all the other silent, embarrassed men, I couldn't help thinking, What is it exactly that I've got to do, then? When the mother is breathing correctly and walking and focusing and contracting and timing her contractions so as not to go into hospital too early, what does the man have to do?

Apparently the answer to this question is "make sandwiches." That was the only instruction which I wrote down that was definitely aimed at me. In fact, making sandwiches is the only other thing that men are needed for during the entire nine months. One sperm at the beginning of the pregnancy, two rounds of cheese and pickle at the end of it. But my enthusiasm was resilient—if this was all I had to do, then I wanted to get it right. The teacher went back to describing the first-stage contractions, hardly pausing to give me the slightest guidance on how we might best do our bit, so I put my hand up.

"Just going back to those sandwiches a minute, is there a particular filling that's best for a woman in labor?"

"Well, um, nothing too difficult to digest, but whatever your partner normally likes."

"It's just that I thought maybe her tastebuds might be affected by hormones or whatever; there might be something that women in labor often develop a violent aversion to."

"Maybe best to make a selection of fillings, just to be on the safe side. Now, once the cervix has dilated the full ten centimeters—"

"White or brown bread?"

"What?"

"White or brown bread for the sandwiches? You know, I want everything to be perfect for the baby, so I was just wondering which is best. I know brown is normally healthier, but is it easier to digest? I suppose we ought to have brown if we're going for a natural childbirth."

One of the other men picked up the thread and suggested that we make a selection of fillings inside a choice of white *and* brown bread, which seemed like a sensible suggestion, but at that point a woman with large glasses said that she was sorry if the men weren't used to being in meetings that they couldn't dominate but could we shut the fuck up about the fucking sandwiches because we were getting on her tits. The teacher had spent the last hour discussing intercourse, vaginas and breasts, but still blushed to hear such talk.

Because of minor gynecological problems during her pregnancy, Catherine had been allocated a specialist consultant at St. Thomas's. This was obviously very distressing for her; a North Londoner being told that she would have to travel south of the river. But no problems ever arose, apart from having to drive halfway across London in the rush hour with my wife in labor in the back seat. Once we were in the delivery suite Catherine did everything that she had been told and breathed and pushed and waited and pushed again and produced a perfect little baby girl. I did everything I was supposed to do as well, but the sandwiches never came out of the bag. Of course I dabbed her forehead and said, "You're doing really well," and, "That's really brilliant," and things like that, but that's not the way I normally talk, so it can't have sounded very convincing. But then nothing about that day was very normal. Having this alien finally pop out of her was quite the most surreal experience of my life. The baby was handed to Catherine and she immediately seemed comfortable and confident with it. Her overjoyment gland had secreted gallons of the overjoyment hormone and she burst into tears. And although I was deeply moved by that moment, I secretly felt guilty that I was clearly not deeply moved in the way that she was. So I managed a wan smile, unsure whether I should try and cheer her up or pretend to cry as well. I think I was probably in a deep state of shock.

Although that was the moment I technically became a father, it didn't really sink in for another couple of hours. Catherine was asleep and I was slumped in the leatherette chair by her bed. A toy coughing noise started to come from the cot and, since I didn't want Catherine to be disturbed, I nervously picked up the baby myself. She seemed so fragile and tiny, and I carried her to my chair as if she were some priceless antique vase.

"Hello, little girl, I'm your dad," I said. And then for the next hour or so I held her in my arms, just staring at this perfect little model of a person while an enormous sense of responsibility welled up within me. This baby was completely dependent on Catherine and me. We hadn't been made to take any exams or attend any interviews, but here we were, suddenly in charge of a child. It felt moving, thrilling, awe-inspiring, but most of all terrifying. As I sat there looking at her, I thought about all those proud parents who had brought their babies round to our house, and I smiled when I thought how foolish they had all been. They had really thought that theirs were the most beautiful babies of all, when it was obvious to anyone that this little girl in my arms was by far the most beautiful creature the world had yet seen. I was sure that everyone would recognize this fact once they saw her. She was so innocent, so unspoiled, so new. I wanted to protect her from everything in the world and show her all the wonderful things on earth at the same time. When she eventually became restless I walked her across to the window and, while dawn was breaking over London, I looked down over the city from high up in St. Thomas's Hospital.

"That's the River Thames down there, little girl," I told her. "And that's the Houses of Parliament. That clock there is Big Ben and that big red thing going over the bridge is called a bus. Say, 'Bus.' "

"Bus," said a babyish voice to my astonishment. Either I had fathered a genius or Catherine was awake and watching me. The baby had been growing increasingly uncomfortable and Catherine took her from me and placed the baby on her breast where she fed as if they had both been doing it for years.

Catherine and I had agreed on the name Millie for a girl weeks before the birth. But now that a baby girl had actually come along I felt an urge to name her after my late mother. I shared the idea with Catherine, who said it was a beautiful thought.

"Your mother sounds like a wonderful person, and I wish I had met you earlier so that I could have known her. It would be a lovely thing to name this baby after the grandmother she will never meet; it's a touching and poetic idea. The only trouble, my darling husband, is that your mother's name was Prunella."

"I know."

"Don't you think the world is a cruel enough place into which to bring a new human being without lumbering it with the name Prunella?"

We agreed to sleep on the idea and we took Millie home two days later.

Once in the house, we put the baby in the middle of the lounge and I thought, Now what do we do? That was when I realized that I had only revised for everything up to this point. So much of our focus was on the day of the birth itself that I'd only given the slightest thought to what happened after that. Nothing had prepared me for the way she would totally disrupt my life. Not even every parent I knew telling me that the baby would totally disrupt my life prepared me for how much the baby would totally disrupt my life. It was like having your most difficult and demanding relation come to stay with you *forever*. In fact, it would have been easier to put up with my ninety-year-old great aunt coming into our bed at three in the morning; at least she might have gone back to sleep for an hour or two.

When I first started to feel like a parent that night in the hospital, I was already lagging a couple of hours behind Catherine, and now the gulf between us continued to grow. I felt redundant almost from the outset. Normally, when there had been something that Catherine had really wanted, I had been the one who got it out of the box and wired up the speakers. But when we took this baby home, I was the useless one who had no idea what to do. There seemed to be no logic or system to follow. Sometimes Millie slept and sometimes she cried all night. Sometimes she would feed and sometimes she would refuse. There were no rules or routine, no rhythm or narrative to her—for the first time in my life I seemed to be confronted by a problem which had no solution. Life was out of control; I had no idea what was making this baby scream and what course of action should be taken, whereas Catherine just seemed to know. She could tell when Millie was hot, cold, hungry, thirsty, grumpy, tired, sad, whatever. Although the baby didn't seem to cry any less when she applied the appropriate remedy, I never dared question the confidence with which she told me the reason for the baby's distress. Millie was supposed to fill me with joy and fulfillment, but my strongest sensation was an overwhelming anxiety. It was anxiety at first sight. I wasn't in love with the baby, I was "in worry" with it.

But with Catherine it was like first love all over again. It was an overwhelming, all-consuming, total obsessive love. Her every waking thought was of Millie.

"Mind the red car," I would say in a panic as she drove along, staring at her baby strapped in the back seat.

"Aah. Millie's got a little hat that color," she would say dreamily.

"Ow! I've cut my hand open with the bread knife."

"Ooh, show Millie; she's never seen blood."

"Did you read that article about the USA trying to force Europe to import its bananas from American multinationals?"

"Millie likes bananas."

She put Millie's name on the answerphone. "Hello. If you would like to leave a message for Catherine, Michael or Millie, please speak after the tone." Being a baby who was as yet unable to use the phone or speak English, it was not very surprising that Millie didn't get very many messages of her own.

Everything came back to the baby. I was in a shop buying a new stereo and Catherine said, "Well, I think you should buy these speakers because they've got a really good bass sound and that's supposed to help relax the baby." Obviously the most important criterion when buying myself a new stereo is which one is best for relaxing the baby. I already had my heart set on another pair of speakers, but God forbid that I should appear indifferent to the needs of The Baby. "These are better," I said. "The edges are rounder—she won't hurt herself if she falls against these." And Catherine was delighted with my choice.

Suddenly I never seemed to be doing anything that I actually wanted to be doing. This struck me on our first family holiday together. I realized it wasn't a holiday at all. That having Millie crawling around a rented cottage with extra-steep unguarded stairs and loose electrical sockets and a real log fire spitting out glowing splinters was even less relaxing than sitting at home watching her stuff half-chewed rusks into the video. My first holiday as a parent was when I realized I had become a teenager again, that I was grumpily being dragged along from playground to children's farm and it was all completely stupid and pointless and pathetic. "Look, Millie, look at the llama eating the hay." Yup, she definitely glanced at the llama then, so that was worth it. Why couldn't we just have stayed at home in London? I wouldn't have minded taking her out of the front door every now and then and saying, "Look, Millie, look at the dog crapping on the pavement." She wouldn't have been any less impressed. But no, we had to drive all the way to Devon and stay in a freezing-cold cottage so the poor disoriented baby could wake up every two hours and then be strapped into the car seat again because there was a children's farm eleven miles away where they had llamas and not enough high chairs and a swing not dissimilar to the one at the bottom of our road. All that effort wasn't for her; it was for us. We had to do too much just to convince ourselves that we were doing enough.

And then, of course, there were the nighttimes. I remembered how Catherine and I used to cuddle up and fall asleep with our bodies still wrapped together. Then Millie came into our bed—quite literally between us. We had tried having her in a cot at the bottom of the bed, but Catherine found that she slept more soundly with Millie at her side, once she no longer felt compelled to sit up in panic at every moan, gurgle or indeed every silence. The baby would drift in and out of sleep feeding at Catherine's breast—the very breasts that I was no longer permitted to touch—and I would lie there awake, resentfully thinking, Honestly! Has that baby no idea who those breasts are for?

I found it hard to sleep through the constant snuffling and kicking of the baby while I perched precariously on the edge of the mattress. On a couple of occasions I actually fell right out and landed face down on the wooden floor. I discovered that it was quite hard to sleep through this as well.

"Shhh, you'll wake Millie," whispered Catherine as I checked to see if my nose was bleeding. After a few wakeful nights, Catherine suggested I slept downstairs on the sofa. So now she didn't sleep with her husband anymore, she slept with her new love, The Baby. She seemed to have become completely immune to the feelings of anyone except The Baby. She was besotted, spellbound, obsessed. It was like when she first fell in love with me. Except this time it wasn't with me.

Millie had pushed me out. She had taken my place in the bed, my social life and my time with Catherine; she'd even robbed me of my birthday. "What a perfect birthday present," everyone said to me when she was born on the day that I turned thirty. That was the last birthday I ever had. A year later, on our "joint" birthday, Millie got a shape sorter, a ball that bounced in funny directions, a trolley with colored bricks in it, a plastic bath toy, a baby gym, a squeaky book and about thirty cuddly toys. I got a photo album in which to put pictures of Millie. Happy Birthday, Michael! "Sorry it's not very much, but

I didn't have time to go to the shops," said Catherine as she filled a bin liner with all the packaging from the toys she'd bought Millie from the shops.

I would have liked to go out that night, but Catherine said it felt funny to leave Millie on her first birthday. I pointed out that Millie was not only fast asleep, she was also completely unaware that it was her birthday and, if she woke up, would be perfectly happy to be settled again by Catherine's mother. But Catherine said she wouldn't have enjoyed it and so neither would I, so we stayed in and watched a program about gardening.

To cap a memorable evening Catherine asked me to pop down to the supermarket for some nappies and, since it was my birthday, I treated myself to two cans of lager and a packet of Cheesey Wotsits. But then, as I returned home, I noticed all the lights were out. I knew immediately what Catherine had done. My wife, God bless her, had secretly organized me a surprise birthday party. The nappy mission had just been a way of getting me out of the house. I checked my hair in the car mirror, let myself in, tiptoed into the lounge and went to switch on the light, ready to appear surprised and delighted as everyone shouted, "Happy Birthday, Michael!" I braced myself and flicked the light switch. I probably did look really surprised. The room was completely empty. So was the kitchen. I went upstairs and Catherine was fast asleep in bed. I went back downstairs, flopped onto the sofa, drank a can of lager and flicked between the television channels. My Cheesey Wotsits had a free *Star Wars* card inside, so that was some consolation. "Live life to the max," said the ad on the telly, so I drank my second can of lager before going to bed.

I had thought my youth and freedom would last forever. When I was eighteen I'd left home and rented a shared flat, thinking that at long last I was free, that now I could do whatever I wanted—forever. No one had told me that this emancipation was only temporary, that I'd only enjoy total liberty for a very brief period of my life. I had spent my childhood doing what my parents wanted to do and now my adulthood seemed doomed to be spent doing what my children wanted to do. I was back in the jug again; my home had turned into a prison. I could no longer come and go as I pleased; there were bars on the upstairs windows, security gates on the stairs and monitors and locks and alarms, soon there would even be a stinking potty to be slopped out. This baby that had arrived was part warder and part prison bully. She would not permit me to sleep beyond 6 A.M., after which time I was her gofer, her lackey, fetching and carrying just for her amusement. She would humiliate me by throwing a piece of cutlery to the floor and then demanding that I pick it up, and when I obeyed her she would do it again.

Any prisoner dreams of escape. Mine happened subconsciously at first. I would lie in the bath and allow my ears to slip under the water so the soundtrack of crying babies and angry shouting would become a dull and distant babble. Once, when Millie was asleep in the buggy, I offered to push her out across Hampstead Heath so Catherine could have a lie-down and relax in an empty house. As I pushed the buggy up and down the only steep hills in London, I realized that the reason I had made this apparently generous offer was just to get some time to myself, because now I needed to escape from Catherine as well. She made me feel as if I always did everything wrong. I headed for the Bull and Last and had two pints sitting in the pub garden, feeling more relaxed and carefree than I could remember. Millie stayed asleep the whole time we were out, and soon all my cares and tensions were washed away on the foamy tide of beer. When I arrived home I felt completely serene and at peace with the world, until Catherine's furious face at the window brought me back down to reality with a disappointing bump. Oh no, what have I done wrong now? I thought to myself. I decided I would try to ignore her obvious displeasure, but as I cheerfully strode up the front path with my hands in my pockets she came to greet me at the door.

"Where's Millie?" she said.

"Millie?"

"Yes, your daughter that you took for a walk on the heath . . ."

I now know that it is possible to run from my house to the Bull and Last pub in four minutes and forty-seven seconds.

I suppose that on that occasion I have to accept some of the blame. Most of the blame. But Catherine seemed to find fault with everything I did with the children. I dried them with the wrong towel, I mixed their babymilk with the wrong water and I put the wrong amount of lotion on their bottoms. I got the impression that Catherine found it quicker and easier to do everything herself. I would dutifully be there at dressing time, feeding time and at bath time, hoping that I might be of some use, but generally I just got in the way. I was offering to be hands-on, but in reality my hands were just hanging down by my sides, not quite sure what to do with themselves. In babyland she was queen; I was Prince Philip, hovering awkwardly in the background making stupid comments.

Was it like this for all fathers? Is this why, for thousands of years, men had made themselves scarce: to be spared the humiliation of being second best at something? Before long, my absence became routine. I would tend to be held up at meetings; I was no longer in a rush to get home in time to be told off for putting plastic teaspoons in the dishwasher. If I was working out of town, I would always seem to end up on the later train back to London, and wouldn't get home until after Catherine was fast asleep.

One day I came home late and crept into the room that I had persisted in clinging to as my recording studio. Then I saw it. A whole wall had been covered with *Wind in the Willows* wallpaper. Where there had previously been a Clash poster of Joe Strummer smashing a guitar, now there were little nursery drawings of Ratty and Mole in tweeds and plus-fours. That was my parenting Kristallnacht, the moment I knew I was being driven out.

We had always agreed that when the baby went into "the nursery" I would have to rent a room away from home for my work, but the move was one of those far-off problems that I preferred to put out of my head. Just because I agreed I would move my stuff out didn't mean that I was actually planning to do anything about it. I pointed out that finding somewhere suitable would be a long and complicated business.

"There's a free room going in Heather's brother's house in Balham; you can rent that in the short term." Catherine was way ahead of me. The following weekend we packed up all the things that I would need in my new recording studio, and a little bit more. By the end of the morning the hallway was blocked with a large pile of boxes containing my entire youth. CDs, tapes, music magazines, my autographed Elvis Costello baseball cap and all the ironically naff mugs that I had bought before we moved in together. Two birthdays ago I had given her a chrome CD rack in the shape of an electric guitar; that appeared on the pile by the front door as well. I got the feeling there was a side to me that Catherine was looking forward to expunging from the family home.

"Oh, you've got to have your Beatles mirror in your studio. It'll look great there and it doesn't really go in our bedroom," she said, taking it down off the wall with a little too much relish.

And so I started commuting to a little room in South London. It was only half an hour down the Northern Line, but it felt like a whole world away. If Catherine needed to speak to me she could ring my mobile, except when I was really up against it, when the mobile was switched off. It seems I was often really up against it. Nothing improved our marriage like being apart. The more time I spent at the studio, the more we liked each other. I had always worked unconventional hours and, with a sofa bed that folded out between the amps and keyboards, I continued to do so. As far as Catherine was concerned, the longer I was in my studio, the harder I must have been working, and she was proud to have a husband who could work such long hours and yet still come home and put so much effort into his family.

"Where do you get your energy from?" she asked as she lay on the bed after her bath and watched me swinging Millie round by her arms. "Well, a change is as good as a rest," I said modestly, thinking to myself that a change *and* a rest was even better. I gave the kids a quick bath in their mum's perfumed bathwater while she lay on the bed and finished the bottle of wine. She assured me that she wasn't too drunk to tell Millie her bedtime story and proceeded to read perfectly, only ripping two of the tabs on the *Pocahontas* pop-up book. Soon Millie and Alfie were asleep and the house was at peace. Catherine lay on our bed, wrapped in a giant towel, soft and talcum-powdered and still glowing warm from her hour-long soak. She gazed up at me.

"If we're going to have more children, it would be good to have them close together, wouldn't it?"

This particular come-on was somehow left out of the *Erotic Guide to Sexual Seduction*. She looked irresistible, but two children was enough for me.

"Well, Alfie's only nine months; there's no need to hurry," I said, avoiding a confrontation. But Catherine had always known she was going to have four kids and she had a very persuasive argument in favor of trying for another one right now, namely that she was lying naked on a warm soft bed. We hadn't made love for three weeks and four days, and here she was pressing herself against me and kissing me wet kisses on my lips. I won't pretend that I wasn't very tempted, but I knew I had to be strong. Without any contraception it would simply be too much of a gamble. For a few minutes' pleasure I was not prepared to risk yet more years of sleepless nights and all the marital tension and continued deception on my part that another baby would bring. Any way that you looked at it, it just wasn't worth it. I was not going to have five minutes of ecstatic sexual intercourse with my beautiful wife.

As it turned out, this last bit was true—it was only a minute and a half. I cursed my weakness as I held her close and climaxed. Lots of men apparently shout obscenities at that moment, but I moaned, "Oh fuck!" Not as in, "Wow! That was amazing!" But more in the sense of, "Oh fuck! What have I just done!" Sex was the crime and I'd just blown my parole. I had let this double life develop, thinking it would just be a temporary measure, that soon the kids would reach the age when we could emerge from the war zone of babies and then I could start being a normal husband and father. Fortunately, the chances of Catherine conceiving so quickly were slim. She was still breastfeeding once a day and so I reckoned it was safe.

Two weeks later, Catherine told me she was pregnant.

3

Have a Break

WHEN CATHERINE had been expecting our first child, one of the books I had read suggested that, in order to appreciate what my wife was going through, I should fill a balloon up with water and wear it strapped to my stomach for a day. To demonstrate how supportive I was, I actually attempted this exercise. I followed the diagrams and tied the squishy balloon around my waist and then walked around the kitchen with one hand on the base of my back, trying to look radiant. Afterward, I felt I could look my wife in the eye and say that now, at last, I finally understood how it felt to have a balloon filled with water stuffed under your jumper. I only did it for an hour. My waters burst suddenly while I was pruning the roses.

A good father-to-be is supposed to empathize. In fact, I read that occasionally the most sensitive of men genuinely experience some of the actual *physical* symptoms of their partner's pregnancies, although having an eight-pound baby pop out of their vaginas was obviously not one of them. "Couvade syndrome," as it's called, happened to me with Catherine's first pregnancy. In the first six weeks or so, as Catherine started to put on weight, through some deep spiritual sensibility I began to gain weight as well. Amazingly, since we had stopped playing squash together and stayed in ordering takeaway pizzas and tubs of Ben & Jerry's ice cream, my waistline had started to expand at approximately the same rate as hers. Truly, nature is a wonderful thing.

All these concepts and suggestions left me feeling that I was supposed to try and make myself more maternal. That's what they wanted me to be: a backup mother. I ought to be feeling what she felt; I ought to have the instincts that she had. I almost felt guilty for not blubbing when my milk seemed a bit slow to come in. No wonder I felt that I was no good at it, because it was an aspiration that was impossible to achieve. My wife was always going to be a better woman than I was.

I suppose we were quite a conventional couple in the way we slotted into our gender stereotypes. Catherine had decided she wanted to put her acting career on hold while the children were small. She didn't feel she was getting anywhere, despite the fact that after Millie was born she was no longer being cast as "passerby" but had progressed to "passerby holding baby." So she resolved to become a full-time mother. "Ah well, that is the toughest role of all," said her annoying father a hundred and twelve times. What Catherine found disorientating was how guilty she was made to feel for not being a promotion-hungry career woman. When she told people that she'd given up work, they froze into embarrassed silence. She said she didn't want to go to any more drinks parties unless she could ring a handbell and wear a placard round her neck saying, "Uninteresting." Being with the baby was what she wanted and so I was happy to support her decision, even though I had always enjoyed her occasional appearances on television, not to mention the occasional appearance of the checks that had landed on the doormat.

We had always liked to think of ourselves as artistic and Bohemian, me the musician and her the actress, but in reality we were no different from any of the accountants and insurance brokers who lived in our road. We lived in a small two-bedroom house in Kentish Town which the estate agents had described as a "cottage." This meant that you could just about fit the pushchair through the front door, but then getting past it yourself was such a physical impossibility that you had to sleep in the front garden. I can vouch for the fact that there wasn't room to swing a cat in our house because I once caught Millie trying.

Because we aspired to live in a neighborhood which was quite close to a postal code which was next door to a borough which was quite near a desirable part of London, we had no choice but to live in a tiny house. I remember climbing inside the kiddies' playhouse at Toys "R" Us and thinking, Blimey, this is roomy! How we were going to fit another baby into our home was quite beyond me, but if the old lady who lived in the shoe had managed, then I suppose we would have to try our best. I never really understood that nursery rhyme until I moved to London. If that had been today, some developer would have bought the old lady's shoe and converted it into flats.

The third baby was not due for another eight months and was no more than half an inch long, but it was still able to make its mother nauseous, tired and tearful. I suppose that's an early warning that there's no relationship between the size of a baby and the scale of disruption it can cause. Of course an embryo disrupts your life in a different way to a small baby, and a small baby disrupts your life in a different way to a toddler. But now we had all three of them wreaking havoc simultaneously. Few of us have any memories of our own lives before we were three years old. This is an evolutionary necessity—if we could recall what bastards we were to our parents we'd never have any children of our own. Millie was two and a half, Alfie was ten months, the embryo was four weeks and I felt about a hundred and five. Nothing could have prepared me for how tired I felt, let alone Catherine. Sleep deprivation is a popular torture device used by the Indonesian secret police and small babies. I suppose at least Alfie couldn't kick me in the testicles every time I eventually dropped off. He left that to his big sister, who generally climbed into our bed at around three in the morning. Even when I slept on my own I still found myself lying there with my hands over my groin in the footballer-in-defensive-wall position.

Catherine was always most exhausted at the beginning of her pregnancies, when they were still secret from everyone else. I had to pretend to friends that she kept fainting and bursting into tears because we'd stayed up very late watching old James Stewart movies, but she always insisted that she was coping all right. "Tired? No, I'm not tired," she said as I cleared the dinner plates away, although my suspicions were increased when I came back with the pudding to find her fast asleep with her head on the kitchen table.

Although we had been together five years, I'd not yet learned how to translate the things she said to me. Before her last birthday she had remarked, "Don't get me anything special this year," and I had foolishly taken this to mean, "Don't get me anything special this year." I had failed to decipher the subtle intonation in her voice, I had listened to the lyrics rather than the notes. In the same way she had a dozen different ways of saying, "I'm not tired." Some of them meant exactly that, while others meant, "I am very tired, please insist that I go to bed right away."

I knew she was not her usual self that evening when some Jehovah's Witnesses had come to the door. That's strange behavior, I had thought, she didn't want to talk to them. Normally she would have invited them in, given them a cup of tea and then asked them if they had thought about taking Satan into their lives. She nearly recruited one of them once when she earnestly described the uplifting spiritual catharsis of naked bouncy-castle night.

But tonight tiredness reduced her to a robotic drone; she had carried out the duties required to get the kids into bed, with no energy or enthusiasm remaining for anything else.

Alfie had just given us three terrible nights in a row and we were both completely exhausted and demoralized. I can't say that we had been sleeping badly because I don't actually think we slept at all. The wakeful nighttimes were totally disorientating and we had lost any sense of time; how Catherine's body clock remembered to make her throw up in the morning was completely beyond me.

When she finally lifted her creased face off the kitchen table, I tried to persuade her to sleep downstairs on the sofa with the door closed, where she would be out of earshot of the baby. I wanted her to delegate some of the sleeplessness to me before I went off to work the next morning. But she found this hard to agree to. She was greedy; she wanted all the misery to herself. But I kept on and on at her, and eventually she didn't have the energy to resist my arguments. So I set her up on the sofa with a duvet and pillows before kissing her goodnight and heading upstairs to face the nighttime on my own.

It was like an approaching storm which I entered into with nervous trepidation. Batten down the hatches; we're going into the night. In the days before children came along I often deliberately chose to stay up until morning. It was a fun and crazy thing to do. We'd climb over the railings of Hyde Park and play on the swings. I went to an all-night sci-fi festival at an independent cinema. I went to parties and took speed or coke and sat at the top of Hampstead Heath watching the sun rise over London. Often, when I had a big piece of work in, I liked to spend an evening with Catherine and then, as she went to bed, I would disappear into the studio, put on the headphones and work at my keyboard until dawn. I would have breakfast with Catherine before she went off to her audition or whatever, and then I'd go to bed until she came back again. I loved working at night when it was all quiet and still and you could really lose yourself in your thoughts. A melody would come into my head and I'd think, Where is this coming from? Somebody else has taken over my body and is giving me this tune for free. Sometimes, if I got stuck, I would go for a walk in the dead of the night and just feel the stillness of the city asleep. The nights were my time to myself. Mr. Moonlight she called me. That was Catherine's pet name for her boyfriend who loved to stay up all night. In moments of intimacy and affection she still called me Mr. Moonlight, though now that I was secretly moonlighting on our family life, it was no longer a nickname with which I felt particularly comfortable.

I tiptoed into Millie's room and checked that she was asleep. She looked so sweet and trusting and secure. Carefully avoiding the creaky floorboard, I picked up a couple of soft toys that had fallen on the floor and silently placed them behind her pillow. As quietly and gently as I could, I slowly pulled her blanket back over her. With the care and precision of a microsurgeon, I moved the plastic doll from where it was pressing into her face and laid it on the side of the bed. Then, as I straightened up, my head crashed into the stained-glass mobile above her bed, which set it jangling and clinking, and she opened her eyes and looked at me in surprised disbelief.

"Why are you here?" she said in a dreamy voice. It wasn't an easy question to answer on any level. I told her to go back to sleep again, and amazingly she did.

Alfie was asleep in the pram which, for reasons that had once seemed sensible but now eluded me, we carried up to our bedroom every night. He was sleeping soundly, getting his rest in now so that he would have as much energy as possible for the long night ahead. Silently, and on my own, I prepared for bed, wondering how the next few hours might unfold, like a soldier on the eve of battle. The knowledge that I would soon be disturbed made me desperate to get to sleep as quickly as possible, so that I lay down in panicky concentration, thinking, Got to get to sleep. Got to get to sleep, which kept me awake for far longer than usual. Then finally I was gone.

In the first hour or so my mind would race downhill into its deepest, deepest sleep, but it was during this dreamy descent that I was always violently pulled up, jerked awake by the sudden angry scream of the baby. Tonight Alfie was bang on cue, and though I was suddenly conscious of being awake, for a couple of scary seconds I lay there frozen, paralyzed while my body struggled to catch up and become operative as well. Then, like some bleary automaton, I threw back the duvet, staggered over to the pram and stuck my little finger in his mouth. The crying stopped as he sucked and sucked, and I sat down on the end of the bed, still only half conscious. Rubbing my aching head I glanced in the mirror and saw the hunched, graying figure of an exhausted man, a ghost of my former self, my thinning hair sticking up and my face creased and lined. When he had been born, one of the cards we had been sent featured a black-and-white photo of a muscular man clutching a naked baby to his rippling chest. That was not how fatherhood felt right now. The clock told me that I had only slept for an hour and forty minutes and that it was far too early to give Alfie a feed. After a while the sucking became less frantic; he slowly calmed down as I gently rocked the pram back and forth for good measure. When I deftly removed the digit, he barely reacted.

My finger was a portable pacifier that had worked for both children. Unsurprisingly, they seemed to find Catherine's long, sharp fingernails rather less comforting, and so my little finger was the only oral comfort they were permitted. Early on I had tentatively suggested that we buy them plastic dummies, but Catherine put up the objections that dummies were unhygienic and that they impaired speech development and that we would only be creating a rod for our own backs and it would be impossible to wean them off them and several other secondhand objections. She never mentioned the real one, which was that she secretly thought dummies looked common and no baby of hers was going to look common. I couldn't offer an argument against a conviction I dared not accuse her of, and so the only pacifier that our children ever had was my upturned little finger. The dummy was me.

To keep little Alfie asleep I knew I had to keep gently rocking the pram, so inch by inch I maneuvered it to a position beside the bed. Now, at least, I could lie down. I was probably only making it worse for myself. Like an alcoholic going to the pub for a glass of water, I was taunting myself with my proximity to the thing I craved most. But I was just too tired to sit upright, so I lay on the edge of the bed and, with the blood draining from my outstretched arm, I slowly pushed the pram back and forth. As long as this motion was maintained at an enthusiastic enough rate, Alfie would grudgingly lie there in silence and I could pretend to myself that he was going to sleep. But he was made of stronger stuff than I was. The rocking would become increasingly halfhearted; growing slower and weaker until the moment my exhausted arm finally flopped down by the side of the bed. This was his signal to resume crying and then, independently of the rest of my comatose body, my arm would take hold of the pram handle and start pushing it back and forth once again. This pattern was repeated over and over again; for the next hour we took turns to almost drift off. Then eventually I stopped. Silence. Could it be that at last he was finally going to let me doze off and let my weary, demoralized body finally have some rest? All I could think about was sleep.

Oh sleep, I just need to sleep, I would give anything just to have eight hours' solid, uninterrupted sleep. Not this violent bungee jumping in and out of half-consciousness, but real, deep, deep, proper sleep. That's the only drug I need: sleep. Tune in, turn on and drop off. If only I could find a dealer and score some snore; I'd pay good money for it, I wouldn't care if it was illegal or who it had been stolen from; I'd rob my mother's purse to pay for it, I've just got to get a fix of sleep; I'd snort it, smoke it, take a big tab of it, inject it—I'd share a needle if that was all the sleep I could get hold of, and then I'd mainline a massive dose of pure unrefined sleep and just lie back as the hit washed over me, feeling my brain go numb and my body relax, and then I'd just close my eyes and I'd be gone, zonked out, out of this world; there's no drug like it and I've just got to have some sleep or I'm going to die; maybe if I kill myself that'll feel like sleep; please, please, please, I've got to have some sleep; I'll steal the sleep from Catherine; yeah, she doesn't need it; that's it, I'll have her sleep; in the morning I'm going back over the river and I'll tell her I've got to work and I'll get into my room and turn my mobile off, I'll take off all my clothes and I'll fluff up the feather pillows and I'll pull the duvet over my head and I'll feel the heaviness of my limbs on the soft mattress and I'll just feel myself going, going, slipping away, and then I'll have such a massive shot, when I've had that fix I'll feel so great, like an athlete, like the heavyweight champion of the world, like I could run a marathon, but I'm falling asleep now and it feels so good; it's all I want; please let me sleep, baby, let me sleep; I need it now, I can't wait; I've got to sleep now and I'm going, I'm going . . .

Was I dreaming or did I hear a tiny moan from the pram? I held my breath lest even my breathing should disturb him. Sure enough, there followed another barely perceptible half moan and my heart sank. The pattern was always the same. The moans would be weak at first—intermittent, unimpressive attempts to stir, like somebody failing to start a car with a flat battery. But as I closed my eyes and tried to ignore them, eventually the moans would develop into bleats, and then a bleat would break into a coughed-out cry, and then the cries would become more punctuated and insistent, until the engine finally started and roared and revved as the baby screamed with a strength that belied its tiny size.

I lay there awake, listening to the angry crying, unable to summon the enthusiasm to pull my heavy frame upright again. Catherine would normally have leaped up long before now because she didn't want Millie to be woken up by the baby, but I was never particularly convinced of the likelihood of this. It was one of those fussy overprotective worries that Catherine was always coming up with. There was the creak of a floorboard in the doorway.

"Alfie waked me up," said Millie weepily, standing in the half-light, clutching a chewed blanket.

"Oh no." I sighed. I picked up the baby to stop the crying, prompting Millie to hold her arms out for me to lift her up as well, which I did. And then I just stood there in the lonely nadir of the nighttime, balancing two small crying children in my arms, my tired body nearly buckling under the weight, wondering what on earth to do next.

I thought about how there was only one thing worse than children that refused to sleep and that was the self-satisfied parents of babies who did. They believed it was down to them. Whenever Catherine and I were at our most exasperated we would be forced to listen to her stupid hippie sister Judith smugly explaining to us what we were doing wrong. I wanted to pick her up and scream at her, "It's because you were lucky, that's all. Because you happen to have had a baby that sleeps. It's not because you had a water birth or fed him organic baby-food, or *feng shui*-ed the fucking nursery. It's just the luck of the draw."

Catherine and I had tried everything with Millie and Alfie, and now I was reduced to empty threats. "Just wait till you're teenagers," I told them, "then I'll get my revenge. I'm going to pick you up from your friends' in a purple flowery shirt and I'll do the twist at the school disco and when you bring home your first dates, I'm going to produce those photos of you as babies wriggling in the nude on the carpet." But my threats meant nothing and now the stakes were raised. I hadn't wanted Catherine to be roused because she desperately needed to sleep. With both her children awake she was more likely to stir, and when she did and saw that I had allowed Alfie to disturb Millie, too, there would be an argument and I wouldn't hear the end of it until Catherine had her head in the toilet bowl the following morning. Millie being awake was a disaster on every front. Apart from anything else the process of feeding and changing a baby in the small hours of the morning was a precise and precarious operation. Generally speaking, having an irritable two-and-a-half-year-old at one's side was a hindrance rather than a help.

"I want to watch *Barney* video," said Millie.

We were not particularly severe parents, but one regulation that we did agree on was that Millie could not get us up in the middle of the night to watch children's videos. This was fine as an abstract regulation, but it didn't take into account the fact that Millie had the personality of Margaret Thatcher. She was not someone you could negotiate with, meet halfway, bribe or persuade. She would take up a position and you could see in her demonic eyes that she was completely persuaded by the total and absolute rightness of her cause, and at this moment nothing would shift her from her unwavering belief that she was going to watch the *Barney* video.

One of our child-rearing books had said that the clever thing to do is not to confront a toddler head-on, but to outwit her by changing the subject or distracting her with the unexpected. Imaginative distraction techniques are for when you are not feeling tired and irritable. I presume that this feeling comes back when the toddlers have grown up and gone to school.

"No! You're not watching the *Barney* video, Millie," I snapped. On hearing my firm refusal Millie threw herself to the ground with all the agony of a bereaved parent. She repeated her demand one hundred and forty-seven times while I proceeded to try and change Alfie's nappy, but I opted to ignore it. It was fine, I was in control, I was just going to ignore her and not let her get to me.

"FOR GOD'S SAKE *SHUT UP*, MILLIE!" I yelled. Deep down I knew that one way or another she would get to watch the *Barney* video before morning. I was still fighting to put a clean nappy on Alfie, but he wouldn't keep still. The lotion I'd been trying to smear on his red bottom had landed on the front of the nappy, where the sticky tape goes, so the nappy wouldn't hold together. I cast it aside and decided to start again, looking around to see where I had put the pack. It was now that Alfie chose to urinate. A great arc of wee shot up over his head, as if someone had suddenly turned on the garden sprinkler. I attempted to catch the last few drops with the old nappy, but it was a pointless exercise as he had already sprayed most of it in all directions and now his vest and Babygro were both soaked.

Millie was now emphasizing her repeated proposal that she watch the *Barney* video by hitting me on the arm every time she said it. I was unaware that in her other hand she was clutching a bright-red wooden building block, and at that moment her other arm swung round and she hit me full in the face with it. The sharp corner caught me just above the eye. The pain shot through me, and in a flash of temper I picked her up and threw her too roughly onto the bed and she banged the back of her head on the wooden headboard. Now she was really screaming. Frightened by the volume of his sister's cries, or maybe just out of a sense of sibling solidarity, Alfie started screaming at full pitch as well. Almost panicking, I tried covering his mouth with my hand to shut him up, but unsurprisingly this didn't make him more relaxed and he spluttered and wriggled his head and I backed off. And then I felt fear and shame that the boiling sense of anger and frustration within me could have been capable of covering the baby's mouth completely and holding it there until he was completely silent and still.

I left them both to scream and turned and punched my pillow as hard as I could, and then I punched it again and again, and I shouted, "WHY DON'T YOU FUCKING SHUT UP! WHY DON'T YOU JUST LET ME GO TO FUCKING SLEEP!" And I looked up and saw that Catherine was standing in the doorway surveying the scene.

She had that look on her face that suggested I wasn't coping very well. She picked up Millie and told her that she was taking her straight back to bed, and because of some special code that she must have used, Millie accepted this state of affairs.

"I was just going to do that," I said unconvincingly. "Why can't you just let me deal with things *my* way?" She didn't reply. "You're supposed to be getting some sleep," I shouted after her as a defiant afterthought, as if she had got up and wandered into a perfectly normal situation.

"Did Alfie's crying wake Millie up?" she asked me directly when she came back in.

"Yeah. I mean, I got straight up and everything, but he was just inconsolable."

"Oh great, she'll be really ratty tomorrow." She gave an irritated sigh, and then I noticed that she'd come in with a warmed bottle of milk for the baby. "Why hasn't Alfie had his bottle?"

"It wasn't time."

"It's three o'clock."

"Yes, it's time *now*, but it wasn't time when he started crying. You said not to feed him before it was time. I was only doing what you said."

Catherine picked up Alfie from where I had changed him and popped the plastic teat of the bottle into his mouth.

"*I'll* feed him," I protested. "I said I'd do it tonight. You go to bed and go to sleep." She handed me the baby and the bottle and, instead of returning to the sofa bed downstairs, climbed into our double bed, where she could spend her break from feeding Alfie in the middle of the night watching me feed Alfie in the middle of the night.

"Don't hold it right up like that or he won't take it," she heckled from the sidelines. Because of the tone in which she told me this information I felt compelled to ignore her and sure enough the baby wriggled and started to cry.

"What are you doing? Why do you deliberately do it wrong?"

"I wasn't doing it deliberately."

"Give him to me," and she got out of bed and took the baby and I sulkily climbed under the covers and sat there, angry and indignant, as she gave the bottle to Alfie. The baby sucked rhythmically and happily, comfortable and relaxed in his mother's arms, and when the sucking began to slow as Alfie fell into a stupefied sleep, Catherine would gently tap the soles of his feet to stir him. It was as if those tiny podgy feet had a little secret button that only Catherine knew about which made the head end start feeding properly. And even though I was lying there feeling injured and resentful, there was a little part of me that thought it was marvelous that she knew how to do that.

She eventually resumed her place in bed beside me and I decided against pressing the point that I could cope perfectly well on my own.

"I've only had an hour and a half's sleep," I moaned, in the hope of some sympathy.

"That's more than I've had recently," she parried.

Now the baby was fed, changed and warm. Now, surely he would sleep. We lay together, stiffly and silently, both knowing that the other was listening for the first grating moan to come from the pram. Like patients reclining on a dentist's chair, it was impossible to relax because we were waiting for that moment when the drill hits the tooth—the first fretful cry that told us that the baby's pitiful precipitation was beginning again. When it came I said nothing, but I felt Catherine flinch beside me. It was nobody's turn to get up and so, as the moans grew more regular and insistent, neither of us moved from our hopelessly optimistic sleeping positions, like a couple trying to sunbathe in the pouring rain.

"Let's just try leaving him," I said as the cry broke into full-blown wailing.

"I can't do that when you're working and I'm here on my own."

"Well, I'm here tonight, so this can be the night that he learns we won't always go running to him."

"I can't."

"Just till the clock says three fifty."

I said that at 3:42. I got up to close the door so that Millie would not be woken up again. Catherine said nothing, but lay there facing the glowing digital display on the radio alarm as the baby bawled its tightly wound, breathless cries.

After what seemed an age—3:43—Catherine angrily put the pillow over her head. I think it must have been intended to demonstrate something to me because I noticed her lift it slightly above her ear so that she could still listen to Alfie crying. I had thought the baby's volume needle was already on the red line, that his little lungs and tinny voice box could not produce any more power, but at 3:44 the screaming suddenly went into quadraphonic hypersound, doubling in power, anger and volume. If it had been a *son et lumière* this would have been the moment when the fireworks went off and the chorus stood up. How could he suddenly find such energy? Where did he get the stamina and strength of purpose from at that time of the night when we, his parents, with twenty times his weight and strength, had been ready to throw in the towel hours ago?

Now I understood why mothers used to worry that the big metal nappy pin must have come unclasped and was piercing the flesh of the baby's thigh, because that was the extreme level of pain Alfie was expressing. Even I was worried that he must have a safety pin sticking right through his skin, and we used disposable nappies.

The furious bawling continued throughout 3:45, still at full pitch, but there was a gear change that produced shorter, more erratic noises. They were taut, painful, bewildered cries that screamed, "Mother, Mother, why hast thou forsaken me?" And though her back was turned to me, I guessed that by now Catherine was probably crying, too. I had tried to make her leave the baby to cry in the first few months when she had still been breastfeeding. As the baby wailed, Catherine had sat up in bed with tears pouring down her cheeks and Pavlovian milk spraying out from her bosoms. At that point I had suggested she go and get the baby. I was worried that one way or another she might dehydrate completely.

If she was crying now I'd feel as if I had caused it. Now I was the torturer; I had brought this poor mother to a darkened room in the middle of the night and forced her to listen to her own baby screaming and writhing in apparent agony. Though the cries maddened and infuriated me, they didn't break my heart as I sensed they did hers. It was clear how much it hurt her to listen to it, but I couldn't feel what she was feeling. I was able to step back from it, to close off the side of my brain that was aware that our baby was unhappy, and now I was forcing Catherine to try and do the same. I was trying to make her be more like a man. Perhaps this was my subconscious revenge. In the daytime she made me feel that I should be more like a woman, that I should instinctively understand all the moods and needs of the baby in the way that she did. The daylight hours were definitely hers. But now, at night, it was my turn. I had made her read the bits of the books that agreed with me; I had shown her written proof of what I kept saying to her: that she shouldn't rush straight to the baby every time it cried, that she had to try and steel herself, to lash herself to the mast and endure her baby's sobbing while it learned to fall asleep on its own. But though she was prepared to entertain the abstract theory of this idea, it was something she could never implement in practice.

Here at last was an aspect of parenting that I was better at than her. Here was something that I could do and she could not. I suppose there's an irony that my particular area of expertise involved leaving the baby to cry in its pram, but I needed something to feel good about and this was it. I was better at lying there and doing nothing than she was. This reversal of power was a subtle one and might even have gone unnoticed if it hadn't been highlighted, so at 3:46 I gently and sympathetically asked her if she was coping all right.

"Yes," she snapped, irritated at being patronized.

"I know it's hard," I went on in my most consoling and understanding voice, "but soon you'll be glad I made you do it."

She said nothing, so I drove the point home. "Try and be strong; it's for baby's good as well in the long run."

Then a grossly unfair thing happened. She agreed with me. "I know," she said. "You're right; we've got to win this."

"What?" I said, in consternation.

"We can't go on like this every night; the baby making me an exhausted wreck. We have to take control."

This wasn't what I was expecting at all. I had thought she was about to leap out of bed and run to the baby and say, "I'm sorry, Michael, I'm just not as strong as you. I can't help it; I'm sorry."

I tried to cling on to my superior status as tough paternal supervisor. "I don't mind, if you really feel you have to go to him."

"No!" she said insistently. "We've got to be strong."

"You're very brave, Catherine, but I know you want to go and pick him up."

"No, I'm not going to. We're going to win this."

"Do you want me to pick him up for you?"

"Don't you dare! Leave him to cry."

And I just lay there listening to the baby wailing, and with my last scrap of pride and status taken from me, I felt like joining in.

Alfie did learn to send himself off to sleep, and we felt a sense of triumph and achievement, as if a milestone had been reached. An hour later it seemed that he had forgotten the lesson completely and needed to learn it all over again. We took turns to push the pram up and down the bedroom, we diagnosed colic and wind and every other ailment we'd read about on the tatty noticeboard at the health center. Then we suddenly panicked that he might be crying so much because he had meningitis, and I ran downstairs and got the torch. If the baby shows an aversion to bright light, that's a definite symptom of meningitis, and sure enough, to our utter dismay, this baby that had been lying in a darkened room all night recoiled from having a 200-watt torch shone in his face. Meningitis is a killer; it's infectious. What if Millie had it as well? We ran into her bedroom and shook her awake in order to shine my super-powered spotlight into her eyes. She recoiled as well. And drowsiness, that's another symptom. Both our children had meningitis! A disorientated Millie was placed in front of the telly while we quickly looked up the other symptoms in the book—headache, temperature, stiffness of the neck. Neither of them seemed to be suffering any of these. And then we realized that if Millie was happy to stare at the light coming out of a television screen then she couldn't have meningitis.

"Come on, Millie. Off to bed."

"But I'm watching Barney."

"You know you're not allowed to watch television at night-time."

Her bottom lip stuck out and she started to cry, and we couldn't help but be aware that there was perhaps a slight injustice to shaking a child awake at five o'clock in the morning and putting her in front of the television, only to tell her she wasn't allowed to watch television. So I spent the hour before dawn sitting up with Millie, watching a giant cuddly green and purple dinosaur being hugged by a lot of sickly American children.

Breakfast was tense. It didn't require Catherine's morning sickness to make it tense, but the sound of her throwing up didn't particularly lighten the mood. By this stage we were both so irritably irrational that I was convinced she was just affecting the vomiting to try and demonstrate that she felt worse than I did. These were the times when we needed some space apart, when I needed to go and hide out in my cave. Catherine's father had converted the shed at the bottom of the garden into a little office, which was his private refuge, where he could sit in quiet, peaceful meditation, planning the next massacre of the woodlice. But I had the whole of South London to myself. Having been born and brought up in North London, Catherine would be no more inclined to travel to the depths of Balham than she would consider trekking to Kazakhstan. She had a vague idea of where both of them probably were, but she could not begin to contemplate what sort of visas, maps and local guides you would need to get to such places.

It would have been better if I'd headed across the river there and then; Catherine would be a lot happier once I was out of the way. But there were a few practicalities that had to be sorted out first: I wanted to at least mix the babymilk, then I had to find my phone charger, gather a few things together in my holdall and then we had to have a full-blown marital row. It was approaching with all the depressing inevitability of a Cliff Richard Christmas single.

"Level it off with a knife," she said as I measured out the milk powder.

"What?"

"You're supposed to level the spoonfuls off with a knife, so you get exactly the right amount."

"Catherine, what is the worst that could happen if the babymilk is fractionally stronger or weaker? Will Alfie get food poisoning? Will he die of starvation?"

"You only have to follow the instructions," she said, prickling.

"You mean I only have to follow *your* instructions. Why can't you just trust me to measure out a few poxy spoons of babymilk without watching me like a bloody hawk?"

And then we were off. The fight was nobody's fault, it was just the unavoidable collision of an exhausted couple cooped up together in a poky little house, like battery hens locked up for too long in the same tiny cage. But before long all our anger and frustration was being clumsily knocked back and forth. I hurled obscenities at her and she threw a large paperback at me. It was a book called *The Caring Parent* and it flew straight past me and hit Millie on her leg. Millie looked rather bemused and carried on playing, but I made such a meal of my sympathy for her that she decided perhaps she ought to cry after all, and then I was able to give Catherine a hateful glare and say, "Look what you've done." Then, to emphasize who was the caring parent in this marriage, I comforted our distraught toddler by sitting her down to read her a Beatrix Potter book.

"You naughty kittens, you have lost your mittens," said Mrs. Tabitha Twitchet. Then the cuddly pussy cat apparently added, "You're always so fucking moody, aren't you? You're the only woman who ever managed to be pre-menstrual twenty-eight days a fucking month." Millie looked as if she didn't remember this bit from the book, but then looked reassured when I continued, "Just then, three puddle-ducks marched by . . ."

The argument followed its usual symphonic narrative, each movement building on the last. Catherine said that I never told her anything, that I never talked to her about my work or what I was up to. I told her that whatever I did with the children it was always wrong, that she would never permit me the dignity of just doing things my own way. I was shaking now. I couldn't look at her, so I angrily busied myself by washing up some plastic plates, focusing my pent-up anger on domestic work. I suddenly realized that Catherine had already washed them, but I carried on anyway, hoping she wouldn't notice.

"I've already washed those plates," she said.

Eventually she told me to fuck off back to work, and I made an unconvincing job of saying I'd been planning to hang around a bit longer to help her.

"What's the point?" she said as I put my jacket on. "I've got to go out anyway, walk to the shops, buy some more babymilk, take Millie to playgroup, blah, blah, blah. It's all so bloody *boring*," she said.

"But it doesn't have to be boring. I got you that Sony Walkman so that you can listen to Radio 4 when you take the kids to the swings, and you hardly ever use it."

"It doesn't work like that, Michael. You can't just provide instant answers to my problems like they're a bloody trivia question. I don't want you to try and stop me being bored. I just wish sometimes you could be bored *with* me."

This was such a strange concept to me that I was completely lost for words. She wanted me to be bored with her. The woman who had the greatest sense of fun of anyone I had ever met. The woman who had told a Dutch hitchhiker that I was completely deaf and then spent the next hour trying to make me laugh by telling him how useless I was in bed. I wanted that Catherine back; I wanted to rescue her from the body-snatchers and go back to the days when all we had wanted was to spend every second of the day together. Now we were like a couple of magnets, one side drew us together and the other side forced us apart. Alternately attracting and repelling, adoring and then resenting.

It was just as I went to leave that she hit me with another body blow. "Michael, I don't mind the fact that you're never here, but I do mind the fact that you don't *want* to be here."

How did she have the time to lie awake and think of lines like that?

Attack was my only possible form of defense. "That is *so* unfair," I snapped, raising my voice to give the impression that now she had really overstepped the mark. "You think I choose to be away from the kids this much? You think I don't rush home to see them as soon as I can? You think I don't go to bed feeling miserable at three in the morning because I'm not going to see them wake up? I can't see them as much as you do because I have to go out to work. I have to work all day and night to pay for a wife and two children and a mortgage we can barely afford. And when you want a dishwasher, the money is magically there, or new clothes or a holiday or a stupid bidet that cost four hundred pounds but is only used as a receptacle for storing plastic bath toys. The money is always there, and it's there because I work so hard for it."

I was genuinely fired up now, and Catherine seemed at a loss for words.

"It's not easy, you know, going to my studio exhausted, then working thirty-six hours at a stretch to get compositions ready by their deadlines, writing one piece while pitching for another, working nonstop on my own in a cramped studio on the other side of town, crashing out on a lonely bed so that I can get up and carry straight on with it. But I have to do it so that we can afford to have a decent standard of living, so that we can feed and clothe our children, so that we can afford to all keep on living in this house. I have to work this hard because it's the only way we can stay afloat."

I picked up my holdall and strode angrily toward the front door for a triumphant exit. Lying on the doormat was an envelope the shape and size of which I had come to recognize. I snatched it up and stuffed it in my bag. I didn't need to open it to know what it said. It was another warning letter from our bank. They wanted to know why the mortgage had not been paid for four months.

4

Because I'm Worth It

ONE WAY or another I was always going to be woken up by children. My radio alarm said 3:31 and for a moment I wasn't sure if it was morning or afternoon, but the noise of kids being picked up from over the road convinced me it must be P.M. Your kids would have to be pretty hyperactive for you to leave them at school till half-past three in the morning. Although I had once again broken my own record for sleeping in, I still felt like I needed another twelve hours. When you've been deprived of any proper shut-eye for days, a massive shot of sleep only makes you crave it all the more. All that rest had drained me, now I was tired and groggy, as if emerging from a general anesthetic. How Sleeping Beauty managed to sit up with such a twinkly smile after a hundred years was a mystery to me. I pulled the duvet over my head and tried to drift off again.

Hedgehogs; they had the right idea, I thought. When they felt the time was right to have a massive kip they just found themselves a huge pile of sticks and leaves and crawled inside. Obviously it was a shame that this generally happened to be around November 5, but the basic principle was a sound one. Why couldn't humans hibernate, I wondered. We could turn in at the end of October, sleep right through Christmas and the New Year, and finally get up, having set the radio alarm for some time in mid-March. If it was still raining we could press the snooze button and lie in for another couple of weeks, just getting up to catch the end of the football season. Right, I thought, I'm going to try and do that right now. Nope, no good, I was wide awake. I sat up and clicked on the kettle.

I remembered all that spare sleep I'd had when I was sixteen, seventeen, eighteen. I'd spent it so recklessly. If only I could have put it in a sleep bank, saved up for a sleep pension later in life. "Michael! Get out of bed," my mother used to shout up the stairs at me. We spend the first few years trying to get our children to stay in bed and then, before we know it, we're trying to get them out again. It's hard to think of a period when we actually get our sleep right. Small children wake up too early, teenagers don't wake up at all, new parents don't get any sleep because of the noise their children make, and then a few years later they can't get to sleep because now there's no noise of their children returning home at night. Then, when we get old, we start waking up as early as we did when we were toddlers, until finally we fall asleep forever. Sounds quite attractive sometimes, except they'll probably bury me next to some nursery school and I'll be woken from the dead by kids screaming and crying and jumping on top of me at all hours.

I made myself a cup of tea and switched on the television, flicking around, trying to find some commercials to watch. As always there were far too many programs between the adverts. First up was an inspired interpretation of George Gershwin's "Summertime"—a Paul Robeson soundalike sang, "Somerfield . . . and the shopping is easy. Lots of parking, and the prices ain't high." The next ad was for a shampoo, in which a French footballer told us why he used L'Oréal. "Because I'm worth it," he said. That's why I'm still in bed at half-past three in the afternoon, I thought, because I'm worth it. Because I can, and because there's no harm in it. Then there was an advert for a building society which said, "Remember your home is at risk if you do not keep up repayments" and I quickly switched channels. I'd pay off my overdue mortgage payments soon enough. It would mean a few months of working as hard as Catherine thought I did all the time, but I estimated that I could clear the backlog before the baby was born.

My thoughts had strayed back to our unborn baby as I watched an *Open University* program on BBC2. It was about some nutty institute in California where pregnant women went to have algebraic formulae and quotes from Shakespeare shouted down a tube pressed against their bumps. Apparently the fetus spends much of its time in the womb asleep, but they're even trying to stop that now. "It's never too early to start learning things," said the teacher. Like the fact that your parents are completely mad.

But that must be the soundest sleep of all, I thought, tucked up tight inside that dark, heated waterbed, with the muffled heartbeat hypnotically pattering away, before all the worries of the outside world start to churn over in your subconscious. Everything provided; no need to leave the comfort and security of your fleshy nest. Was that what this was all about? Was my secret refuge in deepest South London an attempt to return to the comforting simplicity I'd enjoyed in the nine months before I was born? I lay down again and curled my naked body into the fetal position, and realized that was how I naturally preferred to fall asleep. My dark, cozy little hideaway had everything my first sleeping place had had. Not literally, obviously; my mother's uterus hadn't had a large poster of the Ramones stuck up with Blu-tack, but practically and spiritually speaking, this little den was an artificial womb of my own. An umbilical cord of tangled electrical leads hung down beside the bed—the electric blanket that brought me warmth, the kettle lead that provided my fluids, the fridge cord for nutrition. The drumbeat from Jim's stereo pulsated rhythmically through the wall and the daylight that seeped through the red-patterned curtains gave a veiny pink effect to my window on the outside world. The only way to escape from the tyranny of babies had been to regress into a prenatal state myself.

I told myself I shouldn't feel guilty that I sometimes found my family so oppressive. I reassured myself that what I was doing was no worse than the behavior of the rest of the men of my generation. Some fathers stayed at work far longer than they really needed to. Some fathers worked all week and then played golf all weekend. Some fathers came home and went straight to their computers for the rest of the evening. These men were not there for their wives and families any more than I was, but at least I wasn't deceiving myself about it. The simple fact was that, for the time being, everyone was better off if I wasn't at home all the time. The problem was that the less I was there, the worse I was at it, and the less I seemed to want to be there.

In all the adverts that I'd arranged the music for, the families always had such fun; they always looked so comfortable with each other. Even though I worked in the industry I still hadn't seen through the lies. Obviously I knew that Lite 'n' lo wasn't really a delicious alternative to butter, but it hadn't occurred to me that they were also lying about the happy smiling kids and parents laughing round the breakfast table together. If that had been my childhood, then the mum would have picked up the butter knife and threatened to stab the dad with it.

The adverts told us we could have it all, we could be great dads and still go off snowboarding and earn lots of money and pop out of the business meeting to tell our children a bedtime story on the mobile phone. But it can't be done. Work, family and self; it's an impossible Rubik's cube. You can't be a hands-on, sensitive father and a tough, high-earning businessman and a pillar of your local community and a handy do-it-yourself

Mr. Fixit and a romantic, attentive husband—something has to give. In my case, everything.

But on top of all this, I had another reason for not wanting to spend hours and hours with my children just yet. It was something that no mother or father was brave enough to admit, a guilty secret that I suspected we all shared but dared not mention for fear of being thought bad parents:

Small children are boring.

We all pretend that we find every little nuance of our offspring wonderful and fascinating, but we're all lying to ourselves. Small children are boring; it's the tedium that dare not speak its name. I want to come out of the closet and stand on top of the tallest climbing frame in the country and proclaim to the world, "Small children are boring." All the other parents would look shocked and offended as they pushed their toddler up and down on the seesaw for the one hundredth time, but secretly they would feel a huge sense of relief that they weren't alone. And all the guilt they had felt because they secretly hated spending the entire mind-numbing day with their little two-year-olds would suddenly be lifted when they realized they weren't bad, unloving parents; there was nothing wrong with them, it was their children. Their children were boring.

Tolerating tedium is not something I'd ever had to do before. If I wasn't enjoying a holiday I would come home. If I was bored by a video I would fast-forward it a bit. I wished I could just point the remote control at the kids and fast-forward them a couple of years; I knew they would be more interesting by the time they got to four or five. Catherine was more patient than me; she didn't mind waiting a few years to see a return on all that time and love she was investing.

I wandered into the toilet and drowsily went to lift the seat, until I remembered that, in this household, it was always already up. I tried not to think about Catherine. This was supposed to be my time off. My urine had the sulfurous musty smell that reminded me I had eaten asparagus the night before. Catherine had cooked my dinner and she knew I loved asparagus. Even my wee reminded me of her.

I guessed that today, like most days, she would be seeing one of the mothers she had met through Millie's playgroup. Catherine had described all the various species of mums to me. There was the guilty career mother, who was so overenthusiastic on the one day she was able to come along to playgroup that she completely drowned out everyone else singing, "The wheels on the bus go round and round." There was the born-again stay-at-home mother who had previously been a very successful businesswoman, but had then thrown herself into motherhood with exactly the same competitive ambition. Instead of being promoted on a regular basis she just had another baby every year, which she felt allowed her to feel superior to all the women around her. There was the mother of Satan, who was totally unaware that she had given birth to the most evil being in the universe and blithely chatted away to you while her two-year-old kept smacking your child in the face and then casually remarked, "Aaaah. They seem to be getting on well together." Then there was the eco-mum, who talked quietly and gently to her child about why he shouldn't talk with his mouth full as the four-year-old sucked away at her breast.

Catherine had befriended all of them. I was constantly impressed by how women made friends with each other so easily. When I was in the playground I found myself engaging in an elaborate paternal dance in which I subtly tried to steer my kids away from the other children being supervised by their dads, lest the two of us should be forced into the embarrassment of actually attempting small talk. Even if communication became unavoidable, we would still not speak to each other directly, but would employ our children as a third party. So if Millie was deliberately blocking the slide, my way of apologizing to the other father would be to say loudly, "Come down the slide, Millie, and let this little girl have a go."

The other father would let me know that it was all right by replying, "Don't push the little girl, Ellie. Let her go down when she's ready." And no eye contact between the two adult males would ever have to be made. While somewhere over on the other side of the playground, his wife and mine were already discussing how soon they'd had sexual intercourse after giving birth.

Now I found myself socializing with all the new couples we had met through our children. Catherine and the mothers chatted and chatted, our children were the same age and played happily together and the other fathers and I would have nothing in common whatsoever. The previous Sunday I had found myself forced to talk to a man called Piers who relaxed at the weekend by wearing a blazer.

"So, Michael, how do you find the handling on the Astra?"

He'd noticed that Catherine and I had driven to their house in a Vauxhall Astra and evidently thought this would be a good opening subject for a conversation.

"The handling? Well, er, do you know, I've never really understood what that means. What is the handling, exactly? Because for years I thought it was something to do with what sort of handles you had on the doors, but it's not, is it?"

Piers looked at me as if I was mentally retarded and took another glug from his personalized beer tankard before he took the trouble to illuminate me. "How does it hold the road?"

So that was what it meant. What a completely bizarre concept. Piers was asking me how our family car "held the road." Gravity; that's how it held the road. That can't be the right answer, I thought to myself. So what was it that I had failed to notice about my car? It did everything I asked it to. When I turned the wheel to the left the car went to the left, when I turned the wheel to the right the car went to the right.

"Fine," I said. "Pretty good actually. Yeah, the handling on the old Astra's pretty good."

"What have you got, the SXi or the 1.4 LS or what?"

"Hmm?"

"The Astra. What model is it?"

I wanted to say, Look, I don't know or care what fucking model it is, all right? It's a car. It's got two baby seats in the back and lots of stains from spilt Ribena cartons on the upholstery, and there's a tape of Disney singalong songs permanently stuck in the cassette player.

"Er, well, I don't know that much about the technical side of cars really," I said pathetically, and Piers regarded me as if I'd just been introduced into Western society from a remote tribe in Papua New Guinea.

"Well, it's pretty straightforward—is it fuel injected or not? That's what the 'i' stands for: 'injection.' "

There was a pause. Every day I had opened the boot of the car, but I couldn't remember which letters I'd seen there. SXi sounded quite possible, but then so did LS. Which one was it? I had to say something.

"Millie, don't snatch!" I blurted out and ran to take a doll from Millie that Piers's daughter had just willingly handed her.

"But she gave it me," said Millie, looking confused.

"Really, Millie. Try and play nicely. Come on, let's ask little Hermione to show us all the toys in her bedroom." And I went upstairs with a couple of two-year-old girls, glancing back at the other dad with a mock long-suffering "kids, eh?" expression and then I hid in the child's bedroom for forty minutes rather than attempt to continue any conversations with the grown-ups downstairs.

"She's really nice, isn't she?" said Catherine as we drove

away three hours later. "I invited them to lunch at our place next weekend."

She heard my world-weary sigh and said, "That's what I like about you, Michael. For you there are no strangers, only friends you haven't taken a dislike to yet."

It was all right for her. The women were always nice; it was just their husbands who were made out of cardboard. She weaved the car in and out of the demonic traffic on Camden Road.

"How do you find the handling on the Astra?" I asked her.

"What?"

"This car, the Astra. How do you find the handling on it?"

"What are you talking about, you boring bastard?"

I felt reassured that I had definitely married the right woman.

I could never see any friendships developing out of the families Catherine met at Millie's playgroup, although I was slightly put out when I learned that Piers and several of the other dads had gone for a drink together one Sunday evening and I hadn't even been offered the chance not to be friends. I chose my mates in the same way as I chose what clothes to wear. In the morning, my jeans and sweatshirt were there on the chair by the bed, so I made do with those. And then, sitting in the chairs in the next room of my flat were Simon, Paul and Jim, and so I spent the rest of my day with them. It wasn't a question of what I liked or what suited me, it was just whatever was most convenient. Male friends seemed to just drift into my life, and then drift out again when the reason for seeing them had passed. I'd often worked with blokes I'd really liked and we had gone to the pub together or whatever. We had probably meant to keep in touch, but you can't just phone someone up two months later and say, "So, do you fancy just going for a drink?" They might say they couldn't make it that night and then you'd look stupid.

So at the moment my best friends were the other three men in this flat.

"All right?" I muttered as I wandered into the living room.

"All right," they all mumbled back.

It was great to catch up on all their news. I read an out-of-date tabloid for a while. There was a story about a married couple in France who were both over a hundred years old but were now getting a divorce. They were asked why they were separating after so long. Apparently they'd wanted to wait until all their kids had died.

Since it was the Easter holidays, neither Paul nor Simon had to go in to work and so all four of us were left hanging around the flat with nothing to do. It was fascinating to watch the other three wasting time as if they would have the luxury forever. They were so much better at doing nothing than I was; they didn't work so hard at being lazy. Jim was stretched out on the sofa and had apparently spent the last three hours trying to work out how his palm top could save him time. Paul was pointedly reading a grown-up newspaper, while Simon was sitting at the kitchen table doing nothing at all. He often did this. It was as if he was waiting for something. Waiting to lose his virginity, Jim said.

Simon had learned the secret of eternal adolescence. There were times when he was so awkward and self-conscious that he was unable to talk in normal phrases and sentences. He had developed a whole parallel mode of communication which was expressed purely in trivia questions. Today, instead of saying, "Hello there, Michael, I haven't seen you around for a few days," he gave a little excited smile and chirped up with, "Capital of New York state?"

"Albany," I dutifully replied, and he gave out a little satisfied grunt to suggest that all was well with the world.

"B-side 'Bohemian Rhapsody'?" he continued.

" 'I'm in Love with My Car.' You won't get me on a piece of music trivia. It happens to be my specialist subject."

"OK, so which line from 'Bohemian Rhapsody' was the title of a song that reached number one in the same year?"

I was thrown into a mild internal panic at hearing a music question I didn't know. "Get lost. You just made that up."

"No, it's a well-known fact," chipped in Jim.

I tried affecting indifference. "Oh, I don't know, er, 'Scaramouche, Scaramouche' by Will Doo and the Fandangos."

"No."

"That only got to number two," said Jim.

Inside, my mind was racing through the lyrics of "Bohemian Rhapsody," trying to find the title of another 1975 number one. There wasn't one, I was sure of it.

"Do you give up?"

"No, of course I don't give up." But I decided that instead of wasting any more time I would go into my room and do a bit of work. An hour later I came out and said, "I give up."

"The answer is, 'Mamma Mia!' " Simon informed me triumphantly.

I was stunned. It wasn't fair. I would have got it if I'd given myself a bit longer. "You said a line. That's not a line, that's just a phrase. It doesn't count."

"All hail, the trivia king," said Simon with his arms held aloft.

An outsider might be impressed by just how much Simon knew. He knew that the Battle of Malplaquet was in 1709 and that the Dodo had lived on the island of Mauritius. However, on the debit side, he did not know the answer to questions like, What are you going to do for a living? He did not know that his parents were rather worried about him or how on earth he was ever going to get a girlfriend. He did not even know that he was a bit smelly. Fortunately, the question, Is

Simon a bit smelly? had never come up in the science and nature category in Trivial Pursuit, although, if it had, he would have been far more distressed about getting a trivia question wrong than he would have been to learn that everyone thought he stank like a soggy PE kit that had been left in its bag all through the summer holidays.

Paul had remained aloof from the quiz, but when the final answer was revealed he just said, "That's right, yes," and nodded wisely. Perhaps he was unable to take part himself because all his energy was required to pull off the near impossible task of reading a newspaper in an annoying way. When he held up the paper it was not in order to read the articles, it was to declare, "Look at me, I'm reading a broadsheet." The silence would be punctuated with affirmative grunts when he wanted us to know that he agreed with the editorial, or slightly too audible tuts when he read some distressing news from the Third World. The cryptic crossword was completed with an almost constant running commentary of satisfied verbal ticks and world-weary sighs.

"Are you doing the crossword, Paul?"

"What? Oh, yeah. Nearly finished it actually," he replied gratefully, unaware that Jim was gently mocking him.

"Is that the easy or the hard one you're doing?"

"The cryptic crossword. I don't bother with the other one."

"Wow!" said Jim.

The late afternoon eventually turned into early evening and Paul started to become edgy and restless, as he usually did around this time.

"Has anyone given any thought to dinner?" said the person who always ended up cooking dinner. There was mild surprise that anyone should be thinking about food before it was actually time to eat. Jim looked at his watch.

"I'm not really hungry yet . . ."

"Well, no, but you have to buy the food and cook it *before* you are hungry so that it's ready at about the same time as you are."

Indifferent silence filled the room.

"Well?" said Paul finally, standing by an empty fridge.

"Well, what?" said Jim.

"What shall we have for dinner?"

"Erm, well, it's a bit early for me, thanks."

"I'm not offering to cook again. I am asking if anyone else has thought about cooking for once?"

The silence was too much for me and I was the first to crack. "All right, Paul, don't worry, I'll do the dinner. I'll go and get some fish and chips or something."

"That's not cooking the dinner, that's getting fish and chips. I don't want fish and chips."

"Indian?" I offered magnanimously, considering that the curry house was another fifty yards' walk.

"Why can't we have proper fresh food cooked freshly here in our kitchen?"

There was another silence while no one volunteered for such an enormous undertaking. Jim contemplated standing over a cooker for twenty minutes and then said exhaustedly, "I don't mind fish and chips, Michael."

"Me neither," echoed Simon.

"OK, fish and chips for three then," I confirmed.

"Well, if you're all going to have a takeaway, I'll just have to cook myself some pasta or something on my own."

There was a moment's pause in which I could sense Jim's mouth watering at the mention of one of Paul's amazing pasta dishes.

"Oh well, if you're cooking some pasta for yourself, Paul, could you do enough for me, too?"

Paul was trying to find the words to express why that didn't feel fair, but he wasn't given time.

"Yeah, I'll have some of that," said Simon.

"Oh cheers, Paul," I said.

Somehow, four men living in a flat together had evolved into a traditional nuclear family. I don't know how it happened, or whether this metamorphosis occurs in every group of people that live together for a while, but we had inadvertently turned ourselves into mum, dad and two kids.

I suppose I was the eldest son, vague, secretive and quiet, who couldn't get up in the mornings on the days when I hadn't stayed out all night. Simon was the youngest child, gauche and unconfident, constantly asking questions to seek attention. Paul was the martyred, long-suffering mum, fussing and worrying for everyone else. And Jim was dad, self-possessed, lazy, mysterious and funny. The confidence that had been purchased at public school gave him a benevolent paternal air which we all looked up to, although sometimes I felt a little uncomfortable having a father figure six years younger than myself.

When I was a child I didn't understand where my dad's money came from, it was just something he always seemed to have, and the same was true of Jim. The only money problem Jim had was spending it all. He bought mini-discs to replace all the CDs that had replaced all his vinyl records. He bought electrical gadgets and designer penknives and new mobile-phone covers. We presumed the money must come from his family, but we were all too polite and English to probe any further when he mumbled evasive answers to comments about his conspicuous wealth.

He had a first-class degree in Italian and Geography, although the only thing he appeared to remember was that Italy was shaped like a boot. He then decided that a Ph.D. might be useful, and he was quite right; it saved him any embarrassment when people asked him what he did. Jim was doing a Ph.D., and would be doing it until the day he died. Procrastination would have been his middle name if he could ever have been bothered to get that far. And he would constantly drive Paul mad with his failure to commit to any sort of plan or pre-arrangement. On a Saturday morning Paul might suggest, "Do you fancy going to the National Film Theatre or something today?"

And in his posh, laid-back way, Jim would shrug indifferently and say, "Well, let's just see what happens."

Paul would then go quiet for a while, anxious not to blow his jittery uptight cover, but when he tried to pitch the idea again, he couldn't help but show the annoyance in his voice.

"Well, nothing will happen unless we get up and do it. Going to the NFT won't just happen to us, we'd have to go down to the South Bank, buy the tickets, go in and sit down. So do you fancy going to the NFT?" asked Paul again, adding, "or something?" as an affected nonchalant afterthought.

"Well, let's just see how the day shakes down."

"The day can't shake down! The day is passive! The day is not going to turn up with a taxi and four tickets to see *The Maltese* fucking *Falcon*," Paul would finally scream. And then Jim would say, All right, keep your hair on, and we'd all tell him to cool it and chill out and we're just hanging out, all right, and he'd storm off and come back an hour later with all the household groceries, including pretzels, olives and fancy Czech lager, which he knew we all really liked.

It really wasn't fair that everyone liked Jim and nobody liked Paul. Paul was a teacher in a tough London school; overworked, underpaid and undervalued. Jim was an idle, privileged Trustafarian, living off inherited money and doing nothing with the huge head start that life had given him. But despite this, I still preferred Jim to Paul, because the rich layabout had a sense of humor and the impoverished public servant did not. Jim made me laugh, and shamefully this was enough to make me forgive him anything. If I had been born in fifteenth-century Wallachia, I probably would have defended Vlad the Impaler on the grounds that he was quite witty on occasion. "All right, I grant you, he does impale quite a lot of peasants, but you can't help liking the bloke. I mean, getting the carpenter who makes his sharpened stakes to do one extra spike 'as a surprise for someone' and then impaling him on it, OK, you could argue it was a bit mean, but hats off, it was a great gag."

Within the complex dynamics of the household was the added musical alliance between Jim and me. We had quite similar tastes in music, although he had this slightly irritating affectation that he liked jazz. I had no time for jazz. Music is a journey; jazz is getting lost. Jim's laziness hadn't prevented him from becoming a rather accomplished guitar player, and the two of us had combined to form our very own super-group, pooled from the enormous wealth of musical talent that was available to us within the four walls of the top flat, 140 Balham High Road, London SW12.

One day, Jim had said, a new rock pilgrimage would be added to the hallowed destinations of Graceland and the Cavern. Rocks fans will flock to this legendary address and stop in quiet contemplation, for it was here, in those early days, that two musicians struggled against the odds to create what became known the world over as "the sound of Balham."

It was, of course, many years since I had truly believed I was ever going to make it as a pop star. Two things are certain in the world of rock music. One is that image is more important than talent, and the other is that in the year 2525 they will re-release the single "In the Year 2525." I was now approaching my mid-thirties and my girth was expanding as fast as my hair was receding. It was hard to imagine anyone who looked less like Kylie Minogue. I knew the pop industry wouldn't be interested in a fat old dad like me, so Jim and I recorded songs together just for the fun of it. There was no sense in which we hoped our tracks would ever be released as singles; they were laid down for our own amusement, just for fun. Although, since I had some reasonable recording equipment, I thought we might as well post them off to the odd record company occasionally just for the hell of it. I mean, I knew they were never going to offer us a contract, but there was nothing to lose by sending them off for a laugh. In fact, only that morning a tape had been returned with a note that it wasn't the sort of thing that particular label was looking for at the moment, and that was fine, that was what we expected. Bastards.

Although my ambition had faded I still had a recurring daydream that I was sitting at my keyboard one day when I suddenly got a phone call from some top A & R man.

"Is that Michael Adams, *the* Michael Adams, composer of the Cheesey Dunkers jingle?" he says.

"Yes?"

"Well, I work for EMI, and I think that riff has all the makings of a number one hit. If we could just change the lyrics from that Chinaman saying, 'Very cheesey if you please-ee,' to a young girl singing, 'I want to feel your sex in my sex; right now, give me sex,' I think we've got an instant smash, no mistake."

I knew it looked like a long shot, but I wasn't able to completely give up hope, so I wrote the songs and Jim wrote the lyrics and we recorded them in my bedroom and the history of rock and roll remained unchanged. Particularly since the task of getting down to recording our definitive demo tape kept getting put back by more important things, like watching daytime television or changing the screen saver on Jim's laptop. I had managed to team up with someone who was even less motivated than I was. Jim wasn't driven, he was parked.

However, the night before we had agreed that today we would lay down our two new songs, so at the end of the day we finally set about doing a day's work. While Jim tuned his guitar,

I did my best to convert my room from a bedroom to a recording studio, picking up socks, turning on amplifiers, folding up the sofa bed, adjusting microphone stands.

"What are you called?" said Simon, hovering by my doorway, hoping he might be allowed to jump on board.

"We haven't really settled on a name yet," said Jim. "Have you got any ideas?"

Alarm bells went off in my head. Oh no, I thought, we're heading toward that debate again: the eternal what-shall-we-call-our-band? discussion. It's one of those perilous lobster-pot conversations that you must never, ever get into. For once you have ventured in there is no way out again; the fatal words "What shall we call our band?" when said in this order actually form an incredible magic spell that can make a whole afternoon disappear.

"Oh come on," I said, "let's get this demo recorded. Once we start talking about band names we'll never get any work done."

There was a general nodding and responsible acceptance of my suggestion, then Jim, who was just writing the label for the DAT, chipped in, "OK, but what shall I put on the label in the meantime?"

"Well, I still quite like the Extractors."

"The Extractors? No, it sounds too punky. Like the Vibrators or the Stranglers."

"Ah ah ah," I said, laughing. "No way. We're not getting into this again. Just put our surnames, for the time being. Adams and Oates."

"Sounds like Hall and Oates," said Paul, who had wandered in trying to pretend he wasn't fascinated by the process of laying down our first single.

"People will think, Oh, wow! Oates has split up with Hall and got a new partner, and then they'll realize that it's a different Oates and chuck the tape in the bin."

"All right, our first names then: Michael and Jimmy."

"Sounds like two of the Osmonds."

"Stop, stop. We're getting into that conversation again."

Everyone agreed and I switched on the gear and plugged in Jim's guitar. There was a brief silence while the equipment was firing up and, as an afterthought, I added, "Just put band untitled for the time being." The moment I said it I knew it was a mistake. I closed my eyes in weary anticipation.

"Band Untitled. I quite like that," said Jim. There was a murmur of agreement around the room and I tried to say nothing, but it was impossible.

"No. I meant put 'band untitled,' meaning our band doesn't have a name yet, not here's a demo from a new group called Band Untitled."

"Band Untitled. It's got a ring to it, hasn't it?"

"Yeah. It's catchy, isn't it."

I had to nip this in the bud. "I'm sorry, but there is no way that we are calling ourselves Band Untitled. It's the worst name I've ever heard."

Simon had a worse one.

"What about Plus Support?" he said.

There was a groan from Jim and me who, as experienced musos, knew that every band in the world had at one time or another thought that it would be incredibly wacky and original to call themselves Plus Support.

Simon's enthusiasm was undimmed. "Because, you see, whenever you see a poster for a gig, it already has your name on it. You could turn up and tell the organizers, We're Plus Support. See, our name's on the poster!"

"Yeah, and when you get famous the posters will say Plus Support plus support," said Paul, "and you'd have to play twice." He laughed.

Throughout all this Jim and I were shaking our heads like wise old sages.

"Yeah, but what if you develop any sort of fan base?" Jim butted in. "They see 'Plus Support' on the poster and go along to see you, only to find that not only have you apparently changed all your songs, but also every single member of the band has moved on. Either that or they see your name on the poster and presume it's not Plus Support, but some other band plus support. It's the worst possible name for a band in the history of rock music ever."

"Apart from Chicory Tip," I volunteered.

"Oh yeah. Apart from Chicory Tip."

I think it was then that I realized we were deep into the conversation of no return. I had been unable to prevent it. Like one of the good fairies in *Sleeping Beauty*, I had shouted and forewarned in vain as they walked trancelike toward the spindle.

"Band names are easy," said Jim, despite all the evidence. "Just read something out of the paper."

"Euro-commissioners renew demands for GATT inquiry."

"Hmm, catchy!"

"Just pick out a phrase."

"Nordic Biker Feud."

"I like it."

"Sounds like some God-awful heavy-metal outfit. Like Viking Blitzkrieg or Titan's Anvil."

"The Beatles," announced Simon cheerfully.

"What?" said the rest of the room in disbelief.

"You said just read something out of the paper. There's an article here about the Beatles."

"Why don't you call yourselves Aardvark, then you'll be the very first entry in the *NME Book of Rock*," suggested the English teacher.

"Or A1," said Simon, "just to be doubly sure."

"A1? People will keep ringing us to order a cab."

"What about the Acid Test?"

"Oh God, no," I said. "It reminds me of that crappy band the Truth Test who used to support us in Godalming. They've still got my bloody mike stand."

Then the conversation moved on to the next stage, as it always did—the quick-fire round when hundreds of names were put up and knocked down in record time.

"The Smell of Red."

"No."

"Elite Republican Guard."

"No."

"Bigger than Jesus."

"No."

"Charlie Don't Surf."

"No."

"Come Dancing."

"No."

"Buster Hymen and the Penetrations."

"No, Simon."

"Dead on Arrival."

"No."

"Who's Billy Shears?"

"No."

"Things Fall Apart."

"No."

"Caution: May Contain Nuts."

"No."

"Let Fish Swim."

"No."

"The Detritus Twins."

"No."

"Big Bird."

"No."

"The Man Whose Head Expanded."

"No."

"Little Fat Belgian Bastards."

"No."

"The Sound of Music."

"No."

"Semi-detached."

"No."

"Mind the Gap."

"No."

"The Rest."

"No."

"The Carpet Mites."

"No."

"Chain Gang."

"No."

"Ayatollah and the Shi'ites."

"No."

"The Snakepit Strollers."

"No."

"Twenty-four Minutes from Tulse Hill."

"No."

"Ow!"

"No."

"No, I mean, Ow! I just got a splinter off this chair."

After a while your brain becomes numb from continually searching for an original combination of two or three syllables, and through mental exhaustion you end up just mumbling incomprehensible noises. "The blub-blub-blah-blahs."

"What about something sort of royal?"

"They've all been done. There's been *Queen, King, Prince, Princess*; there's only the Duchess of Kent left. You can't name a cutting-edge rock band after some posh bird whose only claim to fame is getting free tickets to Wimbledon."

"I know," said Simon excitedly, unjustifiably getting our hopes up, "What about Hey!"

"Hey?"

"No, not Hey? Not Hey with a question mark. Hey! with an exclamation mark. You know, like Wham! Sort of attention grabbing."

Nobody ever actually took the trouble to reject this idea; it was too mediocre a suggestion to warrant a response. Instead it was simply ignored to death, and Simon looked rather hurt when he realized that everyone had just carried on suggesting other names without even bothering to acknowledge his. For another hour or so, endless suggestions were released like clay pigeons, and then blown to smithereens by one of us. We rejected, the Scuds, Go to Jail, Rocktober and unsurprisingly St. Joan and the Heavy Heavy Dandruff Conspiracy. Until, with a certain gravitas that comes from knowing you finally have the right answer, Jim said, "Lust for Life."

"Lust for Life," I repeated with impressed contemplation.

"It's an Iggy Pop track," said Paul.

"I know."

"And a film about Van Gogh."

"I know."

Paul pompously put up these objections only to be disappointed to learn they were not objections. We said it a few more times and agreed that Lust for Life it was. Two and a half hours it had taken us, but finally we could do some work. I switched on the mike and adopted the persona of the announcer at the Hollywood Bowl.

"Ladies and gentlemen, tonight playing the first gig of their sell-out U.S. tour; they're number one all over the world, all the way from Balham, England, it's Lust for Life."

Jim and Simon applauded and whistled, and then Simon held up his cigarette lighter. Paul struck a posture of unimpressed aloofness by just sitting there and reading *Time Out.*

"Anyone fancy going to a gig tomorrow night?" he said rather cryptically.

"Why, who's playing?"

"I was thinking of going to the Half Moon in Putney." He waved the advert under our noses. "There's a new band playing called Lust for Life."

There was a pause.

"Fucking bunch of plagiarists!" spat Jim. "They've nicked our fucking name!"

No music was recorded that night. At one point I did say, "Come on, guys, let's work," but that was rejected as sounding too much like Men at Work. The worst moment had been halfway through the debate when my mobile had rung and I'd answered it to find Catherine on the other end.

"What do you think of the name India?" she'd said.

"There's already a band called India," I'd replied, confused. And then I'd tried to repeat the sentence, emphasizing the word "band" as if to say, Well, there's already a *band* called India, but that's not to say you couldn't call a *baby* India. It didn't really matter because I knew the name suggestion was just an excuse to ring and make the first contact after our row.

She made me miss home. My flatmates had been so infuriating all day that now I wanted to go back to Catherine again. With Paul's stupid tantrums about the way Jim made tea or the way I didn't cook dinner, Simon's tedious questions and Jim's impossible procrastination and a whole evening spent discussing bloody band names again, they were driving me mad. And then a terrible realization struck me. It was something I hadn't foreseen when I'd run away from my family to get a bit of sanity: that the surrogate family I'd adopted were just as unbearable as any other. That every time I got to that far-off field I would look back at where I'd just come from and it would suddenly seem far greener than when I'd left it. That wherever I was in my life I would always want to be somewhere else. That I had gone to all this trouble, deceived the woman I loved and got myself into debt, only to find that the things which annoyed and oppressed me followed me around. It wasn't Catherine or the children that were the problem. It wasn't even Jim, Paul and Simon. It was me.

5

It's Good to Talk

I AM FIFTEEN YEARS OLD and standing outside a theater close to Piccadilly Circus. Sixty other fifth formers have just slunk off two coaches to see *Hamlet* by William Shakespeare. They look awkward and self-conscious in their jackets and ties. They have all given my English teacher a check from their parents, but they haven't had to pay full price because my mother works at the theater and can get us all discounted tickets. Well, that's what I'd imagined and had carelessly told my English teacher. Actually, my mother only had a part-time job at the theater, cleaning costumes, and couldn't get us a discount at all. And so no tickets were ever booked.

I'd wanted to be helpful. When he had said the name of the theater, I'd recognized it, put up my hand and told him about Mum, and he had said, half joking, "Well, maybe she could get us all discounted tickets, Michael." And I'd said I was sure she could, and it had just snowballed from there. I don't know why I didn't say anything in the weeks before. I didn't want to disappoint him, I suppose. I really liked Mr. Stannard, and he seemed to like me. I didn't tell him when he said, "Your mother has definitely booked these tickets, hasn't she?" That probably would have been a good time to tell him. I didn't tell him as he was giving out the letters about the school trip for everyone to take home to their parents. And when he was doing a list of who was and wasn't going to see *Hamlet*, I didn't tell him that actually none of us were. I didn't even tell him as everyone clambered onto the coaches.

The two coach drivers took turns to overtake each other on the dual carriageway and all the children cheered. All the kids except me. Only I knew that we were all completely wasting our time and that it was all my fault and that my dreadful secret would soon be exposed. But still I didn't say anything. When all sixty-four of us were standing in the foyer of the theater and Mr. Stannard was arguing with the lady in the ticket office and he turned to me and said, "Michael, you said your mother had definitely booked sixty-four tickets?" I did tell him then. I adopted the air of someone who had meant to give him a message but had allowed it to completely slip my mind. "Oh, that's right. Oh, I meant to say . . . um . . . she's not entitled to a discount so I didn't get her to book any."

My feigned indifference failed to persuade him that this was not a big deal. That night's performance was sold out, the theater manager explained and Mr. Stannard turned to me and completely lost control. They say that the fear of a moment is often worse than the moment itself. Not in this case; my fear was completely justified. I think even the other teachers were embarrassed at the way his face went bright red and his body shook and he spat as he shouted at me. I just stood there, unable to think of anything to say in my defense, shrugging my shoulders silently in response to every question he screamed at me. The veins were standing out on his forehead, and as he yelled two inches from my face, I could smell stale cigarettes. He was so angry with me that he got his words mixed up. As his fury reached a crescendo he shouted, "And now, now, the, the, the entire fifth form aren't going to miss *Hamlet.*"

"Yes they are, sir."

"What?"

"You said they *aren't* going to miss it."

"No, I said they aren't going to *see* it."

"No, you said they aren't going to *miss it*, sir."

I may have ruined the evening for sixty-four people, but I was definitely right on this point.

"Don't tell me what I did and didn't bloody say. I said *see it.*" His quivering purple face was still just a couple of inches from mine and a bit of his spit landed on my nose, but I thought it better just to leave it there.

One of the other teachers tried to calm him down. "Actually, you did say *miss it*, Dave."

And then Mr. Stannard turned to Mr. Morgan and started shouting at him instead, which all the other kids thought was quite exciting because we'd never seen teachers shouting at each other before.

The stupid thing was that the only reason I hadn't told him was because I hadn't wanted to upset him. As a long-term strategy this had never been very likely to succeed. Eventually we all went out and sat around under the statue of Eros for hours, waiting for the time when the coaches were due to pick us up again, and I sensed that Mr. Stannard didn't like me anymore and it started to rain.

"Well, if we all die of pneumonia we can thank Michael Adams," he'd said bitterly, which I thought was a bit unfair because it wasn't my fault it was raining.

"You stupid dingbat, Adams," said my classmates.

" 'Oh! that this too too solid flesh would melt, Thaw, and resolve itself into a dew,' " said Hamlet. I knew how he felt.

"Michael, you have a tendency to put off problems until they are no longer problems but have developed into full-scale disasters," my headteacher announced the following morning as I stood before his desk. And this was pretty much the gist of what my bank manager said to me sixteen years later when

we spoke on the phone about my outstanding mortgage payments. He made a date for me to come and see him and sort it
all out, and to prove that his analysis of my character was entirely correct, I failed to turn up for the appointment.

I sat down in my bachelor pad and worked out how much
I needed to pay to get up to date with the mortgage on my
family home. I wrote out how much I owed on all my credit
cards and various hire-purchase agreements. In a column next
to these I wrote out how much money I had coming in over the
next couple of months. I tried bumping the second figure up
a little bit by including some unspent record vouchers I'd had
since Christmas, but it didn't look any less depressing. I stared
long and hard at the two amounts, trying to think of the most
sensible and realistic course of action open to me. And then I
went out and bought a lottery ticket.

The day when I was going to have to start working like a
slave was fast approaching. In the meantime, I resolved to
make some economies. I'd try to put less toothpaste on my
brush and I'd start buying peanuts instead of cashew nuts.
There had been another household expense in my South
London flat that had been niggling me for some time, but I
hadn't been quite sure of the most tactful way to raise it. The
cost of our telephone was split four ways, but closer examina-
tion of the bill revealed that well over half the calls were made
by Sordid Simon calling up his favorite obscene sites on the
Internet. I was subsidizing his ritual self-abuse. It's awkward
enough when you feel someone should pay a little bit more
toward the bill in a restaurant, but telling a flatmate they owe
you a lot of money because they spend half their spare time
having sex with their right hand, well it's not the sort of thing
that's covered by the *Debrett's* book of social etiquette. But the
evidence was there in black and white, the itemized bill showed
the same number over and over again, and for how long Simon
had been connected to it. On February 9, for example, he had

called it at 10:52 A.M. and it would appear that he had masturbated for seven minutes and twenty-four seconds. That had cost us all thirty-five pence, not including VAT. Later on that day he had called it for twelve minutes and twenty-three seconds, but then I suppose you'd expect it to take a little longer second time around. There were pages and pages of calls, listing the dates, times and duration of his time spent surfing the Net. Actually, surfing is too glamorous a word for what Simon did on the Internet. He *lurked* on it, he *prowled* it, he *hung around in the bushes* of the Internet.

I raised this problem with the others and we agreed we would have to confront him about it. We were keen to get the conversation over with as quickly as possible, hoping we could discuss the financial principle without getting into the nitty-gritty of what he was actually watching. We should have known better. Despite what we might have imagined to be embarrassing circumstances, Simon seemed to be delighted to be the center of attention and positively welcomed the chance to hold forth on the one subject in which he was a real expert.

"It's really very good value," he explained brightly. "For the price of a local telephone call you can see people having sex with gorillas."

"Ah, the wonders of modern technology," said Jim.

"Or any of the primates for that matter, except orangutans. But they're quite rare, aren't they?"

Simon was completely oblivious to our discomfort and enthusiastically chatted on and on about the fascinating world of hard-core pornography.

"You're a seedy little runt, Simon," I told him and he seemed quite pleased, as if he had presumed that my opinion of him was far lower. I wasn't so much annoyed by the fact that Simon was obsessed with pornography as I was by the fact that he didn't feel the need to be the slightest bit secretive or embarrassed about it. All men are preoccupied with sex, but at least the rest of us make some attempt to hide it. He chatted about his fixation as if it were a charming little hobby, like amateur dramatics or painting watercolors. "It's good to talk," said the advert for British Telecom. Or whatever else you did to run up a phone bill.

In the hope that we might share his enthusiasm if only we saw what we had been missing, he showed us some of the pornographic sites he visited. They featured three or four awkwardly contorted people who looked like they were playing Twister in the nude. "Left hand on red dot; right foot on yellow dot; left breast on black penis." Except that I remember playing Twister had always been great fun, whereas these people's faces suggested they were in a great deal of pain. I found these photos simultaneously revolting and compelling. Like car crashes and anchovies, you knew they were horrible but you couldn't help double-checking just to make sure they were as sickening as they'd seemed the first time. But my first impressions were generally correct. Most of the images were about as erotic as color photos of open heart surgery. There was a sequence of photos that told the story of a dinner party turning into an orgy. The transition seemed quite effortless.

"There it is again, you see," said Simon.

"What?"

"One thing leading to another. Look, picture one, they're being introduced. Picture two, they're chatting a bit. Picture three, she's got his cock in her mouth. I mean, what happened between pictures two and three—that's what I need to know. How does one thing lead to another? If that was me, it would be picture one, 'Hello, hello.' Picture two, 'Chat, chat.' Picture three, she'd be slapping me around the face and leaving."

He called up another Internet site that was stored under "Favorites" and giggled slightly as the next photo slowly downloaded. The computer gradually revealed the picture from the top downward, as if it were playing with us, toying with the idea of showing it all, but then holding back and teasing us by disclosing a little more. The woman revealed was undeniably attractive. She had a pretty face, perfectly formed breasts, well-rounded hips and long, smooth legs. The only thing that spoiled it for me—and maybe this is just me being fussy—was that she had a large erect penis. I know that, as a man, we often unreasonably expect women's bodies to fit into some preconceived stereotype, but I think the absence of a penis and testicles is one prerequisite I would probably have to insist upon.

Amid the exaggerated groans, I told Simon that his relationship with this computer wasn't healthy, that it was all one-way sex, with no love or foreplay, and we all agreed that in future he should at least take the computer out to dinner or something before they got down to it.

Eventually a new house rule was proposed: Simon should only be allowed to masturbate in front of his computer during off-peak hours and at weekends. He protested, pointing out that the calls were discounted. Apparently, when he registered with BT Friends and Family, it turned out that his best friend was his Internet server, which seemed tragically appropriate. It wasn't as if this best friend ever called him. But the rule was passed and now we could leave Simon alone again.

"All agreed," said Jim, "but could I just see that picture of those blonde twins mud wrestling again . . ."

The reason we held Simon in such low esteem is that he naively presented us with so much to find distasteful about him. He didn't keep his dark side to himself. He told people things. It was both a failing and a virtue; he may have been a worm, but he was an honest and unpretentious worm. I felt confident that he wasn't a secret cannibalistic serial killer, because if he had been, he would cheerfully have informed us all about the practical details of cooking human flesh. He was that rare thing, a person with no secrets.

I had lived my life with an instinctive secrecy that had even made me pause before saying, "Here," when the teacher called the register. Jim, Paul and Simon had no idea that when I wasn't with them I was a husband and father. That was just the way I preferred things to be. Soon after I'd started renting my room, the other tenants had moved on, and there didn't seem any need to illuminate my new flatmates about my unconventional domestic arrangements. I didn't generally lie. I just deceived by omission. Catherine once joked that the reason I never talked about what I'd been doing was to avoid lying about it. How I'd laughed. Obviously, I was compelled to launch an extended defense of my masculine silences. I mumbled, "Is not."

My reticence was in her interest as well as mine. I learned early on that if the mother of your children has had a boring day, it isn't particularly tactful to tell them every detail of what a fun and interesting time you've been having. They much prefer it if you've been bored, too. So on the days that I came home to a scene of exhausted ennui, I would do my best to at least play down any enjoyment I'd had while I was out. That Friday I returned to find Millie watching a video while Catherine was on her knees cleaning out the oven, trying to rock Alfie in the baby seat with her foot at the same time.

"How was your day?" she asked.

"Oh, you know, pretty boring."

"Did you have lunch?"

"Well, I grabbed something."

"Where?"

"Where? Erm, well I popped into this sort of awards lunch thing."

"An awards lunch?! Oh, that sounds fun."

"Well, it was no big deal. You know advertising; there's an awards lunch somewhere most days. Really tiresome, actually."

"So did you go back to your studio to do some work?"

"Erm, no. I wouldn't have got much work done: I'd had too much champagne. Well, I don't know if it was real champagne; it tasted a bit cheap actually, so I kind of stayed there all afternoon."

"Oh, that's nice for you."

"Well, I was obliged really. You know, contacts, networking, all that boring stuff."

She put her head in the oven again and I double-checked that she was cleaning it, not committing suicide.

"You weren't up for an award were you?" said the echoey voice from inside.

"Er, sort of."

"Sort of?"

"Erm, well, yes, I was. Best original backing music—for that bank ad I did last autumn?"

"Blimey. You kept that quiet."

"Well you've got enough on your plate without me boring you about my work," I said unconvincingly. She paused while she scraped off the last of the crusty grease and I hoped the cross-examination would end there.

"So you didn't win, then?"

"Erm. Well, yes, I did win, actually. Yeah."

I heard her head bump against the inside of the oven. And then she came out and looked at me in disbelief. "You went to an awards lunch and won an award?"

"Yeah. A big silver statue thing. I went up onstage to collect it and everyone applauded and it was presented to me by John Peel and he shook my hand and afterward we chatted for ages."

"John Peel? I hope you didn't ask him if he remembered your flexi-disc?"

"Catherine, John Peel used to get thousands and thousands of tapes and records every year, I'm not going to expect him to remember one flexi-disc that he didn't play in the late Eighties, am I?"

"So he didn't remember it, then?"

"No, he didn't. No. But he's even nicer than he sounds on the radio and everyone kept coming up and saying congratulations and looking at my award and taking photos."

And then I realized I'd rather blown my martyred cover, and so I belatedly attempted to claw it back.

"But you know, apart from that it was really tiresome. It's all so phony. And the award weighed a ton. It was awful walking the length of Park Lane carrying this three-ton award and trying to get a cab."

"Sounds like hell," she said, looking up from where she was crouching on the floor. Her face was marked with burned fat from the inside of the oven, which had covered her clothes and clogged up her hair. Alfie started to cry gently in the background because Catherine's foot had stopped rocking the seat.

"Erm, I was maybe thinking I might have a bath," I ventured. "But, er, I suppose I could look after the kids for a bit if you wanted to use the bathroom before me."

"Well, I wouldn't want to put you out. Since you've had such an awful day," she said pointedly.

As far as I was concerned, telling people things only ever caused problems. It is always presumed that complete and total honesty is the only way to have a happy relationship, but nothing is further from the truth. When a couple have just made love, the last thing they should do is be open and honest with each other. The woman says, "Mmm, that was lovely." Not, "Oh, that was quicker than I would have liked." And he says,

"Hmmm, it was really nice." Not, "Interestingly, I have discovered that I can heighten my climax by pretending I'm making love to your best friend."

All couples deceive each other to some degree, so what I was doing wasn't particularly unusual. Every father has heard the cry of the baby in the night and then pretended to be asleep as his wife gets out of bed to deal with it. I was more secretive than some men, but far more loyal to my wife than many others. Anyway, I thought to myself, Catherine tells lies. When the Conservatives came looking to canvass me at the general election, she told them that *she* was Michael Adams. She put on this croaky deep voice and asked if you were still allowed to join the Tory Party if you'd had a sex change. The joke rather backfired when the candidate suddenly became very interested in her and we had to hide upstairs every time he came back and rang on the doorbell.

And, of course, she deceived everyone about her pregnancy. She didn't want to tell people for the first three months, so she coerced me into maintaining a front of unfertilized normality. What was so disconcerting about this was that, although I was the practiced liar, when the time came for us to jointly hoodwink everyone else, I realized that she was much better at it than I was. We spent a rare evening out at Catherine's new-age sister's house, listening to Judith's theory that the world was going to end because everyone was leaving on their solar-powered calculators and using up the sun. Judith was a textbook modern hippie. The only time we had been offered meat at her house was years earlier, when we had gone round for a ceremonial meal to celebrate the birth of her child and she had uttered the unforgettable words, "Red or white wine with placenta?"

"Erm, just a little couscous for me, thank you," Catherine had replied. "I had placenta for lunch."

Now that she was pregnant Catherine wasn't drinking wine, and on this occasion I expected her to refuse, but she was way ahead of me. To say no would have been to draw attention to herself and raise suspicion, so she accepted wine along with everyone else and nobody noticed that she never actually drank any. Once I'd recognized her plan, I thought I would do my bit to help and gallantly stepped in to surreptitiously drink her wine for her. All four glasses. It's the sort of self-sacrifice all fathers-to-be should be prepared to make. Our host kept topping up our glasses and I kept emptying both of them. I gave Catherine a sly wink and a conspiratorial smile to acknowledge that I knew what she was up to and that I was discreetly helping her keep up appearances. And then I fell off my chair.

When the time came for us to leave and I was trying to put my arm down the wrong sleeve of my jacket, our host was adamant that we had both drunk too much to drive home.

"Really, I'm fine to drive. I've hardly drunk a thing," maintained Catherine, still anxious not to reveal her secret.

"No, I insist. Michael can pick up the car in the morning. I've ordered you a minicab."

"Yeah. I'll pick up the car in the morning," I slurred. "We can't have you doing it, Catherine, not with you being pregnant."

She was in quite a bad mood when we got home, but then pregnancy can do all sorts of things to a woman's temperament. I suppose the difference between Catherine and me was that she only lied up to a point; she knew when to come clean. If it had been me, I would still have been denying I was pregnant when I was lying in the delivery room with my legs up in stirrups. Apart from her sister and brother-in-law, who had managed to guess after I had let slip that one little clue, Catherine told people that she was pregnant exactly when she had planned to—at the end of the third month. Everyone said congratulations with slightly less excitement and amazement than they had expressed about our second child, which was slightly less than for our first.

"We wanted to have them all quite close together," she said, using the royal "we," and I glanced around wondering who else she could be referring to.

"Aaaahhhh," said all our friends and relations, who patted her tummy as if it were suddenly public property. From now on the little embryo would have to get used to people constantly banging on the walls. I felt quite protective of the miniature baby in there. At twelve weeks the fetus is already the approximate shape of a person. All the major organs are formed. There is a heartbeat, there are lungs that will breathe air, there is a stomach that will digest food, there is a spleen that will, well, do whatever a spleen does . . . get ruptured in accidents.

The embryo has also formed a backbone. I'm glad one of us had. Catherine was still very tired and tearful, so the last thing she wanted was for me to tell her that we were experiencing some temporary financial problems. While she told everyone the happy news, I kept the bad news to myself. To avoid my pregnant wife worrying about threatening letters arriving on the doormat, I decided it was time to act and I finally posted an envelope to the bank. It didn't contain a check for all the money I owed them, but it did request that from now on all correspondence should be sent to my South London address, so that was that problem dealt with.

The only person I still hadn't told about the new baby was my father. Dad had retired to live on his own in Bournemouth and I didn't get round to seeing him that often. He had a very carefully worded answerphone message, which was scripted to give as little away as possible. When I listened to it, I could almost see him carefully reading it off a piece of paper. He said, "The person who you are calling is unable to come to the phone at the moment, although he may well be in." And he imagined that any burglars calling were going, "Drat, drat. If only he'd said he was out, then I would have gone round and done the place over." He had still not seen our little house in Kentish Town, which made me feel guilty every time I thought about it, but he was worried about coming up to London in case there was another poll-tax riot. After he got e-mail we communicated more regularly, because he kept ringing me up to ask why he couldn't get his e-mail to work.

"What about the Net, Michael? Do you do the Net?"

"You don't 'do the Net,' Dad. It's not some new dance craze, like the twist or the locomotion."

"Well, I can't seem to do the Net, either. I think there must be something jammed in my computer."

I could have shared the news of his new grandchild over the phone, but I felt I wanted to tell him to his face. Catherine said that by the time I finally got round to this, the baby would probably have been born, grown up and gone off to university, so I rang him back and suggested that we came down and cooked him lunch, and then afterward I could give him a computer lesson. He was delighted by the idea. "Ooh, that would be lovely, Michael. Now before you come down, is Microsoft something I ought to buy?"

Dad had spent his life making a respectable living as a drugs dealer. He wasn't the sort that had two rottweilers, lots of gold rings and sold crack behind nightclubs in Manchester; Dad never made as much money as those guys because he dealt in the wrong sort of drugs. He sold Beechams Hot Lemon drink and Settlers Tums. I'd tried to imagine him driving round the country and opening up his briefcase for one of his best customers. The pharmacist ripping open one sachet of Alka-Seltzer and dabbing a little on his tongue. "That's good shit, man. But don't you never try cuttin' in any low-grade Enos, man, or I'll see they have to fish your body outta the East River with no head. You dig?" Dad had been the type of drugs dealer who had a company car and a pension plan.

His job had involved a lot of nights away from home, particularly after he met a dark-haired chemist called Janet from Royal Leamington Spa. He went to extraordinary lengths to persuade her to buy his range of products, even leaving his wife and only child for her. So then it was just Mum and five-year-old me. I grew up in the Home Counties in a semi-detached house with a semi-detached dad. After my parents were legally divorced I had to spend my lonely weekends staying at his funny-smelling bungalow. Just as he himself had been an evacuee in the war, so I was shipped off to a strange town, clutching my suitcase and a few hastily gathered toys, a refugee from the war of my parents' partition.

There was nothing for me to do in his grown-up house miles from all my friends, so I played the piano. All day Saturday and all day Sunday for years and years I practiced the piano. There was only one collection of sheet music under the dusty stool, *Traditional Hymns for Pianoforte,* and I played them all over and over again. At first I just tried to pick out the tunes, but over time I became fluent and confident, until finally I imagined that I was Elton John, wearing four-inch platform glitter boots, strutting out at the Hollywood Bowl and launching into my first number one smash hit "Nearer My God to Thee."

"Thank you, ladies and gentlemen. And now a song that's been very good to me; everybody get on down to 'When I Survey the Wondrous Cross.' " And I'd boogie-woogie my way through all four verses, adlibbing the occasional "Yow!" or "Oooh, baby!" after the bit that went "Did e'er such love and sorrow meet, or thorns compose so rich a crown?" Then I took the tempo down a little with "We Plough the Fields and Scatter." I imagined they were holding up their cigarette lighters by now and swaying gently as far back as I could see. Suddenly fireworks exploded all over the stage and I launched into a sequence of my early hits—favorite rock 'n' roll classics like "Onward Christian Soldiers," "Jesu—Lover of My Soul" and the title track from my latest album "I Know that My Redeemer Liveth." That was my encore and I played it standing up and spun around several times as I played the closing bars.

So I could say that, without my parents' divorce, I would probably never have learned to play the piano, studied music at college and gone on to the dizzy heights of having my flexi-disc played three times on Thames Valley FM. Now that I was what Dad called a "pop-music composer" he was very proud of me, and he sometimes rang up to tell me he'd just seen an advert for which I had written the music being broadcast on the television.

"Yes, well, the agency have bought a hundred spots, Dad, twenty of them in peak time."

"Well, they must be pleased with your music, then, if they keep showing it over and over again."

As I carried the kids from the car to his house for Sunday lunch, he came down the path to greet us. It was only ten yards, but he put on his hat for the journey. He had a very good reason for wearing a hat, although he didn't quite feel able to keep it on once he was inside. In the brief couple of years before my dad had split up with Janet the chemist, she had managed to persuade him that he ought to have a hair transplant. Even though his hair hadn't receded very far, he subjected himself to a painstaking and expensive operation in which small clumps of hair were uprooted from the more fertile hair-producing regions and then replanted at the top of his exposed forehead. For a while it seemed the surgeon had pulled off an amazing optical illusion and my father's fringe had returned. But then, behind the fortifications, the original hair continued to recede at the same inexorable rate. Though the tiny tufts of doll's hair heroically stood their ground, all around them the indigenous follicles deserted, leaving the transplanted outpost completely isolated.

Maybe this is what prompted Janet to leave him. His head was by now a classic example of male pattern baldness, a shiny smooth pate stretching from his forehead to his crown, with a straight line of transplanted hair clinging on like clumps of marram grass along the top of a sand dune. It was never ever mentioned.

He hung up his hat and I tried not to let my eyes wander above his. The moment I was in the front door Dad locked on and engaged me. The less I saw him the more anecdotes he stored up to recount, and nothing could deflect him from immediately delivering this month's main items of news.

Top stories on the hour today: Dad's friend Brian has bought a new car in Belgium and made a considerable saving. The queuing system at the bank has been changed and now you have to take a blessed ticket with a number on. And finally, no more printed headed paper, decides Dad, until they sort out the blessed telephone codes once and for all. But first, back to that top story of Brian's new car . . .

Information was fired at me nonstop, oblivious to any preoccupation I might have with childcare or preparing the lunch. I had dropped Catherine off at the supermarket to get some bread and vegetables, so I was left looking after the children on my own as I searched through his cupboards and found some gravy powder. Actually, "powder" is a generous description of what remained when I tore the wrapping away. It was a dark-brown gravy brick which had fossilized sometime around the Cretaceous period. Being a war baby, Dad didn't like to waste anything. Stale bread made perfectly good stale toast. The oil from a tin of tuna was saved in a little egg cup and could be used to fry anything that you wanted to taste of tuna. A few years back, when he'd had a new plastic hip-joint fitted, he'd remarked that he didn't like to ask what they'd done with the old hip bone. I could tell he felt it was a bit of a waste just to throw it away. I could have made a nice stock with that, he'd been thinking.

I tried to put on the roast, listen to Dad and deal with the children, but the combination was too demanding for any mortal.

"Brian was going to get the two-liter Mondeo, but opted for the 1.6, what with all the tax they're putting on petrol."

Millie dropped her beaker, and because I hadn't put the lid on properly, milk started to glug across the kitchen floor. What did Dad say to this? "Don't worry, I'll get a cloth," or, "Let me hold Alfie while you wipe that up?" No. He said, "The 1.6 still has ABS and power steering, but by buying it from a dealership in Belgium he saved three thousand pounds. How about that!" I didn't know Brian, or how much Mondeos normally cost, but I tried my best to look impressed as I searched in vain for the kitchen towels.

"Well, I told him that I'd been thinking of getting a Ford Focus, but I'm not sure if I want to go all the way to Belgium, especially after the way they caved in during the war."

His cat had started to drink the milk as it formed a puddle on the lino, and Millie was trying to pull the cat away by tugging its tail, which made the cat liable to spin round at any second and scratch Millie's face.

"Millie, don't pull the cat's tail."

"She drink my milk."

". . . but Brian said that you can get people to bring them over from Belgium for you, as far as Harwich anyway, but I said I can't pay out any money without seeing the car first; they might bring me a left-hand drive or something and then where does that leave me . . ."

"Hang on a minute, Dad, I'll just clear this up. Stop it, Millie."

But like the creature in *Alien* that locked its tentacles around John Hurt's face, he demanded my full attention and was not going to let go. I tried to nod, as if I was listening, but the potatoes boiled over and the water extinguished the gas ring and then Alfie crawled into the puddle of milk and got his trousers wet and started to cry.

"But they're not just in Belgium, Brian said you can get some very good deals in the Netherlands. I mean, what do you think, Michael? Do you think it would be safe to buy a new car from the continent?"

"It's all right, Alfie. Um, I don't know, Dad. Stop it, Millie."

The cat finally lashed out at Millie and drew blood from her arm, making her scream in panic which, to his credit, Dad did actually manage to acknowledge.

"Oh dear, the cat's scratched her arm. That'll need a plaster. But Brian says they're all right-hand drive, with airbag, ABS, central locking and everything as standard. And you should see his, it's very nice, with a proper British number plate and everything."

Millie could have been sawing her little brother's limbs off with the bread knife but still my dad wouldn't have considered this a valid reason to let up for a second.

"There, there, Millie. Yes, Mummy'll be here in a minute. Don't cry, Alfie, it's only milk. No, I have to wash it, Millie, and then we can put on a *Little Mermaid* plaster . . . Nought percent finance for three years. Really, Dad?"

My sixty-six-year-old dad was really just another infant in need of attention. He even looked like a baby, with his big bald head and food stains down his front. When you are in your thirties, they both want your attention just as much—your new children and your old parents. They are like selfish siblings competing for your love. "Daddy! Daddy! Daddy!" went Millie, but I couldn't deal with her because I was still trying to listen to *my* daddy. My only chance of peace was to time everyone's lunch so carefully that Dad had his afternoon sleep at the same hour as the other children. Maybe I should rig up a musical mobile above the sofa to make sure he went off all right.

Catherine and I eventually told him that he was to be a grandfather again and he seemed genuinely delighted and rang his new lady friend, Jocelyn, to tell her, although knowing Dad he would have a different lady friend by the time the baby was born. After lunch he did us a favor by sleeping for an hour and a half. He left a small patch of damp saliva on the cushion beside his mouth. "That's where you get that habit from," said Catherine and I was mortified. I always took delight in observing aspects of myself in my children, but I was horrified by the prospect of slowly turning into my dad. My only comfort was that I wasn't the kind of man to have a casual affair and recklessly throw away a marriage in the way Dad had done.

As we drove back to London I wondered why it was that so many men seemed to find it impossible to stay committed to one partner? Jim, for example, had had five or six girlfriends since I'd known him. Where was the happiness in that? I mean, really, how could any young man be attracted to the idea of making love to an endless succession of beautiful women? A voluptuous blonde one month, a svelte brunette the next? It just defied explanation.

Jim had just begun a new relationship with a girl called Monica and the following week, when I was in my studio, he called my mobile to invite me down to the Duke of Devonshire to join them. I had been failing to get my computer to print out some invoices and going to the pub seemed about as likely to get the printer to work as everything else I'd attempted. When I arrived, Monica's best friend Kate was in the pub garden with them and so I found myself chatting to her. Kate was pretty and slim and bubbly and carefree and all the things it is quite easy to be when you're not the pregnant mother of two small children. She had a bob of dark-brown hair, which she threw back when she laughed at my jokes, and a white short-sleeved shirt that showed off her tan. This is quite nice, I thought to myself, enjoying the company of attractive young women. Of course, I wasn't going to pursue her, but there was a certain amount of pleasure in chatting and making her laugh. Even if I wasn't going to sleep with another woman ever again, there was a certain excitement to be had in placing myself in a situation where it could at least have been possible. And she warmed to me. She seemed genuinely impressed by the fact that I wrote the music for the Mr. Gearbox ad they played on Capital Radio.

Jim had an open-topped sports car, which his parents must have bought him for learning to tie his shoelaces or something, and so, with the hood down and the stereo blaring out Supergrass, we drove up to Chelsea. Jim and his girlfriend in the front and Kate and me in the back. The wheels screeched as Jim overtook a BMW on a roundabout and Kate squealed with laughter and grabbed my arm for a moment. On the stereo they sang about being young and running free and feeling all right, and I thought, Yeah! Look out Wandsworth one-way system! I was enjoying pretending to be cool. So what if it was nearly dark; the sunglasses weren't there for me looking out, they were there for other people looking in. Suddenly I was as young as the beautiful, posh girl riding beside me.

I felt a tinge of unease as we sped over the river. The Thames ran down the middle of my life; north of the river I was a husband and father, south of the river I was a carefree young man. I once turned down a trip on a riverboat just because I felt I wouldn't know who to go as. Now the young reckless Michael was spreading his wings—all of London was my bachelor playground. We were going to a party, the party of a very rich man for whom Kate and Monica worked in the crazy carefree world of bond yields and corporate leasing. It was the most lavish, glamorous do I'd ever been to. I kept turning my back whenever the photographer appeared in case Catherine spotted me the following week in the pages of *Hello!* The music was supplied by a Japanese man who played Chopin at a grand piano. I'm not sure that anyone else in the room appreciated or even noticed how very, very good he was.

The house was offensively opulent and I felt like I was probably the only guest there who'd had the temerity to turn up without a hyphen in my surname. I attempted to mingle, but none of the circles opened up as I stood on the edges of them, so I stared at the enormous tropical fish tank for a while, but even the guppies seemed to look down their noses at me. All the men were the same—confident, self-possessed rugby captains in their casual gear. Why is it that posh men don't lose their hair, I wondered. Is it in the breeding, or something they put in boarding-school meals? They all had thick, floppy Hugh Grant fringes and bright-red cheeks and loafers and Pringle jumpers and talked about people they knew who were "bloody great blokes." I had more chance of striking up a conversation with the Filipino ladies handing round champagne, and they didn't even speak English. So I ended up talking to Kate for most of the evening. She kept asking me what "song" the pianist was playing, and I told her the name of each new piece and said a little bit about each one. She had just bought a guitar and was having lessons and I told her some good pieces she might try to learn. She was genuinely interested and it was a real pleasure to be able to talk about music to somebody. The fact that she was gorgeous was, of course, an added bonus, but I really wasn't trying to chat her up or make her fancy me. And for someone so beautiful I think she found this quite refreshing. I think it made her fancy me.

A few glasses of wine later, Jim and Monica came over and told us to come down to the basement to see the swimming pool. I thought they were joking, but I followed them into the lift—because you have to have a lift to get to your underground swimming pool—and when the doors opened again I found that we had been transported to an echoey underground paradise. It was like no room I had ever seen. This was the Sistine chapel of swimming pools. This wasn't like the municipal pool I went to with Millie. Nobody had taken the trouble to cultivate green algae between the tiles or leave bloodstained sticking plasters stewing in pools of discolored water; there were no bad cartoons on the wall telling me what I could and couldn't do. Here I could blow all the smoke rings I wanted, if the mood took me.

Jim informed us that the pool was regularly rented out as a location for films and fashion shoots, and it was obvious why. You just had to walk into the room to feel like an actor; like you were someone else, someone glamorous and sexy. There was nobody down there and the lighting was low and sensitive; the only bright lights were deep at the bottom of the turquoise oasis, which drew you seductively to the water. The surface of the pool was completely still and flat, like the seal on a coffee jar, just waiting to be broken.

"Come on, let's go for a swim," said Kate infectiously.

"But we haven't got any swimming costumes," I pointed out, "though they might have some spare . . . costumes . . . upstairs . . ."

The end of my sentence trailed off. Jim, Monica and Kate had all stripped completely naked.

"Um . . . although there's, er, no sign saying that costumes are compulsory or anything." The girls were already jumping in and swimming breaststroke with real live breasts.

Deep down I had a sense that cavorting with naked young women was not top of the one hundred ways to remain faithful to your wife, but I couldn't exactly keep my Y-fronts on and just paddle a bit in the shallow end, so I blushingly followed birthday suit. I quickly dived in and the water washed over every part of me. It felt sensuous and liberating. I manfully swam a whole length underwater, partly to demonstrate my athleticism, but mostly to postpone the problem of having to make casual chit-chat with a beautiful naked twenty-four-year-old. Eventually I surfaced and breathlessly remarked that the water was lovely, which I believe is correct swimming-pool etiquette. We swam a few widths independently and then Jim found a beach ball, which we knocked back and forth in the air. It flashed through my head that there might be some hidden camera somewhere and that Simon was sitting at home watching it all on the Internet. We splashed about trying to be first to the ball and playfully pushing each other out of the way, and then Jim swam underneath Monica and lifted her up on his shoulders. Her skin was brown, except for three white triangles on the parts of her body that were normally covered with a bikini, which seemed to only emphasize the illegality of being allowed to see them. She laughed as Jim struggled to keep his balance.

"Piggyback fight," shouted Monica.

"Come on," said Kate and she looked to me to lift her onto my shoulders and I obligingly did so.

The first time I suspected my wife was interested in me was when she first leaned across and lightly brushed a hair off my jacket. Just that tiny electrical moment of physical contact, that tentative foray into my personal space, had told me that we were more than just acquaintances. Now, as I wrapped my arms around Kate's naked wet thighs and felt her pubic hair bristling against the back of my neck, I thought we had probably crossed that personal space barrier by this juncture. I mustn't let it get too intimate, I thought to myself as she fell forward, pressing her breasts against the top of my head. I had a naked woman literally on top of me, but I was still telling myself I hadn't transgressed the line of actual sexual infidelity. Anyway, it was fun; it was a good laugh. In fact, it was fantastic.

I'm playing piggyback fights with two beautiful, naked women in a luxury swimming pool at midnight; they won't believe me when I'm in my old people's home. Jim pulled Kate off me and we both plunged underwater and her arm brushed tantalizingly against my groin. I tried to stand up, but I was at the point in the pool where the gradient slipped away dramatically and there was nothing there for me to stand on. I was in deep water. I swam back toward the shallow end, toward Kate as it happened, and then I splashed her and she splashed me back. Then the spray died down and I saw that Jim and Monica were standing in the water kissing, gently at first and then more passionately. And I was standing next to Kate. The pool was warm and the lights were low and this secret grotto felt like the only place in the universe. We looked at the other two, wrapping themselves round each other like a pair of overexcited eels, and Kate smiled at me and I stood there self-consciously for a second and smiled back. Her nipples pointed at me like General Kitchener. I felt a sense of heady recklessness; I'd had sun on my body and wine in my belly, and we were young and tanned and naked. I hadn't meant to fly this close to the flame. The moment was heavy with expectation. I had to do something.

"So tell me," I said. "Erm . . . how do you know Monica?"

"Well, we work in the same office, remember?"

"Oh, that's right, you said. Yeah . . . So you, er, so you met her through work."

"Yes."

Jim and Monica were writhing a few yards away and had started to moan slightly.

"I think a lot of people, erm, meet other people at work," I observed.

"Yes, I suppose they do."

There was another awkward pause.

"I like your erm . . . your . . ." I was trying to remember the word "pendant," so I pointed at it in the hope she might help me out.

"Breasts?" she said, rather taken aback, looking down at them.

"No, no, no. Good God no. I mean, they're very nice too—not that I was looking particularly—but now you mention it . . . er . . ."

Why is there never a great white shark to drag you underwater and swallow you whole when you want one?

"No, I meant your necklace thingy."

"Pendant?"

"That's the word. Pendant. I like your pendant."

"Thank you."

"Er, I think I'll just do a few more lengths now," I said, and she smiled a half smile as I rudely left her standing there and took off for the other end of the pool as fast as I could. And as I swam away from her, I wondered what Catherine was doing right now. It was about midnight, so she was probably just feeding Alfie. I hoped Millie hadn't got up as well. I'd meant to tighten the window above her cot to stop it rattling in the wind, in case that was what kept waking her up. Catherine had asked me twice but I hadn't got around to it.

I deliberately didn't look up for the first five lengths, but when I did, I saw that Kate was out of the pool and dressed. I had been so very close to kissing her; I had wanted to press my naked body against hers and kiss her full on the lips; this basement pool had felt like another world, with its own rules and morals. I had traveled deep into the hills of my bachelor Narnia—almost too far to come back.

I couldn't risk getting that close again. I didn't trust myself to be so strong next time, especially if I carried on drinking, so I resolved to leave the party and go back to the flat.

"Yeah, let's," said Kate when I unilaterally announced I was going.

Oh no, I thought, look I'm trying to be resolute here; don't make it harder for me. But as Jim drove down the King's Road she put her arm around me and I didn't feel able to ask her to remove it, so it stayed there, draped over my rigid shoulders all the way back to Balham. The roles were strangely reversed. I was like the nervous young girl and she was the predatory older boy. I was attracted to her, but I knew I had to fight it. My eye was drawn to the gap at the top of her shirt, where I caught a glimpse of the upper slope of her bosom. Bizarrely, this was still exciting, even though I had just seen them bouncing around naked in the swimming pool. For a second I thought I saw Catherine pushing the buggy under the street lights, but as we drove closer I saw it was in fact a tramp pushing a shopping trolley packed with old bags and that two people could not have looked more dissimilar.

Back at the flat I had to play it carefully. We all stayed up drinking and sharing a joint, but as soon as it was polite I announced that I was off to bed.

"Which one's your room, Michael?" said Kate brightly.

And I instinctively answered, "Past the bathroom, first door on the left," as if she were only asking because she was interested in the layout of the house. Then I realized the subtext my directions had given her, so I said a pointed, "Goodnight, Kate."

"Goodnight," she said.

And I thought, Phew!

And then she gave me a naughty wink.

Five minutes later I was nervously lying in bed watching the door handle, waiting for it to turn. I worked out what I would say to her; that she was really lovely and that I found her very attractive, and that I hoped she would understand but I was in love with someone else and that I couldn't betray this other girl. These excuses were mentally rehearsed over and over again until I realized she wasn't coming after all and soon I was fast asleep.

And then I dreamed Kate was next to me in my bed, kissing me on the lips and running her hands through my hair, and it was a nice dream and I wanted it to carry on. I kissed her back and felt her bare buttocks, and this was like a dream that you could navigate because then she clasped mine. I stirred slightly, but the dream didn't end. In fact, it felt even more real. She nibbled my bottom lip and I opened my eyes and Kate smiled at me and kissed me again, and she really was in my bed, all fresh and clean and chlorine-scented, and her body felt different to Catherine, but it still felt good and there were no barriers now. All my defenses were blown away and no one would know, and Kate kissed me long and hard and ran her hands down to between my legs, and I moaned weakly, "Oh God. You won't tell anyone, will you?"

6

Naughty but Nice

AS KATE AND I had sex for the third time that night she discovered that when it came to lovemaking there wasn't much I didn't know. We did every position that I'd seen on Simon's Lover's Guide *video, and then we made love in every position they'd shown in the rip-off sequels. We stood, we lay, we sat, we did it in the shower, on the bed, on the floor and against the wall. Still entwined, I manfully lifted her up and carried her across the room. Since both my hands were clasped to her naked buttocks, she tilted the glass of champagne into my mouth for me. Most of it missed and we laughed decadently as it ran down my chin and fizzed in the space where her bosoms were pressed against my chest. Still carrying her, I pushed her left buttock against the 'play' button on my stereo and it turned on my CD of the* 1812 Overture. *With her right buttock I turned up the volume. Then Tchaikovsky conducted us through our lovemaking. As the Russian national hymn battled symbolically with "La Marseillaise" we rolled around on the carpet, fighting to go on top, playfully scratching and biting each other throughout the Battle of Borodino. I rose with the string section and she moaned with the brass fanfares. Finally the overture reached its crescendo and we climaxed together on the floor; she screamed, "Yes! Yes! Yes!" as the cymbals crashed, the artillery guns fired and Napoleon's army was halted at the gates of Moscow. And then we just lay there throughout the coda, panting on the carpet as the peal of bells rang out across all Russia.*

• • •

Well, that's how I imagined it would have been if I'd gone through with it. I hadn't been able to do it. I couldn't lie there and betray my wife. I think this became clear to me when I held Kate close and said, "Oh, Catherine." I hadn't been able to put her out of my head. Not quite. The compartments in my brain needed slightly thicker walls.

Kate's reaction was not what I expected.

"God. No one's called me that for years."

"Sorry?"

"Catherine. You just called me Catherine. How did you know that I was a Catherine not a Kate?"

"Er, well, Kate is short for Catherine, isn't it. I read that in a baby-naming book. Not my baby-naming book; a friend's. The person who was having a baby."

"I stopped calling myself that when I left boarding school. I hate the name Catherine, don't you?"

"Er, no. No, I don't, actually."

"Which do you prefer, Kate or Catherine?"

"Er, well, they're both lovely. But I'd have to say I prefer Catherine. Sorry."

The moment of passion was gone and I quickly pulled myself together. It was better this way. The reality would never have been so erotically perfect. Sexual climax would have been swiftly followed by enormous regret, guilt, self-loathing, fear and depression. Which is quite a high price to pay for five minutes of sweaty groping in the dark. So I invented a memory of what almost was, which I'd be able to keep with me forever. Kate was very nice about it really. She thought it was rather sweet that I was so faithful to this other girl who I didn't want to talk about. In fact, she was so nice about it that it made me want to kiss her, but I don't think that would have helped clarify where she stood.

"Well, whoever she is," said Kate, "she's a very lucky girl."

"I'm not sure about that," I replied.

We talked for an hour or two and I felt less guilty when she told me that actually she had a bit of a crush on Jim, but was fighting it because he was going out with her best friend. It was just as well we never went all the way, I thought, because I would have been going, "Catherine! Catherine!" and she would have been going, "Jim! Jim!" Eventually I gave her my bed while I slept on the floor with a piece of music by Pyotr Ilyich Tchaikovsky going round in my head as I imagined what might have been . . .

"You're doing it again," said my Catherine the next day.

"What?"

"Humming the *1812 Overture* to yourself."

"Was I? Oh sorry."

We had been sitting in a hospital corridor together. We had been waiting so long that her twelve-week scan felt like it may have to go down as a fourteen-week scan.

"You're very quiet. What are you thinking about?"

"Oh, nothing," I lied. "Just wondering how much longer they're going to be."

"Doesn't matter, does it?" she said, squeezing my arm. "It's nice just to have some time to ourselves without the kids."

"Mmm," I said, unconvincingly. I thought she must be joking. This was her idea of quality time! Sitting for an hour in a sterile-smelling hospital, watching deathly white old people with tubes sticking out of them being wheeled past. For Catherine, *this* was a treat!

"If you're really good," I said, "I'll see if we can get stuck in a two-hour traffic jam on the way home."

"Ooh, yes please. There'll probably be a play on Radio 4, I can just recline the seat in the car, close my eyes and relax. Sounds like heaven."

"Well why not?" I said, seizing the moment. "Why don't we go and sit in the park somewhere and take a book and some wine and spend a couple of hours just doing nothing?"

"Hmm. It would be lovely, wouldn't it?"

"Yes, it would, so why don't we?"

"Just imagine it. Bliss."

"So let's do it."

"That would be just paradise."

She imagined this tiny window of self-indulgence as if it were some impossible dream, a ludicrous fantasy that would never be attainable in her lifetime.

"But it wouldn't be fair on Mum."

"But she loves looking after the kids."

"It wouldn't be fair on the kids."

"They love being looked after by your mum."

She paused because she'd run out of excuses.

"No. I just can't. Sorry."

And that was the rub. She wanted to be with the children for every hour of the day and I didn't, which meant I couldn't see her without the children, except on occasions like this when we were waiting to look at a picture of the next one.

Her legs were tightly crossed and she was rocking back and forth in her plastic molded chair.

"You wouldn't be needing to go to the toilet by any chance, would you?"

"How could you tell," she squeaked painfully as she swigged another half pint of mineral water from her plastic bottle. She'd had it on good authority that you got a better picture of the embryo if the mother's bladder was full. Judging by the number of gallons she was holding in she must have been hoping for a real David Bailey. "And can we have the embryo side-on, looking round and smiling? That's great. And now put your arm round the placenta and give me a big thumbs-up.

Fantastic! Now, last one. I want you to point to the birth canal with one hand, and with the other give me a big fingers-crossed. Ha ha ha, that's lovely."

"I can't hold on much longer," she said. "The moment he presses that thing against my bladder I'm going to wet my knickers, I know it."

"Go for a wee now, then."

"No, I want the first picture of the baby to be a good one."

"Well try not to think about it. Do your pelvic-floor exercises or something."

"I'm already doing them."

I knew she wouldn't wet herself, of course, unless the doctor suddenly announced that he could see twins. It happened to Nick and Debbie, a couple who live near us. They went for the scan and were suddenly told they were expecting two babies. And they thought it was *good* news, bless them. Last time I went past their house I thought I saw the grandparents coming out of the door, but when I looked again I realized that it was Nick and Debbie themselves—six months after the twins were born.

Eventually our turn came and the doctor asked Catherine to lie down. To show that he had every confidence in my wife's personal hygiene, he tore off a huge strip of paper which he placed along the length of the bed before she came into contact with his leatherette mattress. For some reason I wasn't suspected of having any major skin diseases and so was permitted to sit on a chair as I was. He then wheeled across this huge expensive-looking piece of wizardry which he pretended was the ultrasound machine. Of course, fetal scans are all a massive con trick. They don't show you your baby at all. When all the cutbacks were being made in the health service, one of the accountants suddenly realized what a complete waste of money ultrasounds really were. All babies in the womb look completely identical, so what they do these days is just play you a video of a fetus that the consultant made back in the Sixties. That's why it's in black and white. We've all been told to look at the monitor where we've been shown exactly the same footage of the same fetus, and we've all clasped our partner's hand and bitten our lips at the miraculous beauty of our little unborn baby, when really all we are looking at is the gynecological equivalent of that little girl playing noughts and crosses on the test card. The fetus we are actually looking at was born years ago. He's grown up now; he's a chartered surveyor who lives in Droitwich. He still gets the repeat fees.

Obviously, for appearance's sake, they still have to smear ice-cold Swarfega on your wife's bump, rub a shower attachment around a bit and point to a gray splurge on the screen and say, "There, that's the head, see?" when it all looks like the bubbles on a bad animated Sixties underground film. But still you go away satisfied with a flimsy little photo which you believe is of your next baby, and no one is any the wiser when friends say, "I've got one of Jocasta almost identical to that."

I approached the scan like a cynical old hand, exuding the blasé air of someone who already had two ultrasound images framed and artistically placed amid the gallery of black-and-white photos of my kids on the wall up the stairs at home. The doctor turned on the screen and I said, "They're showing the snooker on the other channel," and Catherine told me I had made the same joke when we'd come in for Millie's and Alfie's scans. So I shut up and squinted at the monitor as the deep-sea probe searched the murky depths for any sign of life. But then, when I saw the shape of our third child suddenly emerge, all my skepticism and facetiousness instantly melted away. It was a miracle. There really was a baby in there. It is simply beyond the bounds of ordinary human comprehension as to how such a thing can possibly have happened. How could our two bodies have combined to create a completely new and separate person? How could Catherine's body know how to grow an umbilical cord and a fetal sac and a placenta and create a little human being exactly the right shape and size? How is it possible that such complex biological information can all be innately programmed somewhere inside her while the conscious Catherine still couldn't understand how to set the bloody video? How could one of my sperm transmit so many million messages when I couldn't even remember to tell Catherine that her mother had rung? Millions and millions of years of evolution to get to this point. Species dying out and others emerging all so that this perfect little baby could be born. It was only *one* baby, thank God. Not like the guilty secrets I could feel kicking inside me; they were quints, sextuplets, octuplets. Thank God there was no machine that could see inside me. Now that would be something. A machine that showed us what was really going on inside. Come to think of it, I would have quite liked to have known. The doctor could have pointed to the various blobs on the screen and said, "Oh look, there's your anxiety—that's growing worryingly large. Does your family have a history of anxiety problems?" Or, "Hmm, your ego looks like it may have been damaged there. We'll have to get the nurse to massage that for you."

I looked at Catherine lying there on the bed and thought the two of us couldn't have been more different. Me sitting there quietly, the buttoned-up man with all my secrets inside me, and Catherine, the effusive openhearted woman with her T-shirt pulled up and her trousers unzipped and the scanner squirming around on her exposed midriff so that even the inside of her body was broadcast on the telly for us all to gawp at.

We watched carefully as the doctor plotted the crown-to-rump length and eventually extrapolated from this measurement that Catherine was twelve weeks pregnant. This seemed a fairly uncontroversial diagnosis considering we had come in for her twelve-week scan. Then he chatted at great length about the stage the pregnancy was at and what Catherine should expect to feel in the coming months, and she listened and nodded as politely as she could, considering that she'd done it twice before and all she wanted to do now the scan was over was run to the toilet and have a wee.

Soon we were driving back home and Catherine sat in the seat beside me just staring at the photo of the three-month-old fetus.

"I think it might be safer if I drove," I said nervously.

She pulled over at a bus stop and showed the photo to me again. She loved the baby already. I gave her a tentative kiss. I felt so very proud of her, she was so positive and full of optimism. I undid my seat belt so I could lean across and kiss her properly, and then I found myself hugging and kissing her like a rescued child. I had so nearly let myself slip my moorings and I was so glad to be back with her that I just kept on giving her grateful, silent guilty kisses and hugging her slightly too much.

"Are you all right?" she asked.

"I'm so happy this new baby is coming."

And she was so relieved to hear me say that that she kissed me back passionately. There were no children tugging at our legs or crying in the background; it was just Catherine and me and all the people queuing for the number 31 bus.

Right now we were at the very zenith of our passion cycle. This was the routine emotional loop of our relationship, which came round with all the biological regularity of a menstrual cycle or a biorhythm. It took us from bitter argument to loving, mutual adoration every seven days or so. It fooled me every time. Every week, as we were staring devotedly into each other's eyes, I thought we had finally sorted out all our problems forever. But then a day or two later Catherine would seem inexplicably irritated with me and I'd become defensive and silent, which in turn made her prickly and oversensitive. The tension would build until we reached the nadir of the cycle, when we would explode into argument, saying hateful, hurtful, stupid

things to each other, briefly despising one another as passionately as we had adored each other only days before. Then I
would disappear for a while. I was still in orbit around her, still
in her gravitational pull, but this was the most distant point between us. Then I would re-emerge, shining brightly in her life
for a while, and everything seemed like it was perfect between
us again forever.

If I was ever unsure about what stage we were at in the loop
I just had to check the height of the pile of ironing. The
crumpled clothes would just be a few items at first and then,
during the week, more would be placed on top, until the tower
was in danger of toppling over when we finally had a fight and
Catherine angrily threw herself into the ironing, smashing the
hissing metal onto Barbie and Ken's faces as they smiled up at
her from the front of Millie's T-shirts.

We drove the rest of the way home in a blissful haze and
Catherine miraculously agreed that we should go out that evening if her mother didn't mind staying on and babysitting the
children. Her mum eagerly agreed; she never missed an opportunity to put the kids to bed so that she could send them
off to sleep with another thrilling installment from the ne-
glected copy of *Bible Stories for Children*, which she had given
Millie for Christmas.

Catherine's mother was a Church of England fundamen-
talist, fighting her own holy jihad against anyone who would
not take Jesus into their life, or indeed anyone who wouldn't
help her with the St. Botolph's Christmas fair and jumble sale.

There was a particular shirt I wanted to wear, but discovered that it needed ironing. It occurred to me that I could, of
course, precipitate a row so that I wouldn't have to wait a
couple of days, but on balance I decided it was probably unfair
and against the natural order of things to try to force an argument before it was organically due, and so I painstakingly
ironed the shirt myself. Catherine was amazed and delighted

to see me doing the ironing, and then she realized that I was only doing my own shirt and not ironing anything of hers or the children's and a huge row blew up. Before long she was ironing everything, including the very shirt that I had originally made such a hash of myself.

"Jesus, you're a selfish bastard sometimes, Michael," said Catherine.

"Please do not use the name of our Lord Jesus Christ in that way, dear," said her mother.

I think that was the only time the passion cycle took a couple of hours instead of the full seven days. We never had that evening out together, instead I found myself heading down the Northern Line to Balham. "Mind the gap," said the announcement at Embankment. A few hours later I was back at my flat again, and after I knew she would be asleep I left a brusque message on the answerphone saying that something had come up and I probably wouldn't be able to leave the studio for a couple of days. Lies are like cigarettes—your first one makes you feel sick, but soon you're addicted to them, unaware you are even doing it.

The next day was the hottest day of the summer. The weatherman had predicted that the temperature would be in the mid-eighties, though in London this was probably bumped up another couple of degrees by all the electrical equipment in my studio. It can only have been around half an hour after I had sat down to work that Jim popped his head around the door and asked me if I wanted to come to a barbecue on Clapham Common. The little devil by my right ear said, "Go on, it's a lovely day, have some fun. All this work can wait." And the little angel by my left ear said, "Oh, fuck it, what's the point in even trying?"

The barbecue was already well under way in the semi-wooded hilly area by the Latin American football pitches. There must have been over twenty people at our picnic, all of them about my age—meaning that I was probably seven or eight years older than any of them. Girls with pierced navels laid their heads on the laps of boyfriends in combat trousers, music floated across the grass, a couple of disposable barbecues smoked away and the smell of charcoal mingled with the occasional wafts of cannabis. They were so free they didn't know it. Part of me was nervous about gate-crashing their twenty-something party, as if one of them might suddenly sit up, point at me and say, "Just a minute, you're not *young*!" Lots of the blokes had little beards, so small they hardly seemed worth the trouble. Not me, though—I was far too old for a beard. I hid behind my sunglasses and sat down in a space amongst the stretched-out legs, some of them sporting flared trousers like the ones I remembered wearing first time round. If anyone asked, I couldn't remember when Elvis died. Elvis who? The Falklands? What was that? Typewriters? Never heard of them. Microsoft Windows '95—oooh, yes, I think I just about remember that.

The tragic thing was that while I could remember everything from when I was young, I couldn't actually remember anything from the last few years. This lot would all know what song was number one. When was the last time I knew or cared? I could still list all the Christmas chart-toppers of the Seventies and Eighties—I could tell you every track of every album I bought back then—but ask my brain to store any more new information now and it would refuse. Disk full. It ought to be possible to delete some files to make space. For example, thanks to three hours spent racking my brain after having breakfast with Simon, I knew that St. John's Wood was the only underground station that doesn't include a letter from the word "mackerel." I'd be more than happy to wipe that piece of knowledge from my mind so that I could make room to remember my dad's birthday. But every year I forgot to send him a card, and every time the tube train pulled into St. John's Wood I would now think of mackerel.

I accepted a little bottle of French lager, lay back, closed my eyes and let the sun and alcohol carry me away. A few revelers struggled to their feet and youthfully threw a Frisbee back and forth. Others busied themselves rolling joints or putting overcooked sausages into bread for everyone. Cannabis was passed one way and hot dogs were passed the other; there's probably some modern youth etiquette to it. There was an efficiency to this picnic that made me realize these kids weren't really the lazy no-hopers they affected to be; their bumming about was far too well organized. Anyone at the advertising agencies would be able to tell me the name of this particular tribe. The pierced navels? The clubbers? The Ibiza posse? I think they were expected to drink Pepsi Max and buy snowboards, or care about the planet, but in the most hedonistic way possible. The girls brushed their shiny long hair away from their faces with the backs of their wrists and they all had the healthy glow of well-bred families. Like Jim, they were hippie posh; they'd dropped out, but had return tickets for when they were older. Their parents would have spent the summer doing Ascot, Henley and Wimbledon, and these kids would have had their own summer season, going to the Fleadh, Reading Festival or Glastonbury.

So if I wasn't one of them, which advertising tribe would I be filed under? When Hugo had asked me to write the musical sting for "The saloon car that thinks it's a sports car," he had told me they were aiming at the "Lad Dad." A shudder had run down my spine as I'd felt instantly categorized in two short syllables. "Oh, I know the sort," I had said to him scornfully, simultaneously throwing a glossy men's magazine into the wastepaper bin.

The midday sun felt powerful and I moved into the shade

to prevent my tender forehead from burning. It would be hard to explain how I'd become sunburned from sitting at my keyboard all day. Suddenly, from my bag I could hear my mobile phone ringing. I expected to get groans from all the pierced alternative environmentalists, but they all reached for their pockets and bags as well.

"Hi. It's me," said Catherine.

Her tone was suitably cool considering that we had had a row, but at least she'd made the first contact.

"Are you in your studio?"

I thought I could just about answer that one without lying unnecessarily.

"No."

"Where are you, then?"

I sensed that she might be angling for me to come home for bathtime. I looked around and decided that it wouldn't be a very good idea to say that I was lying on the grass on Clapham Common. Nearby a little boy was wearing a Manchester United top.

"I'm in . . . Manchester."

Some of the people sitting nearby seemed curious, so I smiled at them and mimed a long-suffering tut that the person I was speaking to couldn't grasp this obvious and simple fact.

"Manchester? Really? Whereabouts?"

"Oh. United."

"What?"

"I mean, um, Piccadilly." It had been a bad choice. Manchester was where Catherine had been to college.

"Why did you say united?"

"Sorry, I just associate Manchester with United. As opposed to Manchester City, who wear sky-blue shirts, of course."

"What are you talking about?"

"Sorry. They've just told me to hurry up because this edit suite is costing them five hundred pounds an hour."

"Oh. So you won't see the kids before bed, then?"

" 'Fraid not. It's bloody murder up here. I'm having to rewrite something on the spot. Talk about pressure."

"Oh." She sounded disappointed. "Well, we're just off to see Susan and Piers's new house. I'll speak to you tomorrow."

"Oh, well don't get chatting to Piers about the Astra; you'll never get away."

She was still too cool toward me to laugh, so I asked her to give the kids a kiss from me and we said our goodbyes and hung up. Neither of us said sorry for the horrible things we had shouted at each other the day before, but the ice had been broken and we would speak more warmly again the next day. It was so much better this way; we wouldn't spend two days slamming doors and ruining each other's weekend. I cracked open another stubby lager bottle and passed an hour lazily try-ing to make things out of the shapes of clouds. They looked cloud-shaped to me every time.

The mobile rang again and this time it was Hugo Harrison. When I had completed my last job for him I had put the track on the tape three times in a row, knowing that he would need to listen to it over and over again and so saving him the trou-ble of having to repeatedly cue up the same piece of music.

"Hi, Michael, it's Hugo here. I've had a listen to your tracks."

"Tracks?" I said, confused that he was using the plural.

"Yeah, now I like the beginning of the first mix, the pace of the second one and the best ending of the three is definitely on the last version."

What could I say? They are all completely identical, you stupid prat?

"Right, um, interesting," I stammered.

"Could you have another go at it, incorporating the best bits of all three?"

"Um, well I could try, so let me write that down," I said as onlookers wondered why I wasn't writing anything down. "The beginning of one, the pace of two and the ending of three. Right, I'll do my best, but it might take me a day or two."

"That's OK. Cheers, Michael, gotta dash."

And I lay back making a mental note to send him a tape with just the one version of exactly the same mix, which I knew he'd be delighted with.

More people turned up to the barbecue as the day progressed, including Kate and Monica. Kate had brought her acoustic guitar, which she placed lovingly down on a rug while she brought out seemingly endless plates of sandwiches that she'd made for everyone. Beside me lay a bloke who called himself Dirk, to whom I had already taken an irrational dislike on the grounds that when he took a puff of his cigarette he held the fag between his thumb and little finger, like he was James Dean or Marlon Brando. I knew there were greater crimes against humanity, but at that moment, holding your cigarette between your thumb and little finger was right up there with the worst of them. In any case, my first impression of him was soon vindicated.

Popping a sandwich in his mouth without acknowledging Kate's efforts, Dirk then picked up her guitar and started to pluck out a few notes. Kate looked mildly put out at his presumption, but said nothing. He adjusted the tuning slightly and tutted.

"How much did you pay for this?"

"Only fifty pounds," said Kate proudly. "I got it secondhand."

"Fifty quid? I'll give you twenty for it."

Occasionally you meet somebody who is so unlikable that you can only presume they attend rudeness evening classes.

"Well, I wasn't looking to sell it actually," said Kate, far too politely.

"Bad luck. It's just gone down to fifteen. You missed your chance." And he wedged his cigarette under the strings by the keys. "Fifty quid! For a crappy guitar like this," he muttered to himself as he began strumming. Kate looked at me in disbelief and part of me wanted to grab her guitar off the bloke and hit him over the head with it. But I didn't because I'm not a violent person, it would have ruined the whole picnic and, apart from anything else, it would have smashed into splinters, because he was right, it was a crappy guitar.

I tried to ignore him, but soon he became the center of attention as a few other girls started to sing along to his rather loose interpretation of "Wonderwall." They sounded more like the Von Trapp children than Liam Gallagher, but they weren't helped by this poser getting half the chords wrong. I could contain myself no longer.

"Um, I think that should be E minor seventh there, actually," I said tentatively.

That was the first time he noticed me. He took another affected puff of his cigarette and winced, half closing one eye as he inhaled, as if his Silk Cut were mixed with the strongest Jamaican skunk.

"Don't think so, mate," he replied.

"Yeah, it goes Em7, G, Dsus4, A7sus4."

Suddenly he could tell I knew what I was talking about, but he couldn't back down in front of all these admiring women. There was a new stag in the herd, butting him with his antlers. He paused. Then, instead of continuing with "Wonderwall," he started a different song, one that he had obviously practiced a few more times over the years.

"Oh no," said one of the girls, "not 'Stairway to bloody Heaven.' What happened to Oasis?"

"I'll have a bash at it, if you like," I gallantly offered and there was enthusiastic agreement from the assembled audience. He had no choice but to hand over the guitar, and now the whole crowd was watching to see if I was any better.

"Would that be all right, Kate? If I played your guitar?" She nodded and the tension built as I pointedly and slowly adjusted the tuning. A pause. Then I plunged emphatically into the opening chords of "Wonderwall," strumming with a force and confidence that drew the best possible sound from the nylon strings. The blood drained from Dirk's face as I segued into "The Passenger," "Rock 'n' Roll Suicide" and the tricksiest bit of Rodrigo's *Guitar Concerto No. 2* for good measure. By the time I finished there were cheers and applause and shouts of, "Encore!" and the girls looked ready to ask me if I would father their children. "That's quite a nice guitar you've got there, Kate," I lied as I passed it back to its owner. It was a great moment. If only all of life could be like that. I noticed that when Dirk lit his next cigarette he held it normally. Mission accomplished, I thought.

I suppose the women were so enamored of me because I expressed so much emotion with the music. If I had a guitar in my hand or a keyboard under my fingertips I could say, "I'm so in love" or "I'm so unhappy" and really convey how those things felt. I could never have just said the words. Right now I had to try quite hard not to show how I was feeling, which was revoltingly self-satisfied. I had just defended the honor of Kate's guitar, it was a beautiful sunny day and the egg-mayonnaise sandwiches even had the crusts cut off. Temporary financial setbacks aside, my double life was a well-oiled machine. I had a wife, but I was independent, I had a job in which I could choose my own hours, I had the perfect amount of time with my beautiful children, but I also had my own space and all the time to myself that I could possibly want.

I eased myself up and went a few yards into the woods and wee'd against a tree. The mixture of sun and lager made me feel dizzy and I swayed slightly as I buttoned up my flies and squinted in the brightness of the sun. And then, coming through a clearing and down a little hill, I saw Millie. My little daughter Millie, not yet three years old, wandering about in the thicket forty feet away. On Clapham Common. On her own.

She appeared to be perfectly happy so I restrained my instinct to call out her name. No matter how hard I looked I couldn't see her mother. With mounting incomprehension I just watched her, pottering along, picking leaves and cheerfully singing a little song to herself. It was as if she were a child I didn't know; she was completely separate from me, as if I were observing her through a one-way mirror or on an old family video recording. I'd never heard her singing that song before. She was just another kid in the park, except she was my daughter. It was the same sensation I'd had when I'd seen our third baby in the scan—I could see my child, but I wasn't able to relate to her. She felt distant and surreal.

Why isn't Catherine with her? I wondered anxiously. I hid behind a bush so I could watch Millie without giving myself away. Part of me wanted to run and give her a big hug, but there was so much at risk. She must be lost. I would just keep an eye on her from a distance, until her mother found her, and then silently slip away. I could not afford to make my presence known, this was the only logical option I could pursue. And yet as she came closer I blurted out her name in spite of myself, not quite sure why.

"Daddy!" she replied.

She wasn't particularly surprised to see me hiding there, which threw me slightly, but mixed in with my panic and incomprehension was elation at seeing my beautiful little daughter so unexpectedly. She ran toward me and I picked her up; she squeezed me tight, which was lovely even though I had no idea what I could possibly do next.

"Where's Mummy?"

"Erm . . . she's, she's, she's, she's . . . Mummy, um, Mummy . . ."

Come on, Millie, spit it out.

"She's . . . she's over there." And she pointed to the band-stand a good hundred yards away, through the trees. At that moment I heard Catherine calling Millie's name, with terror and panic in her voice. There was no way out of this situation. Catherine had lost Millie; I had found her. Only an hour ago I had told Catherine I was working in Manchester. My heart was beating *allegro forte* and I said, "Oh dear, Millie, what am I going to do?"

"Green bird," she answered, pointing to the tree. And she was right. Crawling up the tree trunk behind me was a green woodpecker. How about that! In the middle of London! I'd never seen a green woodpecker before.

"Millie! Where are you?" screamed her desperate mother, coming closer. I put her down on the ground and pointed to her mum. "Look, Millie, there's Mummy. Run to Mummy. Tell her you saw a man that looked like Daddy."

I let her go and she ran across the open common toward her mother. As she left I heard her shouting, "Mummy! Daddy said I saw man that look like Daddy."

I saw the moment that Catherine spotted her. In a split second her face went from terror to enormous relief, but then barely paused as it progressed to anger at the terrible ordeal she had just been put through. She was furious with Millie, al-though I knew deep down she was angry with herself for losing her. She had Alfie in one arm, but she ran toward Millie with the other outstretched and then grabbed her and burst into tears. She shouted at Millie for running off like that, and any message that Millie attempted to relay was lost in the anger, hugs and tears, so I was safe for the time being.

Still hiding among the trees I watched Catherine get ready to leave the common. What was she doing down here anyway? She was miles from home; she never came south of the river. I knew that getting the kids ready would be a major operation.

She tried to strap Alfie into the double buggy, but he wailed and struggled and arched his back, demanding that he be carried. Millie was upset at having been told off and was also crying. Her mother took a bag out of the buggy and put Millie in. As she was hooking the bag over the pushchair handles Millie started to become hysterical, screaming and holding her arms out to be picked up, jealous that her little brother was being carried.

Catherine picked Millie up out of the pushchair, and as she did so the weight of the bag slung over the handles tipped up the buggy and, in a violent surprise seesaw action, the whole thing upended. The bag hit the tarmac and I heard the sound of shattering glass. That'll be the bottle of Aqua Libre, I thought to myself. That smelly melon drink she buys with a name that means "free water" and costs a fortune. The designer drink was seeping out of the bag and onto the ground. Still supporting the weight of both children, I watched as she squatted down and, with her remaining free hand, tried to stop the liquid ruining everything else in the bag. Then I heard her swear as she cut her hand. Her hand bled as she tried to put Millie down but, being just under three, Millie refused to see the situation from Catherine's point of view and would not let go. Catherine angrily pulled Millie off, who then lay on the ground and screamed. At each step I had felt that I could see what was about to happen, but I was powerless to prevent it, like watching a series of cars bumping one another on one of those compilation videos of motorway accidents. I really would have liked to have gone and helped, but how could I? How could I suddenly appear in the middle of Clapham Common an hour after I had said I was up in Manchester?

"Checking out the local nannies?" sneered a voice behind me. It was Dirk, still smarting from being outplayed on a cheap plywood guitar.

"Er, no, I was just watching that woman struggling with those two little kids. She's their mother actually. Er, I'd say."

"God, who'd have kids, eh?" he said as Millie lay on the floor sobbing and kicking. I found myself half nodding in tacit agreement and then felt guilty for betraying my own children so casually.

"Look at that little brat screaming. I don't think people should be allowed to have kids if they don't know how to control them."

Suddenly I was fuming. What did he know about it?

"It's not her fault," I said, bristling. "It's hard on your own. And most two-year-olds are like that."

"Look how she's shouting at the poor child. No wonder it's screaming."

"Well, she's probably at her wit's end. Not sleeping and all that."

"Yeah, single mother probably," said Dirk as he headed off back to the barbecue. Catherine was now sitting on the ground crying. She looked utterly defeated by it all. I had never seen her give up like this. Her hand was bleeding and both her children were sobbing, too. And this being London, everyone else rushed past as if she was some drug addict or alcoholic nutter. Wasn't anyone going to step in and help her?

"Are you OK, Catherine?" I said.

She looked up and was so astonished to see me standing there that she immediately stopped weeping.

"How on earth did you get here?"

Since I didn't have an answer to this question I thought the best policy would be to ignore it.

"What have you done to your hand?"

"Oh, I cut it," she said, holding it up.

"Ah, that would explain all the blood dripping onto the tarmac." I wrapped my handkerchief around her fingers and she sat there gazing at me as if I were her fairy godmother and a knight in shining armor all rolled into one. "I can see you cut it, you idiot. What were you doing?"

"Well, I was trying to get all the broken glass out of the bottom of the bag."

"And you say this broken glass somehow cut your hand? Well talk about a freak accident."

She smiled and I hoped the moment had passed when she would have asked what I was doing there in the first place.

"Me and Daddy saw a green bird," said Millie helpfully.

"God, she's still going on about that. We saw a green woodpecker about two months ago." I tied the handkerchief into a knot. "Let's go and get a coffee and I'll buy Millie some crisps or something."

Catherine wiped her smudged eye makeup. "Oh God, Michael, I'm so pleased to see you. I lost Millie. It was awful; she just wandered away from the bandstand when I was changing Alfie, and I ran round behind the café, but she must have gone in the other direction because I lost her for ages. It was terrifying. And then the buggy tipped up and the bottles smashed and I cut my hand open and the kids were screaming and I just couldn't cope . . ."

"OK, forget the coffee, how about a glass of wine?"

"What about the baby?"

"Good point—I'll get one for him, too."

I hoisted Millie onto my shoulders and we headed toward the Windmill Inn, away from the direction of the picnic. If the empty seat in the double buggy had been slightly bigger I would have strapped Catherine in next to Alfie and pushed her all the way there. We sat outside the pub and Alfie sucked his bottle and I sipped my pint and Catherine knocked back her glass of wine in one. It seemed like everything was all right again, for a moment at least.

"So why did you say you were in Manchester?" she asked suddenly.

I only had one crisp in my mouth, but apparently my mouth was so full it was impossible for me to reply.

"Manchester?" I finally said. "What are you talking about?"

"You said you were up in Manchester."

There was a pause in which I tried to regard her as if she must be completely deranged and then I steered my puzzled face into exaggerated realization as a way out suddenly came into my head.

"No, no, no. Manchester *Street*. I said I was in Manchester *Street*. In the West End."

She looked confused.

"But you said you were in Piccadilly."

"Piccadilly Circus, yeah?"

She laughed at her foolishness. "Oh, I'd got it into my head that you'd gone up North for work again."

We shared a good-natured laugh at this mix-up and I breathed a silent sigh of relief that Catherine had forgotten, or was unaware, that Manchester Street was a good couple of miles from Piccadilly Circus. Before she had time to think about this I changed the subject.

"So what are you doing this side of the river? Weren't you worried about the border guards stopping you on the bridge?"

"I was supposed to be seeing Susan and Piers's new house in Stockwell, but we got to the front door and there was no one home, so we thought we'd have a bit of a run about on Clapham Common, didn't we, Millie?"

"Me and Daddy saw a green bird."

"Yes, all right, Millie. You said," I interjected. "Have another packet of crisps."

"What about you?" Catherine asked me.

"Well, after I'd finished in *Manchester Street*, I got the tube from *Piccadilly Circus* to go to my studio and thought I'd walk across the common when I saw you. Coincidence, eh?"

"Yeah, well let's not tell my sister. She'd probably put it down to ley lines or psychic energy or something."

"Oh, that's a good idea. I'll tell her I took a diversion across the common because I could sense the negative vibrations you were sending out. We'll never hear the end of it."

Catherine was laughing again, although there seemed to be a slightly hysterical edge to it. I got her another large glass of wine and Millie her third packet of crisps and Catherine seemed more like the wife I knew; the breakdown by the bandstand far behind her. But then, as the alcohol kicked in, she seemed to become almost too tired to keep laughing. I volunteered to change Millie's nappy and that extracted a brief smile. I laid Millie on the changing mat and set about unbuttoning her baggy pink dungarees.

"Michael?" said Catherine ominously.

"What?"

"I'm not happy."

"Sorry?"

"I'm not happy."

"Is it dry enough? I asked for a dry white wine."

"With my life. I'm not happy."

"What do you mean, you're not happy; of course you're happy."

"I'm not. I felt guilty about it so I kept it to myself, but it's just such a strain. It's like there's something missing that I can't put my finger on."

"It's just the drink talking, Catherine. You're feeling tired and a bit drunk and suddenly you think you're not happy, but believe me, you are one of the happiest people I know. Next you'll be saying you can't cope with the children."

"I can't cope with the children."

"Stop it, Catherine, it's not funny. Millie, stop wriggling, will you."

"I'm not joking."

"You do cope with the children. You cope brilliantly. Millie, lie still."

Catherine shrugged and said nothing. I looked up at her from where I was kneeling on the floor, hunched over the changing mat.

"OK, sometimes maybe you feel as if you can't cope with them, but I'm sure that's normal. Generally speaking you like being with the kids on your own."

"No, I don't."

"Yes, you do."

"No, I don't."

"Well maybe occasionally they feel a bit overwhelming. But, generally speaking, you like having me out of the way."

"No, I don't."

"Yes, you do."

"No, I don't."

"Yes, you do."

"No, I don't."

"Look stop it, you naughty girl."

"Are you talking to me or Millie?"

Millie was wriggling and making it impossible for me to put the nappy on straight.

"Why do you have to make things bloody difficult?" And then I added, "Millie!" just to be clear.

"I want Mummy to do it."

"No, Mummy can't do everything."

"Yes she can," said Catherine. "Clever Mummy can do everything and keep smiling happy smiles all day long, tra-la-la."

"Catherine, you're pissed."

". . . off. I'm pissed off."

"Look, I understand that you've had a lousy day and that

the kids can be wearing, but you have always said how much you love being at home with them."

"That was for your sake," she said. "I thought if you were under all that pressure at work then the last thing you needed was to have me moaning about being at home."

"You're just saying that."

"It's true."

"It's not."

"It is; it's miserable being on my own half the week. Sometimes I feel like I've already done a day's work, and then I look at the kitchen clock and it's only ten in the morning and I think, Only nine hours till they're in bed."

"You're just saying that because you feel miserable at the moment. I know you cope really well when I'm not there."

"I don't."

"I'm telling you you do. I know you do."

"How do you know? How do you know better than me how I cope when you're not there?"

"Well, er, because I know you, that's how. You're a very good mother."

"You used to say I was a very good actress."

"You still are a very good actress."

"I must be if you believe all that happy-families stuff I turn on when you walk through the front door."

I didn't have an answer to that, and then Millie tried to wriggle free again and I lost patience with her.

"JUST STOP IT, MILLIE, FOR GOD'S SAKE. YOU'RE A VERY NAUGHTY GIRL! YOU'RE VERY, VERY NAUGHTY AND I'VE HAD ENOUGH OF IT NOW!"

Eventually Catherine decided it was time to go home and she said that I had better get back to my studio to carry on with my work. But this time I didn't take her up on her offer. Something had penetrated my rhino-hide skin and I sensed that she wanted me to change my plans and come home. She needed me to just be there. She needed me to be supportive. And she needed me to drive the car home because she was pissed out of her head.

We headed back over the river, and I told Millie that Albert Bridge was made out of pink icing sugar, and in the late May sunshine it looked as if it might well have been. As we entered Chelsea the people on the street were suddenly very different to those a hundred yards away on the other side of the river. With their Moschino handbags and Ralph Lauren shirts, they were so expensively dressed that they had to wear their labels on the outside. We would have to drive all the way through the richest parts of London before we came out on the other side and were back among the more impoverished middle classes once again.

Forty minutes later we were back in our *bijou* shoebox in Kentish Town. I put some tea in front of Millie, which after three packets of crisps she quite rightly ignored. Why I didn't cook it and then put it straight in the bin to save time, I don't know. Then I sat down beside her and, with Alfie on my lap, we watched *The Lion King* again, right up to the bit where Simba disappears off on his own to grow up and then finally bumps into his long-lost Nala in the forest. Catherine got herself another drink; I was glad that she was no longer breastfeeding because if she had been Alfie would probably have passed out from alcohol poisoning. We didn't talk any more about what she'd said, although I did notice myself making exaggerated aren't-they-sweet? noises every time the kids did anything as much as throw a lump of food on the floor.

I cooked the kids' tea and cleared up, I cooked our dinner and cleared up, I bathed the kids and put them to bed, I tidied away the toys and even put a load of washing on, but it seemed that nothing could extricate any grateful noises of approval from Catherine, who just lay on the sofa, staring at the ceiling. To her credit, she had known when to stop drinking, which was when the wine bottle was empty. Eventually she announced she was going to bed early and she gave me a hug. "It's not you; it's me," she said meaningfully, and then she squeezed me so tightly she nearly cracked a couple of ribs.

I stayed downstairs for a while and listened to a few of my favorite bits of music on my own. I listened to "For No One" by the Beatles three times, which felt like having someone unlock an impossible sequence of secret doors inside my head. When I couldn't think of any more reasons to stay up I got ready to follow Catherine to bed. I mixed Alfie's bottle of babymilk for the night feed, stood it by the microwave and then checked on the kids. Millie had already vacated her bed and taken my place beside Catherine, so I went into the nursery, climbed into her bed and pulled the Barbie duvet up over my head. I kicked a couple of soft toys out of the bottom of the bed and lay there listening to Alfie snuffling in the cot beside me.

An hour passed and I was still awake. I fluffed up the pillow and pulled up the duvet, but it wasn't the bedding that was making me uncomfortable. The picture of her sitting on the ground crying just kept coming back to me. It was so at odds with the image of Catherine that I had kept in my head when we were apart. Unaware that I was watching her, she had just given up and surrendered. And now that her cover was blown she wasn't pretending anymore.

"There's something missing that I just can't put my finger on," she had said. I tried to tell myself it was just some hormonal depression related to the pregnancy, but I knew if it was that simple I wouldn't be lying awake at two o'clock in the morning. An hour later, I listened as Alfie began to stir. Now that he was nearly a year old he generally only woke once in the night, and although the chances of Catherine being stirred from her wine-induced coma were frankly quite slim, I went downstairs and warmed up his babymilk before he started to cry. I took a swig to check the temperature and then spat the disgusting chalky pond water out into the sink, but it left a bad taste in my mouth. The trick now was to give Alfie a good feed without stimulating him so much that he became wide awake. But as we sat together in the half-light of the nursery and he sucked eagerly on the bottle, he suddenly opened his eyes as if he had just realized something very important. He stared at me as he fed and I risked a gentle, "Hello, Alfie Adams," and he just carried on drinking and staring. He seemed so completely trusting and innocent, so completely dependent on my care that I felt like I had somehow let him down. As I looked into his big blue eyes I imagined for a moment that he knew everything about me, that he understood why his mother felt isolated and abandoned and he was just staring sternly at me as if to say, "What on earth do you think you are doing, Dad?"

"I'm sorry, Alfie," I said. "I'm really sorry." And I was.

7

The Mark of a Man

"IT IS NOT POSSIBLE to maintain your dignity in a ball pit. Once you are lying on your back in the krazy quicksand of brightly colored plastic balls you must resign yourself to looking like a lumbering, graceless buffoon, a sweaty injured walrus of a grown-up who, just by dint of being there, invites being bombarded by a hail of primary-colored plastic cannon balls. There is a special fun smile you must wear, even when the little boy with the bullet haircut who you don't know has just got you right in the face with a ball he has squashed to make it hurt more when he throws it. This is just one aspect of the general loss of dignity that is part of the modern paternal contract. You cannot appear aloof and indifferent when your two-year-old is vomiting his chocolate ice cream all over the floor of a designer menswear shop. There is no sophisticated, tasteful way to wipe the shit off your baby's bottom. Don't ever believe those adverts that tell you having kids will make you look cool, because it won't. There is no Action Man double buggy with pullout baby-changing mat. The mark of a man is no longer splashing on Old Spice and surfing to the chorus of the *Carmina Burana*; it is swallowing your pride and grubbing about on the floor and rolling around in ball pits. It's humiliating, but it's part of the deal."

The crowd of fathers-to-be listened to me in shocked silence. Despite this pregnancy being Catherine's third, I found myself being dragged back to antenatal classes and, on this particular evening, all the men had been sent into a separate room to discuss the ways in which we expected our lives to change after our babies were born.

"Another thing they don't warn you about," I continued, like an irate caller on a late-night radio phone-in, "is what it does to your marriage. Suddenly you niggle at each other and score points and try to make out you've had a much worse time than your partner. Catherine will say to me, 'Have you sterilized the bottles,' when she can see the dirty bottles piled up in the sink. She knows the answer to the question, but by asking it knows she will force me into a guilty admission of failure. But all that does is make me exaggerate how difficult Alfie was while she was out. No, not exaggerate, lie! I will claim that I haven't had a minute spare, and then Catherine will be forced to pretend she had a far worse time with Millie at the supermarket. It's martyr's poker—I'll see your tantrum-at-the-checkout story and raise it with my account of diarrhea in mid nappy-change."

They were as eager to hear about my experiences as I was to recount them. No other man in the room had yet become a parent and they looked to me as the war-scarred veteran, back from battle, full of horrific tales from the front line of fatherhood.

"But the thing that really disappears overnight is your youth. Suddenly your youth is over. I tried to artificially re-create mine," I said enigmatically, "but it hasn't really worked. As soon as you become responsible for someone very, very young, it suddenly makes you feel very, very old. For one thing you are exhausted, both physically and emotionally, and if you have any time to still do any of the things you did as a young man, you will find yourself struggling to tackle them with the weary foreboding of an overwhelmed pensioner. By the time the children start to be less physically demanding you've aged ten years in the space of two or three, so it's too late to get it back anyway. You will look in the mirror at the graying hair and sagging face and you will think, Where the bloody hell did *he* come from? But you don't just look old and feel old in your bones, you *think* old. You fuss and you worry about your children, but you don't realize or care that you're walking down the street with odd socks and your hair sticking up. You become fretful and sensible and organized, and if you ever do anything carefree and spontaneous together it's because two weeks ago you set aside an hour to do something carefree and spontaneous together. The day that baby comes out it's over. Your independence, your youth, your pride—everything that made you what you were. You have to start again from scratch."

The cheery teacher came into the room and clapped her hands together in enthusiastic anticipation.

"Well," she said, "how are we all getting on in here?"

And none of the openmouthed men even looked up from where they were staring silently at the floor.

I found these antenatal classes embarrassing, to tell the truth. It was like I was some backward child being made to do a year at school all over again. At one point our partners had to get on all fours and we had to kneel beside them and rub them on the small of the back, and then the teacher came round to see if we were rubbing our partners correctly. We have classes to help us with the birth of the child; I suppose we should just be grateful we don't have some prim little woman guiding us through the best way to conceive them as well. "Right, now if the women would all like to lie on the floor, perhaps the men could practice stimulating the clitoris. No, Michael, you're miles out there . . ."

And why are there no classes to help us once the children have come out? That's the bit that the adults get wrong, that's the bit where we need real help. "Well done, you gave birth, here's your baby. Now the rest is up to you." I allowed myself a private chuckle at all the naive enthusiasm of the first-time parents. One of the men even asked what sort of filling he should put in the sandwiches, bless him. They were all completely consumed by their child before it had even been born. I wanted to say to them, don't keep coming to these parenting classes, go to the cinema together instead, go out for dinner, just do things for yourselves while you still can. But they compared bumps and bootees and asked us whether it was best to put the baby straight into a cot or whether they should let it come into the parents' bed, and Catherine shrugged and said she still didn't know.

Catherine and I didn't discuss the things she had said sitting outside the Windmill Inn, but it was clear that she had abandoned the pretense that everything in her life was as perfect as I had always presumed. Her frustration was allayed by redecorating the house; she had come out of the tired stage of pregnancy and flipped over into the manic nesting phase. I tried to assuage my guilt by suggesting that she should be resting and that she should leave it all to me, but she really wanted to do something for this new baby, and so she heroically climbed up and down the stepladder, lovingly painting the nursery walls as the paint splattered down onto her growing bump. Obviously there were some things she couldn't do herself, things that needed the strength and technical expertise of a handyman, which was when she would turn to me and say, "Michael, pop round to Mrs. Conroy's and see if Klaus and Hans can give us a hand." I could usually just about manage that.

Klaus and Hans were two German students that lodged next door whom Catherine got round on a regular basis to make me feel useless. On this occasion I had failed to assemble a chest of drawers. The instructions were printed in English, German, Italian, Spanish, French and Arabic. It was thoughtful of the manufacturers to print them in English, but it didn't really make any difference; they made the same amount of sense to me in any language. When I read a sentence like "Attach tab 'c' to retaining toggle 'g' without releasing pivot joint 'f'," a blanket of mist descends on my brain and I am no longer reading instructions, I am just looking at a lot of words. Klaus and Hans put the unit together with the speed and efficiency of a Grand Prix pit-stop team.

"You have a set of Allen keys, Michael, yes?"

"Don't think so."

"Yes you have. In your toolbox."

"Allen keys? Are you sure?"

"Yes. They are in the little compartment with the spokeshave."

"Spokeshave? What's a spokeshave?"

Klaus knew the English for spokeshave. I still don't know what a spokeshave is or how I came to be the owner of one. Klaus and Hans often popped round to borrow my tools, which meant ripping open the packaging in which they'd remained hidden since some long-ago Christmas.

"Is Michael using his power drill at the moment?" Klaus would ask Catherine at the front door. And then I could hear him say, "I don't understand. What is funny?"

But however charming and helpful Klaus and Hans were, I couldn't help but feel vaguely emasculated by the way Catherine came to depend on them. They mended the lawnmower, they unblocked the sink, they stopped the radio alarm I had rewired from giving you an electric shock every time you pressed the snooze button. If I ever came home to find one of them putting a new washer on the tap or whatever I'd step in and say, "Thanks, Klaus, I can take over now." And then an hour later I'd knock on his door and say, "So how do I get the tap back on, exactly?"

Catherine always wanted to change things in our house. It was a kind of permanent revolution; as soon as the campaign to have a new carpet in the bedroom was successful, the next campaign to have new kitchen units would begin. I optimistically suggested to her that the nursery wallpaper would be fine for another year or so, but she asserted that it wouldn't be fair if we didn't make it as nice for the next two kids as it had been for our first two.

"The next *two* kids?"

"Yeah, although sooner or later we're going to have to move to a bigger house, aren't we?"

"A BIGGER HOUSE!" and then I realized that my reaction sounded too much like blind panic and so I repeated the phrase with the air of reasoned contemplation. "A bigger house. Hmm, interesting . . ."

It didn't allay suspicions.

"Why? We're not overdrawn or anything, are we?" asked Catherine, rolling an expensive brand of paint across the ceiling.

I responded with an assertive "No!" in the overemphatic, look-straight-ahead-and-broach-no-debate way that I normally reserved for squeegee merchants offering to clean my windscreen at traffic lights. Catherine generally took little interest in the balance of our financial affairs. She did once attempt to pay off an overdraft by writing out a check from the same account, but generally her only financial worry was that when the sun was shining you couldn't read the screen on the cash dispenser.

I wanted to tell her about the double life I had been leading and explain how I had got into so much debt, but now she had revealed she wasn't happy I didn't have the heart to make things any worse. She said I seemed very quiet, and with an affectionate smile she asked me if I was all right. I said I was fine, which was the word I always used to deflect any embarrassing emotional probing. I could have said I was OK, but that's two syllables and I didn't want to start gushing on about my feelings and getting all Californian about it. Somehow it never felt like the perfect moment to announce, "Actually, darling, this decorating we're doing is a complete waste of time because, guess what? I haven't been paying the mortgage!" They say that honesty is the best policy. Well, that's fine when the truth is all nice and lovely, then it's easy to be honest. What if you're the mystery second gunman in the Kennedy assassination? In that case honesty is clearly not the best policy.

"So, Frank, have you ever been to Dallas before?"

"Yes, I came here once to shoot John F. Kennedy from behind the grassy knoll."

As Catherine had come out of her tired phase so I had entered mine. Suddenly I was working every hour there was in an attempt to make up the mortgage arrears. I wanted to rush home and be with her as much as possible, but financial demands meant that I was trapped in my studio, living the life she thought I'd been living all along. Catherine noticed that I was less patient with the children, that I'd come back to the house and, instead of throwing them up in the air and tickling them, I would flop down on the sofa, exhausted, and then object when they took it in turns to jump on my testicles. What defense could I make for my apparent change in enthusiasm for my kids? "It was easier before. I'd only been pretending to be at work all day."

Although I was gradually earning more, the outstanding mortgage payments bred penalty charges and bank expenses and all sorts of other fees to which high-interest charges seemed to be randomly added. I telephoned round the agencies, trying to get extra work, and I was put on hold and made to wait to speak to people whose calls I'd often forgotten to return in the past. Every day I labored away in my studio, converting favorite tunes I'd been saving for my fantasy first album into jingles to promote low-fat frozen pizzas.

My fatigue from working so hard was compounded by the weight of the secrets I was carrying around with me. The deceit had been tiny when it began; no one would have noticed it. I could barely remember the moment of conception, the moment I released a tiny seed of dishonesty into our relationship. But somehow it had latched on, and then it just seemed to grow and grow until it became as obvious as the bulge under Catherine's T-shirt. When a baby gets to a certain size, it has to come out; the same is true for a lie. By now its gestation had reached such a stage that I was starting to feel contractions. I knew I couldn't keep it in much longer, but I didn't know who I could possibly tell. If I'd been a Catholic I suppose I would have told the priest in confession. If I'd been an old lady I would have found an excuse to go to the doctors and bore them about it for several hours. To whom did people tell their secrets these days? There was no way I was going on daytime television and breaking down in the studio audience while some cut-price Oprah Winfrey put her hand on my shoulder, barely pausing before she trailed the next item. "Women who've slept with their daughters' boyfriends—coming right up after the break."

I had sat alone in my studio, wondering who was my nearest soul mate; with whom was I supposed to share my problems. My mobile rang and it felt good to hear Catherine's reassuring voice.

"Are you OK?" she said, sensing that I sounded preoccupied.

"Fine . . ." And then suddenly it all just spilled out.

"Look, er, Catherine, erm, I've not been straight with you. We're badly in debt and I've been deceiving you about how hard I've been working. Basically I've just been living it up here for the past couple of years while you've been struggling with the babies."

There was a terrible silence. I waited for her to say something, but she didn't, and so I gabbled to fill the void. "I know, but I've changed. I'm working really hard now, and I'm going to make it up to you, I promise."

Still she said nothing. I wished I could have said this to her face, to see how she was reacting; the silence was oppressive. It was so quiet I couldn't even hear the crackle of the phone, which was because there was no crackle of the phone—I'd lost the signal; the mobile had cut off. I didn't know whether she'd hung up in angry disgust or not heard a single word of what I'd said. My mobile suddenly rang again.

"Sorry," she said brightly. "Millie pressed the button down on the receiver. So you're all right, are you?"

"Yeah, er, yeah, I'm fine," I said, breathing an exhausted sigh of relief. "I'll be back in time to see the kids tonight."

"Great," she said. "You just sounded a bit subdued."

"Yeah, well, I just wish I was there already."

At least this wasn't a lie. But today I couldn't go home until I had finished arranging a vital eight-second piece of music that was urgently required to assist in persuading people to visit World of Bathrooms. It was needed first thing the following morning, and I estimated the job would take me a couple of hours, maybe one and a half if it went well. I switched on my computer and loaded up the appropriate program. From the living room came a sudden burst of laughter. My flatmates were obviously enjoying something very funny, but I resolved to ignore it and carry on. The first job I had to complete was the mundane task of importing old PC midi-files into Cubase by manually dragging them across with the cursor. It's even less interesting than it sounds. There was another explosion of giggles, this time even louder. I glanced toward the door, wondering what could possibly be so hilarious. I recognized it as that sort of derisory hyena cackling—amusement that was at someone else's expense—which made it all the more intriguing. There is something magnetic about unexplained laughter; it's not just the simple desire to enjoy a burst of happiness, but the burning curiosity it creates about the cause. When a gunman is holed up in a besieged building, the police always try threats and plea-bargaining and appeals from his mother to lure him out. It would be much quicker if, on the count of three, they all fell about in hysterics; the gunman would be out in a flash saying, "What? What is it?"

I dragged the mouse across the grubby mat; suddenly it seemed heavy and unwieldy. The clock said 16:44, as I was sure it had done for the last three and a half minutes. "Ha ha ha ha ha," screamed the siren voices of my flatmates again, but they weren't going to stop me working; they weren't going to tempt me away. Although, as it happened, I did just need to get a tiny drop more milk to put in my tea.

"What? What is it?" I said as I walked into the living room.

"We're playing Beat the Intro," said Jim. This game was a regular household favorite which involved one flatmate playing the opening bars of an old hit or album track and everyone else then going into agonized spasms as they searched for the name of the song. I had spent many an evening in this flat shouting, "Honky Tonk Women" on hearing the solitary tap of a cow bell, or "Ballroom Blitz" at the sound of a siren.

It was hard to imagine how Beat the Intro could be causing such hilarity, but Jim explained further.

"Paul is stuck on one particular record. So far he has guessed that it's 'Shaddap You Face' by Joe Dolce or the theme to *Steptoe and Son*."

"It's obviously a novelty record of some sort," said Paul.

"See if you recognize it, Michael." Jim, with a suspicious glint in his eye, played the track and I immediately recognized the best song I had ever written, recorded on flexi-disc and played three times on Thames Valley FM.

"Is it 'There's No One Quite Like Grandma'?" said Paul hopefully, and Simon and Jim fell around in further hysterics.

"Not as classy as that," said Jim.

"It's not the Mini Pops, is it?" he asked.

"No, it is not," I said indignantly. "It's 'Hot City Metal' by Micky A. and it was played three times on Thames Valley FM. It was quite innovative at the time," I claimed. Trying not to look too obviously hurt, I put my precious flexi-disc back in its sleeve and went and got myself some milk while Jim continued the game with some more conventional tracks.

As I walked back through the living room toward my studio, Jim was cueing up the next track. There was a few seconds' silence before the music began, and since I was mildly curious as to whether I could identify it, my pace slowed slightly. A gentle guitar strumming started up; the chords were C for one bar and then E minor for one bar, repeating over and over again, and I recognized the song immediately. It was such an obvious and famous intro that anyone would have got it right away. Which was why it was so completely infuriating that I couldn't quite place it for a moment.

"Oh, oh, oh, that's, um. Oh God, that is such a famous track. Um, 1970s, huge hit; it's the Stones or someone, isn't it?"

"Maybe," said Jim sadistically, "maybe not."

"Play it again," I intoned, standing with one leg outside the doorway, pretending to myself that I really wasn't staying. He pointed the remote control at the stereo, the guitar faded up again and I nodded sagely as the record went through its familiar intro, while the Rolodex in my brain was spinning round and round trying to locate the place where I stored the rest of the song. It was just so disorganized in there; I could never find anything.

"Oh, it is so obvious," said Simon unhelpfully.

"Come on," said Paul. They had both already got the track; this round was clearly for my benefit only.

C/C/C/C/Em/Em/Em/Em it went yet again, and then, just

as the answer was tantalizingly within my grasp, Jim paused the track again. "I know it, I know it," I pleaded to my interrogators. "It's, like, Neil Young or someone, isn't it?" I suggested.

This caused delighted jeering laughter from the other three. Being the master of human psychology that I was, I therefore deduced that it probably wasn't Neil Young, or indeed Crosby, Stills or Nash for that matter.

"Give me a clue."

They looked at each other, nodded and then Simon volunteered. "It was the first song ever to get to number one after being re-released."

This was far too big a clue to do anything but make matters worse. Facts such as this one are kept in a different office to the department where tunes are stored. In fact, it was right over the other side of town; it was two buses away. Now I was further than ever from recognizing the song because I was on a huge diversion trying to remember a separate piece of pop trivia. I had been so close to completing the intro in my head, but now the only lyrics I could put to the tune was the haunting couplet:

"This is the first song
To be re-released and then get to number one."

It didn't ring any bells.

"Oh God, this is torture. I can't believe it. I know this song so well," I wailed, now sitting in a chair in the living room with my head in my hands, all thoughts of work forgotten. "Tum-te-tum-te-tum-te-tum tum tum tum te-tum-te-tum-te-tum," I repeated to myself over and over again. But no matter how many times I traipsed up that musical staircase, at the same point I suddenly felt as if there was nothing under my feet.

"There was a sequel to the song recorded eleven years after the original which also went to number one," said Simon.

"Shhh, shhh, shhh. I nearly had it then. It was just coming to me and now it's gone again. Doh!" And then I thought about what Simon had actually said.

"A sequel? To a song? God, what on earth is it?"

"And it was taken from an album of the same name."

"A début album," chipped in Paul, and I felt the solution slipping away from me again. Like a salmon that had taken the fly, I was played on the line until exhausted; they had me hooked and were now enjoying the maximum possible sport. When I realized this I resolved to wrench myself free and, summoning all my will power, I stood up and declared, "Oh, this is ridiculous, I really don't care one way or the other," and then I stormed off down the hall back to my studio to forget all about it. Three and a half seconds later I came back into the living room.

"OK. Just play it once more," I said.

"My name is Michael Adams and I am a triviaholic. I am taking one day at a time, but I find that there are certain social situations where I find it really hard to resist the thrill of a quiz question answered correctly."

In my imaginary self-help group, the other triviaholics are seated around in a circle, nodding and smiling at me sympathetically as I relate my experiences.

"There's no buzz like it; it's like a miniature mental climax, a little cerebral orgasm. But I know that just one will never be enough, and then I'll need another and another, and before I know it all my money will have disappeared on pop-quiz books and I will have lost all my friends after a huge argument about the imprecise wording of one of their trivia questions. I'm trying to give it up, I really am, but it's hard because on every street there's a pub, and I think I'll just pop in for one swift pub quiz and I'm in there all night. So now I have to stay at home and just watch television, but on every channel there's *University Challenge* or *Who Wants to Be a Millionaire?*, and I can't believe that the contestant doesn't know which line on the London Underground map is colored pink."

"Hammersmith and City," blurts out one of the trivia-holics, unable to help himself, and his therapy is set back another six months.

The Beat the Intro round ended up turning into a very heavy late-night session. I did finally get the track I'd been searching for, when after trying a thousand different keyholes the music finally unlocked the memory bank where I'd filed the opening line. " 'Space Oddity' by David Bowie," I declared exhaustedly to the patronizing applause of my flatmates. But the buildup had been so long and the anticipation so great that now I could feel only a vague sense of empty disappointment. The only possible cure was to get the next song more quickly.

It was hours before I was back in my studio, and in the end I didn't finish my piece of music until about one in the morning. I turned off my computer, looked at my watch and realized that I had missed the last tube home. If I'd had any cash I would have got a minicab, but I'd already been reduced to ripping open the charity envelope by the front door to pay the pizza delivery man. I left a text message on Catherine's mobile, which included a sad little face made up of the appropriate punctuation marks. Then I left another text message, stressing that this was meant to be ironic, that I didn't normally do anything as naff as leave sad or happy faces on people's mobile screens, and by the time I'd done all that I probably could have walked the six miles across London to Kentish Town.

Catherine would have had a night no different to many others, but for me the routine had changed. Now I felt disappointed and stupid, like I'd spent the evening putting coins into a slot machine and had then walked away with empty pockets wondering why I felt so unfulfilled. I got into bed and, with a last glance at the photo of Catherine and the kids that had recently been propped up on my bedside table, I switched off the light. Then I lay there trying to work out how a promise to be home in time to see them turned into an apologetic text message.

My flatmates were like the games on my computer: as long as they were there I would be unable to resist being tempted away from whatever I was supposed to be doing. Because of my newfound determination to stop squandering my working day I had recently deleted Minesweeper, Tetris, Solitaire and all the other distractions from my PC. Now, whenever I got stuck I found myself wasting twice as much time loading the games back on to the hard drive before playing them, and then deleting them all over again until the next time. Why was I so weak? Why could I not resist the temptation of mindless diversions? Why did I always get near to the end of Minesweeper, stop concentrating and then blow myself up?

I felt like a man having an affair, only it wasn't an affair with a younger woman, it was an affair with a younger version of myself. Just as some men get back in contact with old girlfriends after they are married, I'd met up again with the twenty-something Michael Adams. He'd made me feel young again; he'd understood all my problems. And we still had so much in common; we liked to do the same things. It was only when I mentioned my wife and children that he would go all prickly and defensive. He didn't want to know about them; he'd always secretly hoped that he came first in my life, that my future lay with him. Like any affair it had quickly become too complex. Now I was trying to break it off, but I was in too deep. I tried to say to the irresponsible, carefree version of myself, "I don't want to lose you as a friend," or "Can't we just see each other every now and then," but he wasn't letting go easily. I told him that I had loved the time we'd spent together, that when the younger Michael and I were playing around I was as relaxed and carefree as could be, but I couldn't handle the guilt anymore; I couldn't handle the secrecy and the lies; I couldn't keep it bottled up any longer.

I got out of bed and turned on the light. I started to write it all down: how I was deceiving Catherine and had been doing so for years; how I had felt excluded when the babies came along; how I had suddenly felt like a gooseberry, gate-crashing a private love affair between Catherine and her children. At first these notes were just intended for myself, but the more I wrote down, the more I wanted to share them with someone, and eventually my confessional turned into an extended letter to my father. I'd never talked about personal things with Dad; I didn't have that kind of a relationship with him. But I didn't have that sort of relationship with anyone else, either, so perhaps this was an attempt to establish one. At least I could be certain that, whatever else, he would be on my side. When you are having an affair, who better to tell than someone you know who's had one, too.

I thought about when Mum and Dad had split up. Because I had been so young I think much of it had been re-created in my head; the memory was now digitally remastered. But I had a vivid sequence of pictures of Mum and Dad shouting at one another and Dad jumping in the car and scraping the gatepost as he sped off, and I knew that wasn't the normal way to drive away from our house. I had a stronger memory of the years following their divorce, when I was frostily handed over from one parent to another, like a spy being exchanged at an East German border post. For years I had spent the weekdays with my mother and the weekends with my dad, playing music and killing time in a soulless bachelor pad. It occurred to me that this was a double life I'd managed to replicate perfectly as an adult.

Mum had said that all she wanted was for me to be happy, and then she'd burst into tears in front of me, which I can't really say did the job. After a couple of years she had a special friend called Keith who would come and stay. Mum and Keith had an elaborate foreplay which involved them both walking around the garden in the late afternoon while he pretended to be interested in all the flowers she had planted. Then she cooked him a meal and Keith would stay the night. I wondered if he wore that stupid cravat under his pajamas as well. They would go to bed at the same time and then they would get up about twenty minutes later and go to the toilet a lot. I used to lie in bed listening to them walking across the landing and then flushing the toilet over and over again. I wondered if perhaps Keith's house didn't have a toilet, because whenever he stayed with us, he always seemed to make maximum use of ours.

It was only later that I realized that they'd been having it off, and then the idea of my mother having sex completely horrified me. When it was explained to me that my parents must have had sexual intercourse in order to conceive me, I remember being disgusted and wishing they hadn't. "But then you wouldn't exist," my friend had said.

"That's fine. I'd rather take that option."

After a year or so the toilet flushing decreased, but the noise was replaced by the sound of Mum and Keith shouting at each other. I was always packed off to bed early because Mum and Keith couldn't wait to be alone so they could get down to another bit of fighting.

Being only eight years old, I didn't really understand that I was disturbed by yet another round of shouting and tears in my home, but I suppose it wasn't normal behavior to stand on the end of my bed every night and urinate against the wall. Every night in the same spot. I don't know what possessed me to do it; it's not as if the toilet was constantly engaged any-more. Mum had builders, plumbers and plasterers round—none of them could ever work out why the wallpaper was peeling off, the plaster was crumbling and the carpet was rotting. I remember being scared that one of them would guess the cause. As if the head builder would suck the air in through his teeth and shake his head. "Ooh dear. No, it's not wet rot or a cracked boiler inlet feed. No, that's yer classic subconscious cry for help by an eight-year-old traumatized by his parents' divorce. I could get my chippy to have a look at it for you, but really you want a proper child psychologist, and my one's on another job."

I decided against putting all this in my letter to Dad because I didn't want him to think I was trying to make him feel guilty for walking out when I was five. Though I bloody well hoped he did feel a little bit guilty for walking out when I was five. There had been a time when I'd hated him for leaving Mum, but now I no longer based my view of people entirely on what my mother had thought. I didn't still think that Liberace had just never found the right girl.

Eventually Keith found someone else's toilet to flush, and for years after she was abandoned the second time, Mum didn't let herself get close to anyone. After that I was her man; I was the one who filled her tank when we pulled into the petrol station. And at the weekends I would obligingly play the role of husband substitute, walking around clothes shops with her, shrugging indifferently as she emerged from the changing room in a variety of equally frumpy dresses. I had to grow up fast; maybe that was partly why I'd contrived a second childhood in my thirties. Finally I left home and went off to college, and Mum suddenly met and married a man from Northern Ireland. I think for the last year of her life she was quite happy. She invited me to the wedding, because she said she thought I might like to meet him, which was thoughtful of her. I can't say I cared for him a great deal; he was all firm handshakes and meaningful eye contact, and he said my name too often when he was talking to me. But that didn't stop Mum from moving back to Belfast with him. I wished I'd made the effort to see her after she moved there, but I never did. And six months later she was walking through the city center when she got knocked down and killed by a speeding car. And that was it. Now there is a big empty space where she should be. In a shop, sitting in a chair, standing in a bus queue; there's an empty person-shaped gap where she would be now if she hadn't stepped out in front of that car.

Telling people about the death of a loved one is supposed to be a therapeutic part of the grieving process. Not in my case. When I told all my college friends that my mother had been killed in Belfast, they all said, "By a bomb?"

I would continue to stare solemnly at the ground and explain further. "No. By a car."

"Oh, I see." And then there was a pause. "A car bomb?"

"No. Just a car. She was run over by a man driving down the street."

"Blimey. That's awful. She hadn't been informing on the IRA or anything?"

"No, of course she hadn't. It was an accident. He was just driving too fast."

"Oh. Joyrider, was he?"

"No, it was just an ordinary car accident. It wasn't a car bomb or joyriders or an IRA execution. It was just a common or garden road accident. They do have them in Belfast."

Every person I had to tell would do the usual embarrassed sympathizing bit, and I'd say thanks a lot and then there was that awkward pause when they felt they had to say something to fill the silence. "You must have worried about something like this happening when she moved to Northern Ireland . . ."

"No," I said sharply. Obviously everyone thought that

Mum had brought it upon herself, I mean, moving to Belfast, well, that's just asking to be run over by a seventy-five-year-old man, isn't it? At the funeral one of her cousins said loudly, "I warned her she'd get herself killed if she moved to Belfast." I finally snapped and shouted, "For God's sake. She was run over. By an old man in a car. It happens in Belfast; it happens in London; it happens in fucking Reykjavik!" And someone said, "All right, Michael; there's no need for that." And another relation put an arm round my mum's cousin and said, "Well, of course, it's a very dangerous place, Belfast."

You can always rely on funerals to bring out the worst in a family.

Perhaps if she had still been alive I would have told all my problems to her, because I certainly had little idea how my father would react to this letter when I posted it. I told him about everything that had happened since the children had come along. How I had spent endless days in my room making compilation tapes while Catherine had struggled through the hardest years of being a parent. How Catherine had thought I'd been working sixteen hours a day when really I'd been having naked piggyback fights with beautiful young girls and boozy barbecues on Clapham Common. How I had tried to have everything—the love of a family and the liberty of a single man, the commitment of children and the carefree wastefulness of youth. There were pages of it by the time I'd finished—frank and emotional outpouring that my father would probably have thought as interesting as I found his news about Brian's discounted Mondeo, but next morning I sent it off to him anyway.

It felt good to have got it all off my chest. As I posted the letter I knew I was definitely doing the right thing. I had no choice but to make myself think that—the postman refused to give me the letter back when he finally arrived to empty the pillar box an hour and a half later. Now that I had shared my secret with someone else I felt as if a huge weight had been lifted from my shoulders. Suddenly everything was crystallized. You cannot break off an affair and carry on seeing your old mistress. Dad had tried that with Janet the chemist and had ended up moving in with her. I had promised Catherine I would be home the previous evening, but I had ended up playing around again. The only way forward was clear to me now: I had decided to move out of the flat: my double life was over. I would set up my studio equipment in the loft or the shed or in our bedroom; it didn't matter, but I couldn't carry on as I was.

As it turned out I never really talked to Dad about the enormous revelation that I had sprung upon him. I suppose the therapeutic act of writing it all down and posting it had been what was important, so in that sense the letter had already done its work. By the time I spoke to Dad again, what he thought of it all no longer seemed very important. Because when Catherine got to read the letter, her reaction rather overshadowed everything else.

8

Just Do It

"MICHAEL, how would you like to have your own record in the charts?"

I'd been building a brick tower for Millie when Hugo had rung my mobile. The trill of the phone jolted me out of my trance, and I realized that Millie had actually wandered off sometime before and that for the past couple of minutes I'd been playing with little bricks on my own.

"My own record?" I said, standing up.

"Yup. With your name on it and everything. Top of the charts. How does that grab you?"

This was obviously some scam designed to talk me into doing some crappy underpaid job for him, and so a cautious voice at the back of my head told me to say I wasn't particularly interested.

"Well, I'd be very interested," I said. "Though, um, in what way would this be my own record?" Hugo proceeded to explain and no amount of phony excitement on his part could convince me that this project would be my personal *Sergeant Pepper*. Through one of his various Soho contacts, Hugo was putting together a CD called *Classic Commercials*. Everyone's favorite pieces of classical music—namely the ones they only recognized because they'd heard them on TV ads—now available together on one great album.

"And I immediately thought of you, Michael. You love all that classical stuff, don't you."

"I'm pretty sure this idea has been done before, Hugo."

"Not for at least eighteen months," he said. "And now there's the technology to re-create the orchestra with all your clever equipment, so we don't have to fork out a fortune to pay a lot of poncey violin players in dinner jackets."

"Well, when you put it like that, I'm really flattered that you want me on board."

I attempted to maintain a disdainful air, but Hugo was determined that I was the right man for the job. "It has to be you, Michael. You're the man that put that tum-tc-tum tune into the instant-tea-granules ad." It was true. I had indeed been the man who had made Verdi's "March of the Hebrew Slaves" synonymous with "the cuppa that's easy as one, two, tea." When Classic FM had its annual vote for their listeners' all-time top one hundred pieces of music I had felt quite chuffed to see Verdi's "March of the Hebrew Slaves" make its first entry in the charts at number nine. If it hadn't been for instant tea granules I doubt whether it would ever have made the top one hundred.

So this was to be the extent of my recording success as a musician. It wouldn't be my own compositions on the CD, it would be my synthetic arrangements of Beethoven, Brahms and Berlioz listed according to composer, title and brand of panty liners that they had promoted. I couldn't help but feel a slight sense that my dreams had been compromised since I'd left music college.

"Why don't you just do a compilation of all the classic overtures as played by mobile phones?"

"That's not a bad idea. We could do that as a follow-up."

We talked about which pieces of music they had in mind and I attempted to explain to Hugo that in reality no technology could adequately re-create the sound of an orchestra, but he was unmoved.

"Just stick on a bit of extra reverb or something we'll give you a budget to get in singers or whatever for the ones like when that fat bloke from the opera is so sad he wants just one cornetto."

" 'O Sole Mio' is not from an opera."

"Whatever."

"You could do it, but it would sound shit."

"Yeah, but the sort of people who'll buy it won't be able to tell it sounds shit."

I told Hugo he was the most cynical person I had ever met and he was genuinely flattered. But by not refusing to do the job I found that somehow I seemed to have agreed to do it. *Commercial Classics* would be a pick-and-mix CD, a collection of cheaply produced orchestral soundbites for people who didn't want to commit to a whole symphony. Although I felt vaguely uncomfortable about the whole idea I sat down to work out which little ditties would make up the list. From the opera *The Tale of Tsar Saltan* there would be Rimsky-Korsakov's famous "Flight of the Black and Decker Paint Stripper." There was "Jupiter" from Holst's *Planets* suite—better known as the theme from the Dulux Weathershield ad. There was the Hovis Ad, sometimes known as the *New World Symphony*. Antonín Dvořák had written this music as a tribute to the United States. I think putting ten seconds of it in a TV ad said more about the American way than his symphony ever could have done. There was the "Dance of the Little Swans" from *Swan Lake*, for which Tchaikovsky had wrought his emotions in his quest to express the convenience, the delicious flavor and sheer absence of calories that is Batchelor's Slim A Soup. And there was, of course, *Beethoven's Blue Band Margarine Symphony.*

Within a quarter of an hour I had scribbled a list of about twenty to thirty pieces of music that had been made famous by their repeated exposure on television adverts. Catherine had overheard my phone call and, despite being stretched out on the floor like a beached whale in a futile attempt to be comfortable, she tried to see what it was that I was writing down. I was embarrassed to tell her about the project, but she understood my reservations.

"Don't do it, then, if you find it distasteful."

"Well I've sort of said that I would now."

"Well ring him back and tell him you've changed your mind."

"But you don't know what Hugo's like. I'll come off the phone having just agreed we should make it a double CD."

Catherine was irritated by my weakness when confronted by people like Hugo. She told me I should stick up for myself and, not having the courage to argue with her, I meekly agreed that I would in future.

"I've got an idea to make some money," she suddenly announced. "A compilation novel." And she started making some notes.

"What?"

"Well, if you can buy all these CDs that bring together the most popular bits of classical music, somebody ought to publish a compilation novel."

Catherine was more of a literary person than me. Every month she attended a reading group where about half a dozen women got together and spent five minutes talking about *Captain Corelli's Mandolin* and the other three hours slagging off their husbands.

"I don't understand," I said. "How can you have a compilation novel?"

She cleared her throat to read out her work in progress. "The action starts in the Wessex town of Casterbridge when the mayor wakes up one morning and notices that he has turned into a beetle. Now Mrs. Bennet decides that he would no longer make a suitable husband for her daughter Molly Bloom so she escapes from the attic where she was imprisoned by Rochester and sets fire to Manderley. 'The horror, the horror!' exclaims Heathcliff as the white whale drags Little Nell beneath the waves to a tragic death, and Tom Jones sits alone in the garden of Barchester Towers knowing he had won the victory over himself. He loved Big Brother."

I chuckled at Catherine's fantastically vulgar idea and pretended to recognize all the references. Inside part of me was thinking, Actually, as someone with absolutely no knowledge of English literature I wouldn't mind reading that.

"Quick, quick!" she said suddenly, placing my hand on her bump. "There. Did you feel that?"

"No," I said. "You're not really pregnant, are you?"

"Ah, you've rumbled me. No, I've just been eating loads and loads of cream cakes." And we both laughed and then suddenly I said, "Wow! That was a big one!" Sometimes when Catherine giggled the baby inside her would give approving little kicks to show that it too was enjoying the moment. I watched the baby's heel or elbow or something ripple across under her stretched stomach like Moby Dick just below the surface. Catherine was now over halfway through her pregnancy. A whole new human being was shaping up. In a few months' time I would be a biological parent for the third time, but somehow I didn't really feel like I was a fully formed father yet. The birth of our baby would be a long and painful business; I suppose there was no reason why I should expect my own transition to be any easier.

The baby now made a neat little bump at the front of Catherine's stomach and the received wisdom was that this made it more likely the baby would be a boy. Folklore and fishwives have provided all sorts of ways to detect the sex of the unborn infant: the shape of the bulge, the nature of the mother's food cravings and, of course, the wedding ring test. This involves lying the mother on her back and dangling her wedding ring on a piece of cotton above her womb. If it sways slightly it's a girl; if it spins it's a boy. Catherine's ring spun and swayed and I spent a week worrying that our new baby would grow up to look like the girl on Simon's computer.

A pregnant woman's bulge needs to be a lot larger than Catherine's for her to be absolutely sure of being offered a seat on the underground, but as yet no woman has ever been twenty-two months pregnant. It would be nearly Christmas before Catherine would get really big, and by then men sitting on the tube would have no choice but to do the decent thing and hold their newspapers so close to their face that she couldn't possibly catch their eye. Or so they thought. But Catherine being Catherine would peer over the top of their papers and say, "Are you comfy enough sitting there or would you like to put your feet up on my bump." I suspected that it was embarrassment that prevented some men from giving up their seats—the thought of talking to a complete stranger on the tube, a person of the opposite sex who they would specifically be addressing because of that woman's gynecological condition; it's enough to make the average Englishman shrivel up and die. I put this thesis to Catherine, and she listened carefully and nodded and then proposed her own carefully considered analysis: "You don't think it might just be because men are all selfish bastards?" Embarrassment was not a concept Catherine really understood, but I suppose that once you've been naked with your legs up in stirrups as a group of medical students look on from the end of the bed, it would take quite a lot to make you blush.

She sat on the floor in front of the telly for another hour or so and I rubbed the base of her back, which had been aching for some weeks. Alfie woke, and though it was too early for his feed I brought him downstairs and gave him his bottle anyway. At every suck Alfie looked surprised, as if he really hadn't been expecting warm milk of all things to follow the previous gulp of warm milk. He started to go to sleep, and I tapped the base of his feet and he started to suck again more fervently; Catherine smiled and said that I had finally learned the knack, and the baby inside her kicked again.

Millie must have woken and seen that her brother's cot was empty and decided she was missing out because she suddenly appeared at the door claiming she had sore hair. Against our better judgment we let her stay with us in the lounge, and the four of us cuddled up on the sofa and watched the opening sequence of *The Lion King* again and when Rafiki held up the newborn baby lion to all the animals and they rejoiced and bowed and cheered, I had to stop myself bursting into tears by turning it into a manic laugh and giving Millie such a tight hug that she said, "Ow!"

I put the kids back to bed and wound up the mobile which played a tinny version of Brahms' "Lullaby," the official theme song of every nursery in the land, chosen for its universal popularity, its gentle melody, but mainly for the fact that its copyright expired two centuries ago. I stroked Millie's head as she went to sleep. These were the moments that I had come home for. I thought about all those men at our antenatal classes, so full of enthusiasm and good intentions. How many of them would allow themselves to become alienated from their families? Would seek comfort in the respect they found at work to make up for the lack of status they suddenly felt at home? We had come halfway out of the dark ages and men were now present at the birth of their children, but how many of those men would be there for the *lives* of their children? Now that I was resolved to changing my ways I suddenly felt like a militant family man, like one of those fervent anti-smokers who had recently been on sixty a day. Why was it so many men really cared about how good they were at their jobs or how good they were at sport, but gave less consideration to being better fathers than they did to improving their batting averages?

Millie's eyes eventually closed and the mobile stuttered to an exhausted halt. I knew that it would be hard for me to adjust to spending more time at home, but the alternative just wasn't viable. I had to learn that it wasn't possible to be in the company of my children and have a different agenda to them. I couldn't look after a toddler and a baby and try to restring my acoustic guitar as well. Sitting down, making yourself a sandwich, going to the toilet—these are all luxuries that you have to forgo. You just have to write off the time and throw yourself into whatever they are doing. You have to head into it. You can't take small children swimming and not go in yourself, and that analogy applies to your entire life once children come along. The water might be cold, and you might not feel like it, but you just have to jump in.

"They're asleep," I said as I came back into the lounge. Catherine said nothing and I realized that she was asleep, too. I'd felt more relaxed with her this evening now that I was no longer mentally vetting every sentence, worrying about what it might reveal. There were just the practicalities of sorting out the flat to be tied up and then my duplicitous days would be behind me. I hadn't told her that I would suddenly be arriving home with a van load of equipment to squeeze into our already cramped home, because if I had she would have successfully dissuaded me. Anyway, a lot of it could go in the loft. The various demo tapes of all my songs could gather dust next to the box of my childhood paintings; they were just more souvenirs acquired on another stage of my journey to adulthood. I would tell Catherine that I was fed up with being away from her and the kids so much and had spontaneously decided to give up my studio and work at home. Which felt quite strange because it was almost true.

Two mornings later I nervously drove a large rented van through the busy London streets and, after a deftly executed twenty-seven-point turn, I parked it outside the flat. I would leave the stereo till last so that I could listen to music as I worked. I selected King Crimson's *21st Century Schizoid Man* followed by Verdi's *Force of Destiny*. I hummed along as I folded all my clothes into boxes. It was funny how the ripped jeans and bomber jackets of my bachelor wardrobe contrasted with the cardigans and slippers I wore at home. One thing that I would never have anticipated was how completely differently I had been viewed by the outside world in my two roles. When I was pushing a double buggy along the pavement old ladies would smile at me and I would smile pleasantly back, but when I walked down the street on my own, I'd forget that I was no longer parading my passport to social acceptability and would absentmindedly grin at some passing lady, who would avert her eyes as if to say, Don't you dare even look at me, you rapist.

There was a huge pile of music papers on top of my wardrobe. I looked back through over twenty years' worth of carefully preserved old editions of the *New Musical Express* and then dumped them into bin liners. I flicked through a few of the interviews with my boyhood heroes—snarling punks spouting nihilistic notions of no future and anarchy, postures I'd once adopted myself. I'd better drop all these newspapers off at the recycling depot, I thought.

I was a dad now and I had kids; they brought enough clutter without me bringing all this worthless history into the home. Although I had attempted to beam myself back to my twenties, I knew now there was no way I could really go back. A few weeks earlier we'd been playing football on the common when a stunning nanny had strolled past with a toddler in her charge. All the men stopped playing and stood staring in her direction.

"She's beautiful," said Jim.

"I think it's a he," I'd said, noticing the little boy's Baby Gap jeans.

I just wasn't cut out to be a "lad" anymore. It was as if I was trying to look cool driving around in a Lotus Elan, but with a "Baby on Board" sticker in the rear window.

I packed away the gear and gadgets which were piled up on the shelves: an out-of-date palm top (without batteries), a prohibitively stiff Swiss army knife, a charger that was only compatible with a games console I had replaced ages ago—all the boys' toys and black plastic detritus I'd accumulated over my years as a thirty-something teenager. It only took another hour to pack all my CDs and books, which left the rest of the afternoon to untangle the seven miles of plastic spaghetti that was spewing out of the back of my keyboard, mixing desk and stereo. Eventually I loaded my musical equipment into the Transit. It reminded me of my days playing in all those bands, and how I had thought that all the humping amps and keyboards into vans would one day lead to a number one hit record. I consoled myself with the thought that when *Classic Commercials* went platinum I could frame that and put it up above the mantelpiece instead. Or maybe pride of place on the toilet wall would be more appropriate.

Finally everything was locked up in the back of the van, ready to be driven over the river. I finished cleaning my room and put the bucket of cleaning stuff back under the sink as noisily as possible and returned the Hoover to its place under the cupboard with a bang and a clatter, but none of my flatmates looked up. There was nothing else to do. This was it. This was the point at which I was saying an overdue farewell to my wilting salad days.

Jim was at the table, failing to work out how to store numbers on his mobile phone, while Paul was almost erupting with frustration, trying to stop himself suggesting that Jim simply read the manual. Simon was slumped in front of the telly watching a nonstop video of goals. Not a video of a great football match, where a goal was a precious and significant thing, but a compilation of lots of different goals, all taken out of context and rendered completely meaningless. It was the sports equivalent of *Classic Commercials*.

"Well, this is it," I said with a self-conscious mock sense of occasion that was the only way to disguise my feeling of a genuine sense of occasion. Although I knew these people were not my soul mates, I thought they might have made a little more effort when it came to saying goodbye. Men have never been very good at emotional farewells. When Scott's expedition was struggling back across the Antarctic and Captain Oates resolved to lay down his own life rather than be a burden to his comrades, he pretended he was just slipping out of the tent to go to the toilet. He would have said he was going off to die, but he couldn't face the embarrassed, indifferent shrug of his friends, mumbling, "Yeah, well, see you about then."

"Yeah, well, see you about, Michael," said Jim as I prepared to stride out into the icy snowstorm of fully committed married life.

"Yeah, bye," said Simon and Paul.

I stood there awkwardly for a couple of seconds. When I thought of some of the great times I had had there I felt sad, almost tearful, but the others seemed indifferent and completely unmoved. Of course, they hadn't had kids yet; their emotions were still in the box.

"Oh, one last thing," said Simon.

"Yes?" I said hopefully.

"Which is the only football club that contains no letters that can be colored in?"

"Eh?"

"When you're coloring in letters—like filling in the 'o's or the 'a's—in the newspaper. Well, which is the only English or Scottish football league club whose name contains no letters that you can color in?"

"Simon, that is the most pointless question I have ever heard," and I paused and heard myself say, "Who is it?"

"Work it out."

"No, it's stupid, I am not going to waste my time and energy even thinking about it."

"OK," he said, "see you about." And he went back to watching his video.

"But just for the record, which team is it?"

"I thought you said it didn't matter?"

"No, it doesn't matter; it is a pointless fact. That is so typical of the level of conversation in this household. Hours and hours wasted talking about something of no significance whatsoever. So Simon, pray, do tell us all which team contains only letters that cannot be colored in?"

"You'll get it eventually."

"I just thought, having raised it, you might tell me which it is."

Simon looked up with a matter-of-fact smile.

"No."

There was a pause. "Well, I'd better be off," and I hovered in the doorway.

"Yeah. See you," they mumbled.

"Ah, I've got it," I said.

"Well done."

"Can I just confirm that I'm thinking of the same club as you?"

"Sure. What team were you thinking of?" said Simon, knowing that I didn't have the faintest idea what the answer was.

"Oh come on, which is it?"

"It's not important," he said without looking up from the television.

"QPR," I blurted out, without really thinking about it.

"Not bad. Except that you can color in the Q, the P and the R."

"Oh yeah."

I sat down at the kitchen table and started firing out the

names of obscure football clubs, only to be told that you could color in the "B" in Bury and the "a" and the "e" in East Fife. A couple of bottles of lager later Monica came round, and when she heard it was my last night in the flat she made a few calls and the crowd who had been planning to go to a club came to the flat instead with bottles of wine and cans of beer. She spontaneously organized the farewell party that I secretly would have quite liked my flatmates to have surprised me with.

By nine o'clock there were about forty people in the flat, drinking cheap red wine out of coffee mugs and jumping about to songs I ought to have recognized. And when I talked to people it was nice when they said, "Oh, you're the bloke who's leaving. Well, cheers for the party." In a way that farewell party was a milestone in my life; it was my paternity bar mitzvah. It was an evening dominated by one overriding thought. Not Am I doing the right thing or Will this make me happy, but unfortunately, Which is the only English or Scottish league football club that contains no letters that can be colored in? I couldn't get it out of my mind, I wanted to forget about it but I was ensnared. This was my big night, I was the center of attention, but it was impossible for me to really enjoy myself because when anyone talked to me I could only pretend to listen while my mind frantically sifted through dozens of lower-division football clubs.

"So whereabouts are you moving to?"

"Fulham," I said delightedly.

"Fulham, eh?"

"Oh no, not Fulham."

"Why not?"

"Well, you can color in the letter 'a,' can't you?"

I danced self-consciously at nine o'clock, and a little less self-consciously two lagers later. Then it came to me; the trick was to think in capital letters. It was a relief to have got it out of the way. I bounded up to Simon, delighted with myself.

"Exeter City," I announced smugly.

"You can color in the 'e's."

"Aha, but not if they're in capitals."

"True, but if you're in upper case then you can color in the letter 'R.' "

I paused and thought about this. "OK, Exeter City written in upper case, except for the letter 'r,' which you write in lower case; look, I'm going to get this . . ." and I wandered off, mumbling clubs from the Scottish second division to myself.

The party wore on and Kate arrived with her new boyfriend, which made me inexplicably jealous. Although I knew I could never have a relationship with her, I think subconsciously I hoped she might keep herself single for evermore, just in case I should ever happen to change my mind. And I didn't like the way Jim gave her so much attention. If I wasn't allowed to be unfaithful with her, then no one else was either. I hardly talked to Simon or Jim all evening. Even then I still hadn't told any of my flatmates that I was married. I had an elaborate story prepared to explain why I was moving out and where I was going, but none of them even bothered to ask.

As the evening drew on, Paul spotted me alone in the corner and came over with two bottles of cold beer, one of which he handed to me. "So, are you staying tonight?"

"Well, no, the van's all packed up now. I'd better make this my last beer."

"So you weren't planning to stay and help clear up?"

"Paul, I'm sorry, I hadn't been planning to stay and clear up, but that's often the way when surprise parties are sprung on you."

"I didn't mean it like that. Sorry."

I could tell that he'd had quite a lot to drink. He seemed to be gearing himself up for getting something off his chest.

"Michael, I know why you never brought a girl back to the flat."

Paul didn't know about the night with Kate, but I wasn't about to start boasting about a mythical night of passion when Kate herself was standing only a few yards away.

"Didn't I?" I said, pretending to rack my brain for examples.

"Oh, come on. Three years of living here; all those nights you stayed out, but never a single girl brought back here. I know the reason why."

I was concerned to find out at this late stage that my secret might have slipped out. I wanted to know more.

"Oh, I see," I said. "Did someone tell you or did you just guess?"

"It's obvious."

"I see. Yes, I suppose there's no escaping the fact that I am just, well, different to you lot."

"Not that different, Mike. Not to me anyway," he said enigmatically.

"You don't mean you've been living a double life as well?"

"Yes. Yes, I have."

He seemed delighted to be able to share this with me.

"Bloody hell! You're a dark horse, Paul."

"Yeah, but I don't think I can keep it secret much longer."

"Yeah, I know what you mean."

"I just thought I'd tell you first because you'd understand. I'm gay, too."

"What?"

"I'm gay as well. And I think you feel the same way about me as I do about you."

"No, no, no, Paul. I'm not gay."

"Don't try and get back in the closet now," he whispered as the babble of the party carried on all around us. "If I can share my secret, then so can you."

"I'm not gay," I repeated.

"You just agreed that you couldn't keep it a secret much longer."

"That was about something else."

"Oh sure. Like what?"

"Well, I'd rather not say, if it's all the same."

"Michael, it's all right to be gay."

"I agree. It is all right to be gay. I think it's perfectly all right to be gay."

"That's good, you're getting there."

"But it just so happens that I'm not."

"You're still in denial, Michael."

"I'm not in denial. I'm just denying I'm gay."

"I'll come out if you come out."

"I can't come out because I'm not fucking gay, all right?"

Paul's confident assertion about my apparent homosexuality had rather eclipsed the bigger picture, which was that he had just told me the biggest secret of his life, namely, not only that he was gay, but that he had a crush on *me*. It suddenly all made sense—all the times he had hoped I would be there for meals he'd cooked, all the bizarre sulks he had got himself into. He had behaved like a jilted girlfriend. And having convinced himself that the apparent absence of women in my life was for the same reason as his own, having constructed this fantasy that built deeper meaning around my careless compliments on his baked fish or new trousers, he was not going to accept my shattering of his illusions without a fight. How could anyone allow themselves to become so deluded, I wondered. And then I thought about how happy I'd always presumed Catherine was back at home.

I said I was delighted for him that he'd finally decided to come out, and apologized if the atmosphere in the flat had ever been at all homophobic.

"No. Jim and Simon made the odd joke, but you always corrected them. That's when I first started to realize."

"Just because I'm *not* homophobic doesn't mean I *am* homosexual, you stupid bugger. No offense."

"Michael, I love you, and I think you love me, if only you could face up to it."

"Forget about me. Go and proposition Simon; he's got to have sex with some living creature before he's thirty." And I pointed to where Simon was failing to make a girl fall in love with him by describing some of his favorite sites on the Internet, hoping against hope that one thing might lead to another. But Paul would not be deterred. "Look, I do know some other gay men; they've given me the strength to come out. They can help you, too. I've told them all about you."

This was too much and my patience just snapped.

"WHAT GIVES YOU THE RIGHT TO GO ROUND TELLING PEOPLE THAT I'M GAY?"

The whole room fell quiet at this news and all heads turned to me for an explanation. Mouths were agape that my "secret" was out. The man who had delivered the pizzas put his beer down and announced that he had better get back to the shop.

"That explains everything," said Kate loudly.

"I'm not gay, actually, everyone. I just was, er, saying to Paul here that he shouldn't tell people I was gay. If, erm, the thought should occur to him."

No one looked very convinced.

"It's OK, Michael. There's nothing wrong with being gay," said an encouraging voice from the back of the crowd.

"I know there isn't."

"Good for you, mate," shouted someone else.

"Then it's a double celebration," shouted Monica. "He's going out into the world *and* coming out of the closet." Everyone applauded and some joker cued "YMCA" on the record player, and my lone protestations were drowned out by everyone suddenly singing and dancing along to Village People. They had put the record on especially for me and thought I was really unsporting not to dance, so in the end I did and everyone took that as a final confirmation of my coming out. Space was cleared for me on the dance floor and I was encouraged and applauded as if I'd suddenly had a lifetime of secrecy lifted off my shoulders. I looked across at Paul, standing in the corner mouthing the words of the song but still not liberated enough to dance along to a well-known camp classic. The next time I looked up, I saw Simon looking rather surprised and offended at a proposition that the very drunken Paul was putting to him.

A little later Kate came across to me and said that it had never occurred to her that the "other person" I had been saving myself for was a man. Now she understood why I hadn't wanted to sleep with her. I think she found this reassuring. I didn't feel I had the energy to go through my denials again so I just thanked her for being so understanding and smiled. I probably wouldn't see any of these people again, so if they were determined to believe I was homosexual, then so what?

After a couple of hours of self-imposed sobriety, my smile began to ache as I watched them all disappear over the drunken horizon. I said goodbye to a few people, but everyone had now forgotten the original reason for the party, so I didn't feel too antisocial for just slipping away. I drove my rented van through the London night and soon I was on Waterloo Bridge, on the old border between my two lives. I looked at the river and the glorious sparkling views of Canary Wharf and the City to the east and parliament and the London Eye to the west. Then I headed up Aldwych, past hunched bodies sleeping in doorways or covered in cardboard. London was just like my life. From a distance it looked great; it's only when you got close you realized how fucked up it was.

Finally I was outside my family home. It was too late to unload now; the van was alarmed and had a couple of padlocks on the back, so I felt safe enough leaving it all till the morning. My home was dark and still as I slipped quietly into the hallway and silently closed the door behind me. Since the children came along, Catherine had become such a light sleeper that I found myself tiptoeing around downstairs, trying not to breathe too noisily.

There was a video tape placed where I would see it on the kitchen table, which meant that Catherine had remembered to record my favorite program. Though I preferred people not to know, nothing amused me more than home videos of labradors skateboarding into swimming pools and toddlers getting stuck in the toilet bowl. Our own camcorder was set up on the tripod, so Catherine had obviously been inspired to film our own kids. I grabbed a beer from the fridge and settled down in the lounge with the television on extra-considerate, almost-inaudible low volume to have a really good laugh at some other people's misfortunes. The first clip featured some fairly obviously contrived setups of people pretending not to be looking where they were going as they walked fully clothed into a river, but their efforts got them five hundred quid, which was enough to pay for their new camcorder, so good luck to them. Then there was a sequence of children being embarrassingly honest—a little boy saying to a very overweight children's entertainer, "You're a big fat pig." And then, when he was told off, he pointed to her with a look of gross injustice that this simple truth could be denied and said, "But she *is . . .*"

Then there was a lavish church wedding. The groom was asked if he would take this woman to be his lawful wedded wife and he said that he would. The bride was asked if she would take this man and she was slightly nervous and struggled to get the words out. She's going to faint, I thought. I can see this one coming a mile off. I was wrong. At that moment, about five rows back, a man in the congregation jumped up wearing a Walkman, and throwing both his arms in the air he shouted,

"GOAL!" I laughed so much I thought I would wake up the whole street, never mind just Catherine. I rewound the tape and watched the clip again. It made me laugh almost as much the second time. Fantastic. I loved this program. The host liked that one as well, but promised the next clip was even funnier. Well, this should be really good, I thought, and I took another big glug of beer. Then the picture went blank and I thought, Oh no, she's cocked up the recording.

But she hadn't. Catherine's thunderous face suddenly appeared on the screen. "You wanker!" she shouted at the camcorder. "You lying, selfish, cowardly, lazy, fucking lying bastard! You want to live away from me and the kids. You want to have your 'own space.' Well you've got it, shitface. Fuck you!"

I ran upstairs. Our bed was empty. The kids' room was empty. Her side of the wardrobe was bare; some toys and most of the kids' clothes had gone, too. There was a barren hotel-room neatness to our bedroom. I stood staring around the space in bewilderment; my mind was in freefall. Then, from nowhere, it suddenly came into my head. Hull City. The answer to Simon's trivia question was Hull City. And my wife had walked out on me and taken our children with her. My marriage was in ruins. Hull City. Of course.

9

Where Do You Want to Go Today

"AND THIS IS the children's room," I said as my father stepped over the unwanted soft toys to look around Millie and Alfie's abandoned bedroom.

"Very nice," he said. "I like all those clouds painted on the ceiling. Did you do that?"

"Er, no, that was, erm, Catherine."

"Oh."

If I had ever given any thought to how I would feel when I finally showed Dad around my family home, I suppose I would have imagined the scene with my family still in it.

"That's where Millie slept and that's where Alfie slept."

"I see, yes. And who is this on the eiderdown?"

"On the duvet? Well, that's Barbie," I said incredulously. I'd lived in a home where Barbie was worshipped as an icon more revered than the Virgin Mary in the Vatican; it was disconcerting to find there were still people who'd never heard of her.

"And, erm, that's Ken, there."

"Is 'Ken' Barbie's husband?"

"Well, I don't think they're married. Ken's just her boyfriend. Or he might possibly be her fiancé, I'm not sure."

An awkward silence hung in the air.

"Actually they've been going out for about thirty years now, so if Ken hasn't popped the question yet she ought to start getting worried." And I gave out a little nervous laugh, but Dad didn't seem aware that I had made a joke. Maybe the area of marriages and commitment wasn't the best subject to josh about at the moment. We stood there for a while as Dad made an effort to look interested in the kids' room.

"I haven't touched anything since Catherine walked out on me," I said with an air of almost affected self-pity.

Dad thought about this. "I thought you said she took the car." No one can focus on the irrelevant detail quite like an elderly parent.

"OK, since she *drove* out on me, then."

"So where were you when she drove off?"

"I was loading up all the stuff from my flat to drive back here."

There was a thoughtful pause. Something was worrying him, but it wasn't the disaster that had befallen his son's marriage.

"So how did she get hold of the car?"

"What?"

"How did she get hold of the car if you were loading up your things?"

I sighed an exhausted sigh to try and make him understand that this really wasn't very important and said through gritted teeth, "I wasn't using the car. I'd rented a van."

"I see." And then he contemplated this for a second. "Because you knew that she was going to need the car to take the kids and all their things to her mother's?"

"No, of course I didn't know or I would have tried to stop her."

"So why didn't you use the car to move your things out of the flat? You can get quite a lot in an Astra, can't you, especially a hatchback."

"Look, it doesn't matter. There was quite a bit of stuff; it would have needed two journeys."

He went quiet for a moment and we wandered into the

other bedroom. I was slightly embarrassed when I realized how feminine the decor was: the flowery duvet, the frilly edge on the dressing table—it seemed so inappropriate now that I was sleeping there on my own.

"So is it very expensive, hiring your own van?"

"What?"

"Is it expensive, renting a van to move all your things?"

"Oh, I don't know. Yes, it cost a million pounds. Dad, it really doesn't matter about the van."

"You're not still renting it, are you, to get around in now that Catherine's taken the car?"

"No, I'm not still renting the bloody van!"

Although I wish I had been and then I could have run him over with it.

My irritation was exacerbated by the fact that I couldn't help but blame Dad for my wife's departure. True to form, Dad had recently left his lady friend for a younger woman. Jocelyn was very bitter; it must be hard being chucked when you're fifty-nine, especially when it's because you're not fifty-four anymore. And in her fury she had forwarded my extended confessional letter to Catherine to warn her what these fickle Adams men were like.

Perhaps this was why Dad seemed to avoid discussing what had happened. When I telephoned him to invite him up I asked him if he had read the letter.

"Oh yes, of course," he replied brightly.

"Well, what did you think?"

He didn't hesitate for a second. "Your handwriting has certainly got a lot better, hasn't it?"

But I needed to know the details of how Jocelyn had found the letter; had she searched through his pockets or opened his drawer or what? I was about to ask him when he said, "It's a shame you didn't invite me up a few weeks earlier. It would have been nice to see Catherine and the children."

Yes, what a shame, I thought. What a shame for you that my wife and children have walked out on me. What a shame that is. Poor Dad, poor you.

"Yes, well, it's a shame that Jocelyn read that letter I wrote to you or Catherine and the kids would still be here."

"Ha. Fair dos!" he said, as if I had just scored a minor point in a school debating club.

"So, did she go through your pockets or what?"

"What do you mean?"

"Jocelyn. How did she get to read my letter?"

There was a pause in which Dad gradually sensed that perhaps he had done something he shouldn't have done.

"No, I, um, I showed it to her."

"You did what?" I shrieked.

"Was that all right?"

"You showed her an explosive private letter from your son, and then you chucked her?"

He looked perplexed and the withered row of transplanted hair at the top of his head moved slightly as he furrowed his brow.

"What does 'chucked' mean?" he said.

"It's what I am, thanks to you. Chucked, jilted, dumped."

"Well, I think that's a bit unfair. I mean, it was you who was deceiving your wife, not me."

At this point a whole row of fuses blew inside my head. "Well at least I didn't fuck off with some pharmacist and walk out on my five-year-old kid."

"That's not fair, Michael. It was more complicated than that . . ."

"I thought I must have done something really terrible to have suddenly been abandoned by you. I thought it was my fault."

"Your mother and I were both to blame for the marriage not working."

"Oh yeah, it's Mum's fault. Of course it is. Blame Mum; it's not as if she's in any position to defend herself, is it?"

"I'm just saying there's a lot you don't know about."

"Well I do know this, that she'd still be alive if you hadn't walked out on her because she'd never have moved to Belfast with what's-his-face, so it's your fault she was run over."

"Come on, Michael; it wasn't me driving that car, was it?"

"It might as well have been!" I yelled, and at the back of my brain a little voice was saying, What are you talking about, Michael? That is clearly nonsense, but I was in no mood to re-tract what I'd just said.

"You left me and Mum for a woman who left you, and so you found another woman and then another and then another. And now what have you got to show for it? One fucked-up son and a ridiculous hair transplant that looks like someone sprinkled a row of mustard seeds across your big, shiny bald head!"

I knew I'd pressed the nuclear button. It was all right to ac-cuse him of being a bad father, of ruining my childhood, even of indirectly causing Mum's death, but no one ever mentioned the hair transplant. You just knew not to. There was a brief mo-ment of silence while Dad stared impassively into my eyes, and then he got up, picked up his coat, put on his hat and walked out the door.

Twenty minutes later I ate the supermarket pre-prepared shepherd's pie that had been baking in the oven for the two of us. I divided it in half and ate my portion, and then I ate the rest of it as well. Then I remembered why I had finally invited Dad to come up to London in the first place. I had been plan-ning to show him round the house, give him lunch, explain the situation with the mortgage and then ask him if there was any way he could lend me a rather large amount of money. So that had all gone according to plan, then.

I was shocked by the things I had heard myself say to him, and at the level of bitterness that had been bottled up for so long. Why couldn't I have had a father like the ones in the adverts? In the Gillette commercial that I'd sung along to a million times, the father and son go fishing together in America somewhere, and dad helps son reel in a salmon; they're easy and comfortable with each other and he's had a really good shave and someone sings, "The best a man can get." That father would never run off with a pharmacist called Janet; they'd never use my dad in the Gillette ad. But then, he did have a beard, I suppose.

Of course my dad had never had a father around when he'd been a child, either. Or a mother most of the time, for that matter. On September 1, 1939, he had been put on a train to Wales, and he didn't see his dad again until the end of the war. I mused that if Dad hadn't been evacuated, then he would have had a father as a role model, which might have made him stay around to be a role model for me, which would have made me a better father and stopped Catherine walking out. So there it was, everything was Adolf Hitler's fault. I don't suppose any of this crossed his mind as he was invading Poland.

That night I just lay on the sofa all evening watching telly, occasionally getting hungry enough to see if the disgusting pizza I'd had delivered was any more palatable when cold. It wasn't, but I ate it anyway. With the television remote control in my hand I flicked through all the cable movie channels, watching three films at once. Trevor Howard kissed Celia Johnson as she got on the railway carriage and then the entire train crashed into the River Kwai. Then Celia tucked up her children in bed and Jack Nicholson smashed down the door with an ax.

Here I was again, trying to watch several stories and so enjoying none of them. I actually felt a strange empathy with Jack

Nicholson in *The Shining*; living in this house, frozen in time, guarding the place till everyone came back, slowly going madder and madder as I tried and failed to work. I don't think I was as bad a husband as he was. I never once tried to kill my wife and kids with an ax, for example, but I don't think Catherine would accept this as a point in my favor.

By now I had spent a couple of weeks living on my own in a child-orientated home. The mobile still spun lazily in the breeze and the blue bird pendulum still swung maniacally back and forth under the rainbow clock, but the little isolated pockets of movement only served to emphasize how lifeless and eerily quiet the children's room seemed without them. I didn't want to change anything; it was all ready for them whenever they wanted to come back. I still had to push open the baby gate to get down the stairs, I still had to negotiate the child locks to open the cupboards. The only slight change I had made was to scramble the colorful magnet letters on the side of the fridge where Catherine had spelled out "wanker" at eye level. I wondered how long she had searched for the letter "w" before making do with a number 3 turned on its side? I was the lonely caretaker for a family show home—furnished accommodation all ready for my wife and children to move into any day they fancied. It had everything they needed, every safety precaution you could buy to prevent any possible damage being done to our precious little ones, except for the one minor mishap of their parents splitting up, of course. To think that we had dragged our kids round all those shops, buying plug guards, video covers, child locks, baby gates and a barrier to stop Millie rolling out of her bed, but we never saw anything in Mothercare to prevent the divorce for which we were heading. OK, so the kids grow up without a father, and Mum will become lonely, poor and bitter, but at least the little ones never fell down those three steps by the kitchen, and that's the main thing.

I wanted them back. I wanted them back so much I felt hollow and numb and sick. I had been round to her parents' house and pleaded with Catherine to come home, but she'd said she wasn't prepared to talk to me because I was a selfish shitbag, because I had betrayed her trust and because it was half-past three in the morning. So the only punctuation in my long and lonely weeks were my meetings with the children, which Catherine icily granted me. We met once a week at the windy swings in Hyde Park as the last few leaves were blown from the trees. We stood in silence, watching the children play, and because the silence was so oppressive I would occasionally shout things like, "No! Not on the big slide, Millie," and Catherine would say, "It's all right, Millie, you can go on the big slide if you want," and though she was looking at Millie, she was really talking to me. These few hours a week were supposed to be my quality time with the children, but I never quite managed to see where any quality came into it. I'd have a tense, self-conscious hour with them and then I knew I had to go back to the house on my own again.

And lo and behold, here was my double life all over again. Long days spent on my own, free to do whatever I wanted, and then short periods spent with my wife and family. Catherine was smart enough to say as much. "This is just what you wanted, isn't it? To see us occasionally and have your own space the rest of the time. You still get to see them and play with them, but you don't have to do any of the boring hard work. All that's different is now you've got a bigger bed to lie in all day."

"That's not fair," I said, and then struggled to come up with a reason why it wasn't. From the outside it might have seemed a similar existence, but whereas before I'd believed I had organized myself the perfect life and had reveled in the best of both worlds, now I was utterly miserable. Because now none of it was in my control, now my hours as a father were begrudgingly meted out to me rather than being generously granted by my good self. Catherine had the power. My secret outpost of resistance to the dictatorship of babies had been betrayed by an informer. Now I'd been exiled to parental Siberia, condemned to solitary confinement with two hours' visiting time a week.

Although Catherine initiated these meetings, she was so angry with me that she could hardly bear to make eye contact. On the first occasion I attempted to greet her with a kiss on the cheek, which turned out to be a gross misreading of terms. As I leaned forward she recoiled and turned away; my kiss landed on her ear and I had to carry on as if that were a perfectly normal place to kiss somebody. I had tried to defend myself by claiming it wasn't as bad as having an affair with another woman, but to my disappointment Catherine said she would have preferred that; at least she could have put that down to some insatiable male craving.

She looked tired; apparently she hadn't been able to sleep very well so close to the kids. I was tired, too; I hadn't been able to sleep so far away from them. Her bulge was now comically large. She was either very, very pregnant or she'd already had the baby and was now hiding a space hopper under her jumper. I would have liked to have touched the bump, to feel it and talk to it, but that particular child was even more out of bounds. I wanted to ask about arrangements for the big day, but was too frightened to ask her where she would like me during the birth. She'd probably say Canada. During the previous eight months, while it had grown into a little person and developed eyes and ears and a heart and lungs and blood vessels and nerve endings and all the other incredible things that just happen by themselves, its parents' love had seemingly withered and died. If only babies could burst forth at the moment of passion in which they are conceived and not nine months later when it's all turned to dust.

"Well? Are you going to go and play with them?" she said, since that was what I was there for.

"Right, yes," and I went off and tried to be as spontaneous and fun a dad as it's possible to be when you are being intensively monitored by their mother who is contemplating divorcing you. Millie was on the climbing frame.

"Shall I chase you round the climbing frame, Millie?"

"No."

"Would you like me to push you on the swings, then?"

"No."

"I've got you!" I said as I playfully grabbed her off the frame. My edginess had made me too rough and I grabbed her too hard or made her jump or something because she suddenly started crying.

"What are you doing?" said Catherine angrily, and she came across, took Millie from me and held her daughter close and looked at me with hatred in her eyes. Maybe I would have more success with Alfie, I hoped. He had taken his first steps a few weeks before—an event that I had not been there to witness—and now he was confidently tottering around, only occasionally falling on his nappy-padded bottom. He took up position beside the metal frame of the swing and banged a little pebble against it. I could feel Catherine watching me, and so I squatted down beside him and, with my own stone, banged the metal frame as well. He liked the noise of the stone hitting the metal bar. He didn't get bored of the noise of the stone hitting the metal bar. When after five minutes I wanted to stop, he became distressed, so I continued to bang the little stone against the metal bar. I looked round and did a mock long-suffering smile to Catherine, but she didn't smile back. I was cold to my bones and my squatting position became increasingly uncomfortable, but the spongy playground surface was too wet for me to kneel, so I teetered there as I was, feeling the blood draining from my legs, going tap tap tap with my bit of gravel on the echoey cold steel bar. I'd always wished I could have known which bits of childcare were bonding and which bits were just completely wasting time.

Eventually I sat down beside Catherine on a bench and attempted to find a way to talk about what had happened. She was living with her mad parents, who were even more overbearing than usual as it was no longer the woodlice-crushing season.

"I imagine it must be quite hard, isn't it? Living with your mum and dad, you know, with the kids and everything."

"Yes."

"So have you any idea how long you might stay there?"

"No."

"You could come home, you know."

"And where would you move to?"

I sensed I wasn't charming her out of her shell.

"Well I'd be there to help with the kids. I've given up the flat."

"Yeah, you don't need it now, do you? Now you've got us out of the way there's no need for the flat, is there?"

As passively and apologetically as I could, I tried to float the idea that maybe I hadn't been quite ready for fatherhood and was only now adjusting to it. At this point her emotional dam just burst.

"You don't think it was hard for *me* to adjust?" she said in a furious, spitting whisper. "Giving up work, giving birth and then suddenly being stuck in a house on my own all day with a crying baby? You don't think that was a big shock for *me* to suddenly be ugly, fat, tired and bursting into tears; trying to breastfeed a screaming baby with blood coming out of my cracked nipples and no one there to tell me it was OK, and that I was doing all right, even when the baby wouldn't feed or sleep or do anything but scream for days on end? I'm sorry it was so fucking hard for you to adjust, Michael." She was crying now, angry with me and for letting herself break down in front of me. "But I never fucking adjusted, because it's impossible. I was in a lose-lose situation. I felt guilty when I thought about going back to work and guilty for giving up work, but there's no one you can talk to about it because the only other women with children at the swings are all eighteen years old and only speak fucking Croatian. So I'm really sorry you found it so hard to be in the same house as your wife when she was going through hell, but it's OK, because you could just leave, you could just fuck off whenever you felt like it and lie around with your mates, having parties and watching videos and leaving your mobile turned off just in case your wife wanted to cry down the phone to you."

When she put it like that, she did sort of have a point. When I'd been on my own I had spent hours preparing carefully crafted arguments, like North American Indians fashioning beautifully decorated arrows before battle. And now she came along like the U.S. Army, fired her great big cannon and blew me away. I offered up my puny self-justification all the same. I put it to her that the only difference between what I had done and what other fathers did was that I had been aware I was doing it.

"What? And you think it does you credit that you were *consciously* deceiving me? Those men are still part of a team," she went on. "They are still operating as a unit with their wives, one at home, one at work. They're still in it *together*."

"They're at their place of work, sure, just like I was. But those men don't really have to go on all those trips or have all those meals out in the evening or play golf with clients at the weekend; they do those things because they don't think it's less important than being with their families."

Everything I said just made her angrier. "So, let me get this straight, you thought all this through and, instead of resolving not to be that kind of father, you went and behaved ten times worse by being absent *deliberately* as part of a plan."

"I thought it would help our marriage."

I could feel most of my excuses dying in my mouth as I said them.

"Well, that worked well, didn't it."

And then she got up and said she was going back to her mum's, and for some pathetic, desperate reason I said, "You're lucky to have a mum," and she looked back at me with contempt. I hated myself for saying it almost as much as she appeared to hate me for saying it. And then as she walked away I thought, Oh well, if we both feel the same way about what a pathetic worm I have become, then that's something we have in common; maybe we could build on that?

After they had gone I sat there in the playground on my own for a while. A young mother with a couple of kids came in and looked at me as if I were some escaped child molester, and when I heard her tell her children not to go near me I stood up and went home.

There was another familiar-shaped envelope on the doormat, though this one had been delivered by hand. I put it, unopened, on the side with all the others. They piled up on the hall table like accumulating evidence against me. Obviously I knew the bank wanted money, but I thought I'd never be able to earn any if I read the threats I feared were contained inside. As long as I was trying to work, then I believed I was doing something about it, and so I just buried my head deeper and deeper into my music. One of the letters came registered post, which seemed a bit of a waste of money. I was quite happy to sign for it; it didn't mean I had any intention of opening or reading it. Sometimes they tried ringing, and when I saw their number flash up on the little screen on our telephone, I'd quickly switch on the answerphone and then fast-forward through their messages. The cross-sounding man wasn't as scary when you speeded him up. He sounded like Donald Duck after inhaling helium.

On some days I would sit at my keyboard for thirteen or fourteen hours but I'd often achieve less than I used to in half a morning. Once upon a time I'd been able to lose myself in music, but that was before I'd been so desperate to do so. It was another couple of months before I was due to put together *Classic Commercials* and so between now and then I had a chance to create my own seminal compositions, which today happened to be a thirteen-second jingle that had to accommodate the line, "Butterness! Butterness! It tastes like butter but the fat is less!"

Hmm, I thought, I think they're going for a sort of butter theme here. It was a shame the advert would be legally required to feature a large caption that flashed "NOT BUTTER" along the bottom of the screen, but that wasn't my problem. The woman at the agency had said they wanted it to be just like the Ken Dodd song "Happiness" without breaching copyright. So it would either sound wrong or be illegal. It had to be completed by six o'clock. I fired up my keyboard.

"Butter. What does that put one in mind of?" I tried out different sounds on the Roland. The oboe setting, the harpsichord setting, the bassoon setting; none of them reminded me remotely of butter, but then I don't suppose new Butterness would have done, either. I listened to the Ken Dodd track and broke it down into its constituent parts. Apparently the jingle was going to be sung by a chorus line of pantomime cows, so I had to try and concentrate on that image as I wrote the music. I had never pretended that my job was of vital importance to the future of mankind, but sitting on my swiveling piano stool, trying not to think about the state of my marriage and attempting to concentrate instead on a load of pantomime cows singing about new Butterness, well, it didn't radically improve my feeling of self-worth. It just didn't get the adrenaline going like really important work. The midwife who would deliver our third child, for example, she'd have no choice but to put all her problems out of her head and focus on getting the baby out safely. Damn! There it was; in one short step I was thinking about our next baby and not concentrating on the jingle for a new low-fat margarine containing dairy solids.

"Ah yes, Butterness. Right, concentrate, Michael, concentrate. Butter." I sang the guide track to myself a few times. Had the agency deliberately engineered it so that I would be forced to sing "Happiness!" over and over to myself when I was feeling at my most miserable? I tried to parody the tune, but I couldn't get the original out of my brain. Concentrate, concentrate. Sometimes, when I had things on my mind, when there was a lot of fluff on the stylus, I could barely hear the tunes inside my head. Today there was so much fluff in there that the needle simply slid right across the vinyl.

It was hard to forget about the children with them all smiling at me from frames on the mantelpiece, so I got up and turned all the frames face down. I went and sat down and decided they looked awful like that, as if I was rejecting their existence or something, so I got up and put all the photos back as they were again.

Hmm. Butter? I thought, Butter. Does Catherine have the legal right to take the kids off like that? I mean, I am their father. How would she have liked it if I'd just whisked the kids away, suddenly announced I wasn't happy with the marriage and left her all alone? I continued to mull this over, and then I looked at the clock and it was quarter past twelve and I hadn't thought about butter or new Butterness for hours, and even if I came up with a suitably similar tune I still had to lay it down and master it, and getting it finished by six o'clock suddenly looked like a very close call. So come on. Butter, butter.

Butterness. "Butterness! Butterness! It tastes like butter but the fat is less!" I said this out loud to myself three times. I tried it again, putting the emphasis on different words. And then I went and made a cup of tea.

The house felt different with only me rattling around in it. I saw it in a different way. This was not unrelated to the fact that I sometimes spent hours just lying on my back on the hall carpet or sitting on the floor underneath the kitchen table. You can do these things when you're on your own. I wandered from room to room with my tea and finally decided to drink it sitting at the top of the stairs.

The cat deigned to vacate its favorite spot among Alfie's soft toys and came to lie next to me on the landing carpet. When we had first got the cat, we had told Millie she would be allowed to choose her name. We then spent the rest of the day trying to dissuade Millie from her immediate and unhesitating choice, but she would not be budged, so we just had to accept it. Cat the cat and I had formed quite a close relationship during my weeks on my own in the family home. I'd buy her treats from the shops and then stand at the front gate shouting, "Cat! Cat!" as passersby avoided eye contact and quickened their pace. She would sit on my lap in the evenings and I'd stroke her under the chin and she'd purr ridiculously loudly. I tied a little ball on a piece of string and played with her, and when she wouldn't eat her food I'd give her some fresh fish and she'd always eat that and it was all very comforting. Until Red Collar Day. Cat didn't have a collar. Until Red Collar Day. She walked in through the cat flap, having been out for a few hours, wearing a bright-red new collar. She sniffed her food bowl, didn't fancy it and went out again. I was devastated. All the time I had imagined she was out there keeping other cats out of my garden or trying to catch the odd sparrow to proudly present to her master when really she had been curled up in front of someone else's electric fire, eating someone else's fresh fish, lying in someone else's lap. The collar had a name tag on it which said "Cleo." That was her name when she was at her secret other home. Cat had a double life. I felt double-crossed, jilted, rejected. Worst of all, I had been satirized by a bloody cat.

Forty minutes later I was still at the top of the stairs, lying on my back with my legs dangling over the first few steps. Cat the cat had wandered away long before, but the patterns on the landing ceiling were fascinating enough to keep me there for another half an hour. Eventually the clatter of the letter box jolted me out of my trance and I hauled myself to my feet. It was a noise that brightened my day; it made me feel there was hope I hadn't been completely forgotten by the outside world. Obviously I wouldn't read anything from the bank, but it might be a minicab card or a pizza leaflet, and it was always nice to read things from people who'd taken the trouble to keep in touch. On the mat was an estate agents' brochure, full of houses that cost over a million pounds. As I flicked through the glossy pictures of beautiful expensive family homes I became convinced it had been put through the letter box by the cat, who had now gone off to bask in the glory of her sarcastic triumph.

But the punctuation in the long and lonely day was enough to drive me back to work and I sat back on my stool. There were various vital jobs that had to be done before I could really get down to work. I tried to see how much dandruff I could shake out of my hair onto the desktop. I felt a spot halfway down my back and spent ten minutes trying various bizarre yoga-like contortions in order to reach it with both hands to squeeze it. I scraped off some of the greasy grayness that had built up on the keys of the synthesizer. I smelled it, then dabbed it on my tongue. That's when I was reminded of new

Butterness. "Come on, Michael!" I said out loud. "Butterness! Butterness! It tastes like butter but the fat is less!" I considered ringing the agency to ask them if they were absolutely dead set on this butter tack. Most of the day had somehow disappeared; I had forgotten to have lunch and now I was suddenly so hungry that I had to eat immediately, but there was nothing in the house except some two-day-old bread and the free sample tub of bloody buggering Butterness that I'd been given.

As I threw away the uneaten crust, I faced up to the reality that I was going to let them down, that for the first time in my professional career I was going to miss a deadline, so I tried to ring the producer woman to ask if they could hang on another day. I was held in a queue for ages and then, when I finally got through, it was to an answerphone.

"Hello, this is Sue Paxton on 7946 0003. I'm not at my desk at the moment, though you may be able to reach me on 7946 0007. If you need to speak to me urgently, try my mobile 07700 900004 or my pager, 08081 570980 number 894. You can fax me on 7946 0005 or reach me by e-mail at s dot paxton at Junction5 dot co dot uk. If you want to try me at home my home numbers are 01632 756545 or 01632 758864, or fax me at home on 01632 756533 or e-mail s dot paxton at compuserve dot com. Otherwise just leave a message."

By the end of all that I'd forgotten what I was ringing about, so I hung up. A few minutes later I armed myself with pen and paper and rang the number again. Then I attempted to reach her by all of the listed means, but each of them just informed me of all the other routes to a reply. By the time I'd tried them all I had wasted another hour. And so I really knuckled down and finally, finally, I managed to get the original tune out of my head and reverse the chords, and suddenly it was going round in my brain; quick get it down, record it before it's gone again, and then the phone went and it was

Catherine canceling the next day's meeting in Hyde Park, and I was furious and powerless and rude and pathetic and I hung up and walked round the house, kicking items of furniture.

Then the phone went again but it wasn't Catherine changing her mind, it was the bank again and I just shouted, "Fuck off!" at the officious bastard and hung up, and then he rang back half an hour later, with the satisfied air of a Nazi Kommandant who has discovered a tunnel, and said that they had sent a letter to inform me that they had authorized their solicitors to execute a warrant of possession, and I know what this means: that I am close to losing the house, but I reasoned and explained, I tell him that keeping the house is the only chance I have of getting my family back, that I have two small children and a third one on the way and that their mother has left me to live with her parents, but she can't stay there forever, not with her mother going on about the grandchildren not being christened, and eventually she'll have to come back home, and that's when she'll see that we can work it out, that's when she'll see that I've changed, and then we'll all be together again because that's all that matters, that's the only hope I've got: that they'll all come back home, but that can only happen if I've still got the house, if there's still a home to come back to, so you see, I have to stay here; they can't take the house away from me now. And he listens silently and patiently. And then he tells me they are repossessing the house.

10

It Could Be You

"SPARE SOME CHANGE, PLEASE? Excuse me, could you spare any change, please?"

I had got into the habit of striding past the homeless who did the backing vocals for the music of London's streets. But today it struck me that I had just coldly walked straight past another human being, and so I turned back and put five pounds in his makeshift cardboard money box. Five quid! And he didn't even have a bit of string with a sad-looking dog on the end.

I was briefly irritated that the recipient wasn't ecstatically grateful for my excessive generosity, that five pounds didn't buy me a happier beggar. For a fiver you expect the executive thank-you plus, with a personalized letter to be sent on to you the following week explaining how your money was spent, with a P.S. asking you to convert your gifts into a deed of covenant. But he thought I was just like all the other rich clean people walking past. He thought I had a nice home and a happy wife and everything else he envied.

I had just dropped the keys to my family home off at the bank. I had walked into our local branch, queued up at the window and given them to the young girl behind the counter.

"Hang on, I'd better get the manager," she'd said.

"No, it's all right, he's had the paperwork. Can't stay. I've got to find somewhere to sleep tonight."

"Oh. Is there anything else I need to know?"

"Er, yeah. The downstairs toilet. You have to give it one slow flush and then flush it again very quickly straightaway."

She looked at me blankly, but as I went to leave she remembered the script.

"Thank you for your custom this morning, Mr. Adams," she said. "Have a nice day."

"Thank you. You're too kind," I called behind me as I went out onto the streets of London, unsure as to where I should go now. And then I just walked around for a while; it was quite surreal really. Normally the pavement is for the irrelevant time in between the various parts of your life, now it was all there was. It made me feel that I didn't have a point. The litter bin had a point; it was for putting paper in. The railings had a point; they were for stopping people from stepping out on the road. But what was the point of me? I wasn't doing anything, I wasn't going anywhere, so what was I for?

I stood there for a while and watched a tangle of old cassette tape which was wrapped around the railings—a thin, brown, shiny streamer, discarded and blowing in the wind. There was probably music recorded on that tape, music that had been composed and structured and arranged, and now it was all unraveled and useless. Somewhere along the way the tape had just snapped. Now I had all the leisure time in the world, but the currency had been chronically devalued. Time to myself was no longer stolen away in little treat-size chunks, it was forced upon me like a life sentence. I had with me a holdall that contained a few clothes, a toiletry bag and the *Time Out* guide to London. All my other possessions and all the contents of the family home were crammed into my next-door neighbor's garage.

"Oooh, you are lucky having a fridge with such a big freezer compartment," said the elderly Mrs. Conroy, trying to be positive as I wheeled it up her driveway. Plastic bin liners were packed tight with soft toys, the telly was wrapped in a Pocahontas duvet and placed inside Alfie's cot. Moving everything out had taken me two days, and by the time I'd finished the garage looked like a squashed, post-earthquake version of our family home. Mrs. Conroy kindly said I could leave everything there for as long as I wanted. Klaus and Hans were no longer lodging with her and had gone back to Germany, so no one used the garage anymore. She had given me boxes to put things in and sandwiches and cups of tea when I was exhausted from dragging sofas and mattresses up her driveway and my own key to the garage for when I needed to pop over and get anything. She didn't ask how I had got so behind with the mortgage; the only allusion she made to everything that had happened was as I locked up the garage and thanked her again before I left. She looked at me sadly, gave me a brave smile and said, "You weren't around much, were you?"

Now I walked slowly along Camden High Street, clutching the few belongings that weren't locked up in Mrs. Conroy's garage. I found myself taking more interest than I normally would have done in the plastic bric-a-brac in charity shop windows. I passed an arcade of slot machines called Loads o' Fun but judging by the emotionless gray faces inside it looked as if the sign above the entrance was slightly overstating it. Estate agents advertised attractive family homes, building societies offered easy loans. Catherine had learned about the unpaid mortgage from the letter to my father, but this didn't prevent me from bringing the subject up again during the long hours spent shivering by the swings. If I attempted to talk about trivia she would always give me monosyllabic replies, so I tried to use the impending loss of our home as a means of forcing her to talk to me.

"I think the bank are about to repossess our house," I had announced.

Obviously I didn't expect her to throw her arms around me, but it was the nearest thing I had to a chat-up line. She looked at me and then looked away again.

"Well, we would have had to sell it when we got divorced anyway," she remarked, as if this were something we had already agreed. It was the first time she had ever mentioned divorce, but hey, at least we were talking now, so I tried to see the positive side.

"Anyway, I could never go back there now," she continued. "I was miserable in that house all on my own."

This was a calculated extra turn of the knife. Though she didn't want to be with me now, I had made her miserable by not being with her then. But I was consoled that she didn't appear mortified by the news about the house. I didn't come away feeling that my achievement in losing the family home had lessened our chances of getting back together. However, this was probably because those chances were currently standing at approximately zero.

As I wandered aimlessly down the main drag, it occurred to me that the fact that I had nowhere to sleep now gave me the perfect excuse to present myself to Catherine as someone she might take pity on. I imagined how she would react. If she'd said, "Well, if you're ever made homeless you could always come and stay with me," I'm sure I would have remembered it. "I've only got a single bed, sweetheart, but hey, that'll make it all the cozier when you cuddle up next to me." No, it didn't ring any bells.

My father was not an option, either. Apart from the fact that he lived in Bournemouth, a surfeit of masculine pride on both sides meant that we hadn't spoken to each other since he'd walked out of my kitchen. Anyway, if I had turned up at his door to tell him I'd handed my keys in at the bank, his anxiety would never have progressed beyond worrying that I'd made sure the keyring was clearly labeled. Then there was the option of the Balham flat. But all sorts of things had happened there since I'd moved out.

Monica had finished with Jim, who had then waited a decent interval of hours before asking out her best friend, Kate. Within a few weeks he had decamped to her flat in Holland Park, which had all the facilities that Jim required to continue his Ph.D., although Sky Sports 2 was a little fuzzy. Paul had finally come out of the closet and had moved to Brighton to live with his boyfriend, a nightclub bouncer who also worked in the army recruiting office. Simon had then organized three young women to take our places in the house, but when he showed them all his favorite sites on the Internet they had changed all the locks and put all his belongings on the front doorstep.

In the space of a couple of months, all four of us had left the flat. It had been Simon who had told me about all of this when he'd called my mobile phone a few weeks earlier. He was still smarting from his forced eviction and suggested to me that there must have been another reason why the girls didn't like him. He confessed that he had once helped himself to their peanut butter and he thought that this was probably the real explanation.

So my old bachelor pad was not an option, either. In fact, I was struggling to think of anywhere I could go. I thought about all the friends I'd had in my twenties, but I hadn't kept in contact with any of them. On the day your first child is born you might as well go through your address book and whenever you come across any friends who don't already have babies, then just tear out their names there and then. It will save a lot of embarrassment and pointless Christmas cards later on. Of course, Catherine and I had had a wide social circle, but in reality these had just been her friends with husbands attached. Since I'd got married I had lost contact with all my old comrades from college. I certainly didn't blame Catherine for this, she had never discouraged me from seeing the mates I'd had before we moved in together, it was just that I had sat back and lazily allowed her to organize our social diary, and quite reasonably it never occurred to her to make the effort to keep up with my old friends. There was not one couple that I would feel comfortable calling on now. They had made me feel inadequate enough before, with their great big wine glasses and their Italian bread and their wide selection of olive oils lined up on the dresser.

And so, late in a day spent walking aimlessly around, I found myself phoning Hugo Harrison to ask him if I could possibly stay with him for a night or two until I got myself sorted. I didn't really relish having to explain to a work colleague—my main employer really—that I had got myself into dire financial straits, but as it turned out, Hugo was far too insensitive to be the slightest bit interested in any subject of conversation that did not involve the exploits of Hugo Harrison, so he never bothered to ask. He was delighted to be able to invite me up to his flat so that he could have someone to talk at.

His London address was a magnificent penthouse apartment in a high-rise complex near Albert Bridge, with views over the whole of London so that Hugo could look down on everybody. It had once been a block of council flats, but the council had contrived to successfully evict all the local people on the grounds that they had persistently voted Labour. Now the place was highly fortified, with electric gates and security cameras that would immediately spot anyone doing anything suspicious like staying in London for the weekend. Hugo's wife lived in the country with her horses, his children were at boarding school and Hugo spent his weekday evenings in this opulent apartment. As a lifestyle, it wasn't so different to what I'd attempted, except that for some reason this version seemed to have some sort of social legitimacy. But then, Hugo was posh. He might have stood too close to everyone when he was talking to them, but when it came to his own family, he generally liked them as far away as possible.

Although I was receiving charity I was going to have to pay for it by listening to Hugo all evening. And the more he told me, the more I realized why he had this flat. Hugo's hobby was sexual intercourse. I had met golf bores and bridge bores, but this was the first time I had been forced to listen to a sexual-intercourse bore. He told me about his sexual exploits with a presumption that I'd share his attitude that it was all just healthy male behavior. The fact that my wife had walked out on me made me a martyr to the cause, a heroic victim of the war of the sexes. He plied me with drink and, as dusk fell over the twinkling city below, he tried to cheer me up by telling me what a bastard he had consistently been to his other half. I was interested to know what he actually thought of his wife, and so I probed him a little bit on his marriage.

"Oh, she's a good mum and all that," he conceded. "She's always sending things to the kids at boarding school. But she's fat, you see. Big mistake."

"What? Being fat?"

"No, no, she can't help it," he generously acknowledged. "Big mistake on my part. You see, I initially fancied her because she had these enormous knockers," and in case his choice of words wasn't clear enough, he mimed what enormous knockers were and on what part of the human body one might expect to find them.

"But you should never marry a girl with enormous knockers, Michael. When my eldest son started dating girls I only gave him one piece of advice. I said, 'Always remember, son. Big tits at twenty, fat wife at forty.' "

"How charming," I quipped hopelessly. "I'm sure he'll thank you for that later in life."

He refilled my glass and talked about his wife's chubbiness

as if it were some tragic disability that made it impossible to have any sort of sexual relations with her, thereby justifying him playing the field whenever the fancy took him. And judging by his anecdotes this seemed to be quite often. For example, he was genuinely proud of himself for successfully seducing an actress who was very keen to be in a high-profile and lucrative commercial he was casting. What an incredible achievement, Hugo. Clever old you! He recounted how his wife had been up in London and that he'd been supposed to meet her with tickets for the opera. Instead he'd left her standing outside the Coliseum while he'd taken the young hopeful to a hotel room to have sex. It got worse . . .

"I knew the missus would try and ring me, so I set my mobile phone to vibrate, and I was in the middle of fucking this horny little actress, right—I can't remember her name—when suddenly my mobile started jiggling on the bedside table. I looked at the number on the screen and, sure enough, it was Miranda's mobile."

"Oh dear. That must have made you feel awful?"

"What? No, I had this really wicked idea, right? This actress was half pissed, a bit giggly, you know, so I picked up the vibrating phone and pressed it against her . . . you know, her little sex button."

"You did what?"

"Yah. I mean, she thought it was a scream, but she really got off on it, as well. Can you imagine that? So my wife is trying to ring me to find out where the fuck I am, but all she can hear is the ringing tone. Totally unaware that the longer she held on, the closer she got to bringing my mistress to a sexual climax!"

"That's obscene, Hugo."

"Isn't it! My wife gave my lover an orgasm!" And he gave this loud braying laugh, knocked back his drink and slapped me on the back saying, "Another glass of wine, Michael?" When he came back from the kitchen, I asked him if the girl was good in the commercial, and he looked at me as if I was mad and said, "Good God, no. I didn't cast her!"

He continued telling me far too many details about the sex he'd had with dozens of nameless women, but the more lovers that he listed, the lonelier he sounded. For all I knew every single story could have been made up; he was just using me as a sounding board for all his private fantasies. The only definite evidence I'd ever had of his incredible powers of seduction was his visit to a seedy prostitute in Soho. Strangely, that particular conquest was never recounted. I felt increasingly uncomfortable sitting there listening to him. He was drawing me in, trying to make me approve. Like him, I had deceived my wife, and Hugo made me feel that entitled me to life membership of his women haters' club. I was resolute that I was not the same as him. I wasn't a prude, I didn't disapprove of sex, but Hugo talked with such contempt about the women he had seduced that it left almost as bad a taste in my mouth as it must have done for them.

"You only live once, Michael," he said. "And I can't think of anything more boring than just fucking Miranda once a week for the rest of my life."

Finally he poured me a glass of wine and asked me if I'd had any more thoughts about *Classic Commercials,* and suddenly I realized something with complete clarity.

"Er, I've decided I'd rather not do it after all."

"Why on earth not?"

I tried to explain to him. He had said that he wanted a classical album without all the boring bits, so I told him that you have to have boring bits, because what he called the boring bits are what make the memorable bits memorable. "Life has boring bits," I declared slightly too loudly. I tried to make him understand that the vocal finale of Beethoven's Ninth Symphony is moving and powerful and wonderful because of what you have listened to during the previous hour, because of the commitment you have put in. The cellos and basses take you through the previous movements, reject each in turn and then tentatively develop the "Ode to Joy" theme that had been expressed by the woodwind section earlier on. That is why, when it finally bursts forth, the choral climax is one of the greatest moments in the history of music.

Hugo's reaction was, "OK, we can lose Beethoven's Ninth; we'll stick in that bit of Mozart from the yogurt ad instead." So I tried to explain to him all over again that you can't just have the special bits on their own. Art isn't like that, and life isn't like that. I understood that now.

He was bemused by my bizarre principles and soon steered the conversation back to the various ways in which he had betrayed his wife. At this point I got to my feet and announced, "Actually, Hugo, I'm going to head off now. There's a couple of other people I want to look up, so I'll probably stay with them tonight." And before I knew it I was looking at myself in the lift mirror, wondering how I had exchanged a warm bed in a luxury penthouse flat for I knew not what.

"Goodnight, sir," said the uniformed porter who opened the front door for me. It was a very grand entrance for a homeless person to make onto the dark streets of London.

I saw a mock Irish pub and headed for that. Then I sat in the corner and slowly but methodically got myself drunker. There was a self-consciousness to this reckless behavior; I even bought a small bottle of whisky from the off-license afterward, and I've never liked whisky. Catherine had often accused me of having a self-destructive streak, but sitting in that pub with no home to go to, excommunicated from my family and with no friends to turn to, I think I was entitled to feel a little bit

sorry for myself. Then, just to compound my private humiliation, a song came on the jukebox which I recognized from
years ago.

"What's this music that's playing?" I slurred at the barmaid
as she stacked up my collection of empty glasses.

"The Truth Test," she said in a high-pitched twangy Aus-
tralian accent that didn't quite chime with the plastic sham-
rocks on the wall.

"The Truth Test! Oh, not the bloody Truth Test! Are they
famous, then?"

"Are you joking? This song's number one."

"The Truth Test! But they were rubbish! They used to support us in Godalming. I had to lend them my fucking fuzzbox
for Christ's sake."

She attempted a half smile, thought about asking me what
a fuzzbox was and then decided better of it. Somebody put
the same track on again and I decided that was my cue to leave.
Though my wallet was by now empty of banknotes I had found
the scrap of paper on which I'd scribbled Simon's new address
in Clapham, and so I stuffed it in my pocket and started to
walk southward. It was only a couple of miles as the crow flies,
but at least four miles as the drunk weaves, and by the time I
got there I had lost my piece of paper. I stood in the darkness of Clapham Common, going through the same pockets a
dozen times. Twice I checked that it hadn't fallen into my
turn-ups and both times found that I wasn't wearing turn-ups.
What was I supposed to do now? Distant headlights circled
round the common, the biggest traffic island in London. I sat
on a bench. I was drunk, I was tired. Then I finally conceded
what had happened to me and shifted my body round so I was
lying on the bench. An alarm went off in the distance. I put my
holdall under my head, wrapped my coat around myself as
tightly as I could and attempted to sleep. In my drunken state

I actually allowed myself a flippant little smile at my situation. The last piece of post that I had opened at home was a magazine from my old university, and as always I'd turned straight to the "Where Are They Now?" section. Maybe I could have filled it out, "Here I am, pissed out of my head, sleeping on a bench on Clapham Common."

Despite the wind and the occasional mocking laugh from the mallard ducks on the boating pond, I fell asleep quite quickly. I've always dozed off easily when I've had a lot to drink; that's why I was sacked from that summer job driving pensioners to the seaside. But in the middle of the night the drink and the drizzle started to make themselves felt and I came round feeling damp and dehydrated at the same time. As always when you wake up in a strange place, there is a split second while you try to remember where you are. It didn't feel like my bed at home. It didn't feel like the luxury four-poster I had spurned at Hugo's apartment. When I realized that the shivering and aches I felt were due to the fact that I'd been sleeping on a park bench I became so overwhelmingly depressed that I almost felt like throwing myself under the first vehicle that came past, but this turned out to be a milk float, which would only have bruised my leg a bit, and I didn't want another failure to add to the list.

Then in the depressed introspection of the small hours, my mind wallowed into that dangerous quicksand of self-pity. All that I wanted, in fact, all that I had wanted all along, was the love and respect of Catherine. Just to be really sure that the woman I loved, loved me back. In my self-centered universe I had only ever seen her as a planet revolving around me. That misconception was sustainable until the children came along, but then the physics were suddenly exploded. I couldn't accept it; I still tried to force myself back into the center of her life. If I wasn't the reason she had been pissed off at breakfast, I would make sure I was the reason she was pissed off by lunchtime. I would hijack her irritation, make it relate to me. Maybe this was the way all men thought. Maybe the day after Mrs. Thatcher lost her job as prime minister, Denis Thatcher got all prickly and defensive and said, "I don't know why you're in such a bad mood with me."

I lay there, cold and hollow, watching the cars speed by. They became more frequent as London began to wake up; now their drivers seemed in an increasing hurry. Under the feeble glow of the street lights I noticed a shape attached to the railings on the other side of the road. A few yards along from the stripped skeleton of a bicycle frame I could just make out a withered bunch of carnations, a small bunch of cheap garage flowers, now brown and lifeless. There is only one reason why people tie flowers to railings: to mark the spot where someone was killed. Another car tore past, oblivious to the significance of the spot, speeding down the road just as the fatal car that precipitated the pathetic, withered memorial must have done. In the summer, ice-cream vans park along here. I wondered if a child had run across to get an ice cream and hadn't stopped to look, like that time Millie had seen a feather in the middle of the road and run across, and I'd shouted at her so much I had made her cry. She'd never seen me be so angry with her, but really I'd been furious with myself for letting go of her hand and imagining what might have happened.

Then my unbridled mind started to gallop down a path too terrible to explore. What if Millie was run over? What if there were some railing where I had to go and tie cheap carnations. *Don't think about it, Michael. Put it out of your head.* But I couldn't help myself, I started deliberately fantasizing about Millie's death, imagining the scene step by step, watching it unfold, constructing a chillingly plausible fatal scenario in my head.

I'm in the front garden watering the window boxes, and I

have left the front door slightly ajar because I don't have my door keys in my pocket. I'm half aware of the cat slipping through the gap in the door. I don't see Millie following the cat. The cat is on the pavement now and Millie's holding her tail. The cat doesn't like this game, so it runs off across the road and Millie chases after her, running out between the parked cars. There is a big white builder's van with a copy of the *Sun* on the dashboard; the driver's listening to Capital Gold and they're playing "Bohemian Rhapsody," and it's the guitar solo, which always makes him drive faster, and suddenly there's a thud and a screech and a loud pop as his tire goes over Millie, and then the next set of tires go over her as well, and it all happens so fast, but it's in slow motion, too, and there she is on the road behind the van; she's completely still, just a body, a little broken, useless body; and I put on those shoes that morning and we chose that dress together, and now the driver is standing at the side of the road using every swear word he knows to say that it wasn't his fault, and he's pale and he's shaking, and a BMW coming the other way is tooting his horn because the bloody van is blocking the road, and then the builder throws up on the roadside and his radio's still playing and there's a line about nothing really mattering, and then there's a gong and it's over and that's it—Millie's life only lasted three years.

Another pair of headlights shine on the dried-out brown flowers and I come to. My anti-fantasy is so vivid that I want to see Millie now, I want to pick her up and squeeze her tight and not let her go, but I can't. Not because I lost her to a white van, but because I lost her to another more subtle accident: a marriage breakup. Of course it's not the same, and she'll be all right, and Catherine will bring her up well; but she won't love me like I love her; she won't be bothered about me. And though it's a million times preferable to her being killed by a grubby builder's van, I have lost her; we won't live together;

she won't really know me. There has been a terrible accident and I have lost her.

How did this happen? How did this sequence of events unfold? The day that I first deceived Catherine, when I turned off my mobile when I saw my home number on the little screen— that was the cat slipping out of the front door. Then there was the time that Catherine asked me if I'd been working all through the night, and instead of just saying that I'd worked till ten and had been too tired to travel home and then be woken up by the kids all night, I just stared at the ground and nodded, and by failing to put her straight I lied by default— that was like not looking to see where Millie was, not thinking that she might be in danger. Then I lied with increasing nonchalance and lied to myself that Catherine was happy, and I started to deliberately escape from her and the baby—like the cat pulling away as Millie tried to hold on to its tail. And then the cat was over the road and Millie couldn't catch it, and then suddenly, bang, my two lives collide, and Catherine cries and cries and cries and it's all over, it can't be mended. I've lost them, just like Dad lost me. That was another sort of accident, I thought. The affair. My dad had taught me how to cross the road, because he didn't want to lose me; he had told me not to run off the pavement after a football, because he didn't want to lose me; but he didn't see the danger he was putting me in when he went for a drink with that girl he met through work. He just didn't think; like the child running after a cat or a ball, he was excited and he'd run after the pretty girl and then, bang, he had lost his son, his marriage was over and it was all a terrible accident.

The darkest hour before the dawn was lit by the flashing blue light of a speeding police car, though there was no siren to pierce the silence of the winter night. Why didn't they come rushing to marriage breakups? Why hadn't the police car sped after my dad when he had driven away from our family home and said, "That's very dangerous, sir, that child could get hurt." Was it now set to happen all over again?

In my last meeting at the swings with Catherine, I had pleaded with her yet again that I had already given up the flat when she left me, and I think I saw a brief flicker of hesitation, when she was almost tempted to believe me. I had told her how furious I was with my dad for showing his girlfriend the letter.

"Why would he do that?" I had said to her. "Why would he show Jocelyn a deeply personal private letter that I had written him?"

"Because he was proud," she said calmly.

In an instant so much suddenly became clear. It was so obvious once Catherine had said it. Dad had shown my extended confession to his girlfriend because he was so proud to have had a letter from me. I'd never sent him so much as a postcard before; I'd hardly ever called him or been to see him in Bournemouth. It didn't matter what I'd put in the letter; if I'd written to tell him I was robbing pensioners to pay for my crack habit he would have waved the letter around to say, "Look, look, a letter from my son!"

It was my fault that Dad had shown my letter to his girlfriend. It was my fault that Catherine had received it. I'd not been there for the generation above any more than I had been for the one below. So my letter ended up being important not for what it told Dad, or Catherine, but for what it told me. How incredibly betrayed Catherine felt when she learned the truth about my way of life and how desperate my father was for the slightest attention.

Dawn was breaking over the common and I suddenly felt like I had got it. I understood how all this worked; the riddle was solved in my head. You just have to spend time with the people you love. You don't try to change them, you don't get annoyed because they don't behave how you want them to behave, you put up with boredom or tantrums or repetition and you just spend time with them. On their terms, listening to them telling you about cars their friends bought in Belgium, or what they drew at playgroup or whatever. You have to have patience and just be there. Elderly parent or small child; it's all the same. Just pass time with them and then everyone is happy, even you, in the end.

I wanted to see Catherine to share this revelation with her, to tell her that now I knew what I was supposed to do then everything could be all right again. I wanted to join her, be bored with her. In the half-light I struggled to sit up, but I felt nauseous and dizzy. Hangovers usually made me clamor for fresh air, but that wasn't a problem on this occasion. I closed my eyes and pressed my fingers against my temples, attempting a gentle circular rubbing movement as if this had the remotest chance of countering the effects of a bottle of wine, several pints of strong lager and a small bottle of blended whisky.

"You look a bit rough there, mate."

If I looked as rough as I felt I was surprised that anyone would come within a hundred yards of me. Sitting beside me on the park bench was a tramp. A traditional smelly tramp, with a big can of Special Brew in his hand and a huge scab on his chin. The only thing that wasn't traditional about him was that he was Welsh. Scottish drunks, yes, I had seen plenty of those. Irish drunks, yes, they had made Camden tube station their own. But a Welsh homeless alcoholic, that was a new one on me. It was strange how the Scots and Irish seemed to be everywhere—in films, in music, in Celtic dance extravaganzas, even slumped outside tube stations. Here, at last, was a Welshman who was doing his bit to redress the balance.

"Er, yeah, I do feel a bit rough, yeah. I just needed to sit down for a bit."

"And then you just lay down and spent the night here, ha

ha ha ha. This is my bench, see, but you were fast asleep so I let you have it for a night. Drink?" and he offered me a swig from his can of Special Brew which still had a globule of his spittle hanging from the rim.

"No thanks, I never drink warm lager and tramp's gob before breakfast."

I only thought that; I didn't have the courage to actually say it. It was nice of him to offer to share what little he had with me, even if it was the singularly most unattractive offer I had ever had in my whole life. It concerned me that this tramp was so friendly, that he was talking to me like an equal.

"I've not seen you sleeping around here before," he said.

"Well, of course you haven't. I'm not homeless."

"Oh sorry, your majesty," and he gave an exaggerated groveling drunken bow from his position on the bench beside me. "So where do you live then?"

"Er, well, I don't actually live anywhere just at the moment," I mumbled. "But as it happens, until very recently I had two homes," I added, in the hope that this would improve my claim to be a paid-up member of mainstream society.

"So you used to have two homes and now you've got none." He took a final glug from his can and dropped it on the ground. "That sounds about fair to me."

He was right, there was a symmetry in the way things had turned out: the man who had tried to have it all had ended up with nothing. But I resented the way he was trying to bring me down to his level. I wasn't a tramp! OK, I had nowhere to live and I had no money and I'd spent last night on a bench, but however smashed I got on Special Brew I could never have just dropped the empty can on the ground like that.

"I've got a wife and two children, you know, and a third one on the way," I told him, proudly.

He looked me up and down. He looked at my creased,

stubbly face, my sticking-up hair, my crumpled dirty clothes and my pathetic bundle of belongings crammed into a tatty holdall.

"What a lucky girl. I mean, you look like a hell of a catch for any woman."

"Yeah, well, we had a big bust-up, but I'm going to ring her. I'm going to ring her now from that call box over there."

"Go on, then."

"And I'm going to make it up with her because I am not some down-and-out."

"Whatever you say."

"Because I'm not some homeless beggar."

"Sure. Go and phone your wife."

"I would, only . . . Can you spare some change, please?"

With twenty pence scrounged from the Welsh tramp I rang Catherine's parents' number and braced myself for their icy disapproval. But my heart leaped as Millie took it upon herself to answer the phone.

"Hello, Millie, it's Daddy. How are you?"

"All right."

"Have you had your breakfast?"

There was silence from the other end of the phone, which I realized meant she was nodding.

"Have you been being good children for Gran and Grandad?"

More silence; she might be nodding, she might be shaking her head, it was hard to tell. I had to stop asking questions that didn't require her to speak.

"Do you like my hat?" she asked me.

"It's a lovely hat. Is it Granny's?"

"No!" she said as if I was completely stupid. "Granny's not a pirate!"

The call box was eating up my units and, lovely as it was to talk to Millie, a discussion about whether or not Granny was a pirate was not going very far toward rebuilding my life. "Is Mummy there, darling?"

Silence.

"Millie, I can't see you nodding or shaking your head from here. Can you put Mummy on the phone?"

I heard Catherine's voice talking to Millie, telling her to hand over the phone.

"Hello?"

"Hi, it's me. Look, we have to talk, because I know you must hate me and everything, and I can understand that from where you are I can't look like the most wonderful bloke in the world, but I'm not the worst, you know. And the thing is that I love you, and Jesus, men have slept with other women and their wives have forgiven them, but I've never done that. Christ, even when I masturbate I always try and think of you."

"It's not Catherine, Michael. It's Sheila," said the frosty voice of her mother. "Please do not use the Lord's name in that way."

"Oh, er, sorry, Sheila. God, you sound just like her on the phone."

"Please do not take God's name in vain."

"Oh yeah. Fuck, sorry. Can I speak to Catherine, please?"

"No you can't."

"What? No you won't let me, or no she's not there?"

"No she's not here."

Sheila was not going out of her way to be more helpful than she needed.

"Er, do you know where she is?"

"Yes."

"Well, could you tell me where she is, please."

"I'm not sure I should."

"Look for Chr— for crikey's sake, Sheila. She is still my

wife. She's nine months pregnant with our third child. I think I have a right to know where she is."

Sheila paused. And then she told me where Catherine was. And then I shouted something and ran out of the telephone box, leaving the receiver swinging back and forth, and the person waiting to use the phone box after me picked it up to hear Sheila saying, "Please do not use the name of our Lord Jesus Christ in that way."

I ran up Clapham High Street and through Stockwell and past all the tube stops that I used to whiz through when I commuted between marriage and boyhood, but now I didn't even have a pound to ride on the train and I ran and ran and ran and my body hurt and I felt sick, but I kept on running because I had to get to Catherine. I had to be with her now; I had to be by her side because Catherine had gone into labor. At this moment our third child was being born.

11

The Real Thing

A CAR TOOTED and swerved as I ran across the traffic crossing Clapham Road. I had run two miles and felt close to collapsing when I saw the orange beacon of an approaching taxi and maniacally waved my hand.

"Hello." I panted, leaning on the side of the cab. "Look I've got no cash on me, but my wife is in labor at St. Thomas's, and if you could just give me a lift up there I can post you a check for twice the fare."

"Hop in, I've got two meself, little monkeys. I'll get you there double quick and there's no charge. This one's on me."

That's what I'd been hoping he might say. I'd seen it in the movies—desperate man with wife in labor meets policeman or cabbie who bends the rules to help him. This taxi driver hadn't seen the same films as me. "Fuck off," he snarled, and then drove off, nearly taking my arm with him.

I resumed my marathon dash across South London, occasionally swapping my holdall from one hand to the other, and then eventually dropping it in a litter bin. By the time I reached the river I could only run in short intermittent bursts, in between long stretches of anxious, brisk walking. You can never really appreciate exactly how far away somewhere is until you're desperately trying to race there with a severe hangover in time to witness the birth of your child. Stretches of road that in my head were only fifty yards long seemed to go on and on and on, as if I was trudging the wrong way along the moving walkway at Gatwick Airport. The exertion increased my feeling of nausea; I felt dizzy and sick and could feel the sweat running down my back and soaking through my overcoat.

The Thames stretched out on my left with parliament looming out of the mist on the other side of the river. As I jogged exhaustedly along the embankment path, a stampede of cyclists bore down on me, and for a moment it looked like the only safe option would be to climb up a tree. Finally I arrived at the entrance to St. Thomas's Hospital and, gasping for breath, I approached the reception desk.

"Hello, I've come to see Catherine Adams who's giving birth here at this very moment. Can you tell me what floor she's on, please?"

The receptionist did not seem to share my sense of urgency. Still panting, I explained that I was her husband, that I hadn't come in with her because I hadn't been with her when she suddenly went into labor, but that I had to get up there right away and obviously they would want me beside her as soon as possible. And then I threw up in the litter bin.

The hospital receptionist obviously saw people being sick on a fairly regular basis as she was completely unfazed by this. As I rested my head on her desk and moaned, "Oh God," quietly to myself, she called the labor ward to confirm my version of events.

"Yes, he's down here at reception," she said. "He's just been sick in the litter bin and now I think he may be about to pass out."

A conversation ensued of which I could only hear one half. "I see . . . yes . . . yes . . ." but from the tone of her voice I could sense there must be some sort of administrative holdup.

"Well, what is it? Is there a problem?" I asked impatiently.

"They want to know why you have been sick? Are you ill?"

"No, I'm not ill, I just ran here, that's all."

"No, he's not ill. He does smell of drink, though," she

added helpfully, and then she gave me a little disappointed shake of the head to suggest that this detail had just failed to swing it in my favor. Finally she informed me that they could not allow me onto the labor ward, that they understood that Catherine and I were separated and that Catherine already had her sister Judith there as her birthing partner. As if childbirth wasn't painful enough.

"OK. That's fine, I understand," I said calmly. "I'll, um, call round later, maybe." And then I walked slowly round the corner and jumped in the lift up to the labor ward. I came out on the seventh floor and the next obstacle was a big scuffed metal door with a security buzzer on the side. I hung around for a while, pretending to study the poster that said, "How to examine your breasts," and a passing nurse gave me a very strange look. Eventually the ping of the lift announced the arrival of another expectant father, who emerged clutching a large bundle of pre-packed sandwiches which he had bought in the shop downstairs. Excellent, he was heading for the door to the labor ward.

"Ah, the famous sandwiches," I said, thinking it best to befriend him if I was going to try and follow him into the inner sanctum.

"I didn't know what sort of filling was best for a mother in labor, so I got a selection."

"Cheese and pickle," I announced confidently as I moved to stand behind him at the door.

"Oh," he said, looking crestfallen. "That's the only one I didn't get. I'll go and change this for cheese and pickle."

"No, no, egg and cress is even better. In fact, some people think that cheese and pickle increases the chance of a cesarean."

"Really? Blimey, thanks for telling me," and he buzzed and gave his name to the intercom and he was in and so was I.

I adopted the resolute air of someone who definitely knew

where he was going, despite the fact that I kept having to slow down in the hope of glancing in any doors that just happened to open. The labor ward's windowless corridor had the atmosphere of a secret prison in some faraway Fascist dictatorship. Screams of agony came from behind various doors as determined-looking men and women marched in and out clutching metallic torture instruments. I saw a door and had a hunch that was the room Catherine would be giving birth in.

"Sorry, wrong room," I said to the naked lady climbing into the birthing pool. I put my ear to the next delivery room. I could hear a man's authoritative voice. "No, everyone knows that cheese and pickle increases the chance of having a cesarean," he said. At the end of the corridor was the nurse's desk, and I decided there was nothing else for it. I walked confidently past in search of some clue and there on the wall was a large white board with the room numbers and mothers' names scrawled underneath. By Room 8 somebody had scribbled Catherine Addams in blue felt-tip. Adams with two "d"s, as if we were the Addams family. As I caught sight of myself in the mirror, that mistake suddenly seemed quite appropriate. Then I reached Room 8. I tried to flatten down my hair, but I felt it spring straight up again. I knocked gently and walked in.

"Aaarrrrggghhhhhhh!"

"Hello, Catherine."

"Aaaarrrrgggghhhhh!" she screamed again. I presumed she was having a contraction, unless this was just a natural reaction to seeing me.

"What the fucking hell are you doing here," she exclaimed.

"I need to talk to you."

"Oh, that's fine because I'm not doing anything in particular at the moment. Aaaaaaaaarrrrrggghhh!"

The only other person in the room was Judith, who had the disappointed look of an understudy who had just seen the lead return in time for curtain-up.

"Shouldn't there be a midwife or a doctor here or something?" I said.

"She's only five centimeters dilated," said Judith, looking hurt that she didn't even count as an "or something." "They've been popping in and out to see how she's doing. And I've got her sandwiches and everything."

"She never eats the sandwiches."

"Oh." Judith looked even more disappointed.

"Catherine, listen," I said, "I've worked it out. I know what I was doing wrong."

"Oh congratulations, Michael!"

She was sitting up in bed wearing an unflattering hospital gown and she looked almost as hot and disheveled as me.

"I thought you were always pissed off with me."

"I am pissed off with you. Completely and utterly disgusted and appalled by you."

"Yes, obviously you are *now*," I conceded. "But before, when you were pissed off with being the mother of small babies, I thought you didn't love me anymore, and I think that's why I kept running away."

"Aaaarrgggghhhh!"

Judith pointedly edged in to give Catherine an annoying weedy dab on the forehead with a flannel that was even wetter than she was.

"What's that smell?"

"Essential oils," said Judith with a smug nod. "They really helped me when I had Barney."

"They are not essential oils, though, are they, Judith? They are not at all essential. For thousands of years women have given birth without essential oils. Completely fucking superfluous oils would be a better name."

"Stop it, Michael," said Catherine, still recovering from her last contraction. "You lied to me and deserted me and then you think you can just fucking turn up here and every-thing will be all right again. You're bored with being on your own, so now you'd like another spell of being a dad until you get bored with that again. Well, you can just fuck right off!" She was shouting now.

"Erm, would you like me to massage your feet?" said Judith, looking a little self-conscious.

"No, Judith, I do not want you to massage my feet, thank you very much."

"Look, Catherine, everything you say is true. But you were the one who wanted kids so soon. I pretended to want them, too, but that was only to keep you happy. Everything I did was because I was trying to make you happy."

"Oh I see, living it up in your flat was to make *me* happy, was it. There's me thinking this was all about you being a self-ish wanker and now I see that I was the one who was getting everything my own way. Well, pardon me for being so selfish."

"Hang on," I said suddenly. "What's that noise?"

"What noise?" said Catherine, irritated at being halted in full flow.

I heard it again. An eerie distant moan was coming from somewhere inside the room. It was like there was a drugged old man groaning from inside the cupboard, only his batteries were running out.

"There it is again. It's awful. What is it?"

Judith looked hurt. "That's my whale-song tape. It's to help Catherine relax."

"Aaaaaaaaaaargh!" went Catherine.

"Well that's working well, isn't it? A whale-song tape! Oh my God, what a hippie cliché you are. I bet they're not even modern whale songs; I bet they're whale-song classics from the Sixties."

"Gnnnnnnoooooo . . ." went the whale.

"Aaaaaaaaarrrrgggghhhh!" went Catherine again. "Actually, Judith, could you do me a favor," she added, shifting uncomfortably.

"Yes?" said Judith brightly.

"Could you turn off the stupid bloody whale-song tape. I feel enough like a big fat whale as it is."

"Oh, all right."

"And stop rubbing that stinking oil on my feet before the smell makes me puke up."

Catherine and I then argued back and forth while she had the distinct disadvantage of being well into the first stages of labor. There were one or two occasions when I thought I had her stumped because she didn't reply, but it always turned out that this was because a huge painful contraction was washing over her. As we shouted at one another I was vaguely aware of Judith flicking through a natural-birth handbook to see if it explained what sort of crystals or herbs might be waved about in this situation. Catherine said I only cared about myself and I said, "No, I love you, you stupid fuckwit." She called me a self-centered bastard and I said she was a whinging martyr. I had given up trying to grovel because it was getting me nowhere and thought I'd try going on the offensive instead.

"Well you drove me out so *you* owe *me* an apology."

"I owe *you* an apology?" she said incredulously.

"Yeah." I didn't know where this was leading, but I plowed on anyway.

"I owe you an apology? Do you really want to know what I owe you?"

"Er, yeah, all right?"

And that was her cue to punch me with all her might in the middle of my face. I went down like a felled tree, hitting the back of my head on the metal gas-and-air canisters, which were there for pain relief and which really hurt a lot. Then Catherine started crying and whacking me with a plastic bedpan and I rolled into a ball on the ground, and then Catherine started another contraction and Judith pressed the emergency call button.

For the birth of my first two children I had felt strangely spiritually detached from it all. For the birth of my third I was physically removed by two burly men from hospital security. I helplessly hung around the outside of the hospital for an hour or so while happy visitors to the maternity ward bustled in and out clutching flowers and soft toys. There had been one ray of hope that made me want to stay outside the hospital. Catherine had said "I love you" over and over again as she struck me round the head with the bedpan. I had thought she hated me, which I suppose she might have done as well. But as the security guards grasped the back of my hair, bent me double and frog-marched me out of the hospital with my arm nearly breaking up my back, I felt a euphoric serenity, as if my feet were off the ground, which they were, in fact, when the two gorillas threw me out onto the pavement.

After a while I approached a group of visitors and persuaded them to convey a message to Room 8 on the labor ward. I handed them a note that I had scribbled on the back of a piece of card I'd found in a telephone box. They were so full of goodwill to the world that it was easy to ask them a favor, although they seemed less sure about helping me when they turned the card over and saw a photo of a large-breasted topless prostitute with the message "Dominatrix! Let her punish you!" It had been the only bit of card I could find. "It's a private joke," I stammered. "She likes to get her own way at home." The message told Catherine that I would not be far away and would appreciate a phone call when the baby was born. Catherine would not recognize the number as it was for a telephone box by Westminster Bridge. I then spent the day sitting on a bench beside my chosen public telephone. Occasionally people would move toward it, but then they'd notice a large "out of order" sticker on the door, and they'd look at me and we'd share a what-is-this-country-coming-to tut.

Every quarter of an hour Big Ben would strike to remind me how slowly the day was going by. Somehow I had contrived to watch the minutes pass by sitting opposite the largest clock in the world. The London Eye inched slowly round and the tide rose and then started to ebb again. I tucked into my lunch. Before I'd sat down I had approached a shell-shocked couple emerging into the hospital car park with a new baby.

"Congratulations," I said.

"Thank you," they both replied, looking proud and bewildered as mother and baby were helped into the back seat.

"Erm, can I ask? Did she eat the sandwiches?"

"I beg your pardon?"

"The sandwiches you made her when she went into labor."

"No. It's funny you should say that because she didn't touch them."

"Well, would you mind if I took them for the homeless round here. It's part of a scheme we're running."

"Of course. What a splendid idea." And he gave me the sandwiches and fizzy drinks and even a bar of chocolate. And even though she had just given birth and was apparently focusing totally on her newborn baby, a firm voice came from the back seat of the car: "*Not* the chocolate."

My long vigil beside the phone box went through several stages. At first I was pleased with myself for my powers of organization in the face of such apparent adversity. I had a seat with a view over the Thames. My lunch was in a bag on my left. My private public phone was on my right. It was just a question of waiting. But as hour followed hour and the cold gnawed away at my morale, I began to worry. First I worried that Catherine wasn't going to ring, that she would have just torn up the note and I'd still be sitting there long after she had left the hospital. Then I began to worry that the telephone really was out of order, that I had stuck a sign on it without first making sure the notice was definitely lying. I went into the telephone box and dialed 150.

"Hello, BT customer services, Janice speaking, how may I help you?"

"Thank you, that's all I wanted to know."

Then I became anxious that the ten seconds it had taken me to make that call had been when Catherine had tried to ring, and she would have got the engaged signal and wouldn't try again. Should I try and scrounge 10p from a passerby so I could ring the labor ward to find out? But then that might turn out to be the exact moment she chose to ring me. These anxieties spun around and around until I had worn them out and then was left with only genuine, serious worries to fret over. What on earth did I think she should want to ring me for? And anyway, what would I do then? Go back to my bench on Clapham Common? Go and sleep in Mrs. Conroy's garage? The homeless unemployed have more problems than most people, but worst of all they have hours and hours with nothing to do but dwell on them. At least when General Custer had lots of problems he was busy.

Dusk began to fall. The thousands of people who had walked past me in one direction that morning now walked back the other way. The lights on the riverboats disappeared under Westminster Bridge and the headlights on the bridge slowed to a halt. And with the darkness it grew colder and the need to urinate, which I had hoped might go away if I ignored it, now became my overriding and all-consuming concern. I walked up and down in front of my bench, I crossed my legs, I jumped up and down, but it became unbearable. I had to remain within earshot of the telephone box, but I desperately needed to go to the toilet. So that's why telephone boxes always smelled of urine. Eventually I had an idea. I furtively took a discarded empty lager can into the telephone box and decided the deed would be done in there. It seemed like a civilized solution at the time, but I had never measured the capacity of my full bladder before. It never occurred to me that it was about four times the volume of an empty 50cl lager tin. The can filled up in about two seconds, by which time the torrent seemed unstoppable. I couldn't bear the idea that I had been reduced to urinating in a public telephone box, and so I squeezed the end of my penis and painfully turned off the tap. Then I awkwardly nudged the door of the box open with my leg and contorted my body so that I could tip the can out onto the muddy patch of grass outside, while with my other hand I continued to grip my poor aching penis, which was swollen to bursting, like a blocked fire hose in a *Tom and Jerry* cartoon. It was then that the telephone rang.

It made me jump and panic all at the same time. "Hello?" I said into the receiver as urine sprayed like a burst dam all over my trousers. "Oh no!" Then I realized that I had dropped the can as well and it was glugging out all over my shoes. "Oh fuck, shit, bollocks!"

"It's me," said Catherine. "I thought you wanted me to ring."

"No, I did. Sorry, it's just you made me drop my can of piss."

"What?"

"Lager, pissy lager."

I attempted to affect a casual air of normality as urine sprayed uncontrollably down my trousers.

"So, um, what have you been up to?"

There was a pause.

"Having a baby," she replied, matter-of-factly.

"Yes, yes, of course, that's right."

A man was walking past the telephone box and glanced at

me through the glass as I struggled to conceal the fact that I was effectively using it as a public toilet.

"So, um, what have you been up to?"

"You just asked me that."

"Oh yes, sorry. And you said you'd been having a baby. So you see I was listening."

The steaming Niagara Falls inside the telephone box had finally come to a halt and, still clinging onto the phone, I buttoned up my flies with my other hand.

"Well, I've had it," she finally said. She sounded strange. Tired, obviously, but cold and remote, which scared me slightly.

"And the baby's OK?" I asked nervously. "I mean, it's healthy and everything?"

"Yes, completely healthy and beautiful. Seven pounds, three ounces. Born at half-past one this afternoon. It's a boy, by the way, in case you were thinking of asking."

"A boy! Fantastic! And you're OK, are you?"

"Yes. He came out really easily."

"Well, that's the wonder of whale song," I joked, but Catherine wasn't tempted to laugh.

"Look, you'd better come and see us. I have to talk to you. I've persuaded them to let you in now. They've put me in Helen Ward, sixth floor."

"Great, thanks. I'll be there as quick as I can," I said and hung up. I could have added, "I've just got to rinse all this urine out of my trousers," but it didn't seem like quite the right moment. I picked up the half-full lager can and threw it in a nearby litter bin. Out of the corner of my eye I noticed a dosser watch the liquid slosh out of the can as I threw it away, and as I rushed toward the hospital he lumbered up to the litter bin, excitedly anticipating his first taste.

"Good evening," I said brightly to the porter who came into the hospital toilets. I had decided that if I behaved as if it was perfectly normal to stand there in my underpants, holding my rinsed-out trousers under the electric hand dryer, then he might be temporarily convinced. He wasn't. "I spilled some coffee on my trousers, so I've just washed it out," I said, giving him the opportunity to smile and understand. He didn't take it.

Before long I was dressed again. I washed my stubbly face and did my best to flatten down my thinning hair. I looked like an old man, but had the nervous air of a boy on his first date. As I went to pull open the door I noticed my hand was shaking. The elation I felt at the birth of our baby took my private anxiety up another level. One new life had already started today, it was now up to Catherine whether another one could begin for me. It felt like my last chance. I had told her that I would be different, that I'd change. If she didn't feel that we should be together when she had just had our third baby then she never would. I pressed the button for the lift as if I were being summoned to hear the outcome of my appeal. I should have felt excited but instead I felt nervous. She said she loved me, I kept telling myself, but she punched me in the face. These seemed to be conflicting signals. And if she was going to take me back, why had she sounded so cool and loveless on the phone?

The lift doors opened and a joyful young couple came out with a newborn infant; obviously their first, judging by the nervousness with which they were taking it home. I'd forgotten how absolutely tiny newborn babies are, how much they look like something out of a nature documentary. "He's gorgeous," I said.

"I know," said the proud mum, trying to stop the huge blue cotton hat slipping down over the baby's entire face. The event of childbirth is one of the few things that will prompt the British to talk to complete strangers. Newborn babies, puppies and being in major rail disasters.

The lift arrived at the sixth floor and I buzzed my way into Helen Ward. A polished corridor stretched out in front of me. On my right was the first bay, with six beds containing six very different women. Catherine was not one of them. The mothers were all in dressing gowns or nighties, but were too focused on the little packages in their little Perspex cribs to worry about the strange man walking past, looking at each of them in turn. The next bay had another batch of new mums, all so completely unlike Catherine that it just confirmed to me that there was no one else I could ever be interested in. The last bay was next to the television room and the distorted shouting of actors could be heard through the open door.

"Hello, Michael," said Catherine's voice from behind me. There was a little gap between the tatty green curtains that had been drawn around the first bed and I walked toward it. I stepped through the curtain, where Catherine was sitting up in bed wearing an old Radiohead T-shirt of mine. She didn't look happy to see me. In fact, if anything she looked a little scared. I bent down to kiss her on the cheek and she didn't resist.

"Congratulations," I said.

She said nothing and looked back blankly.

"Erm, right, well, where's my little boy, then?" I stuttered, trying to affect an air of happy-family normality, made all the more surreal by the jaunty signature tune of a sitcom which echoed through from the TV room.

Then I looked down at the tiny infant asleep in the crib, wrapped in a hospital blanket and with a light-blue plastic name tag around his wrist. He was so perfect and miniature, with every detail lovingly handcrafted, that it made me want to believe in God.

"Oh, he's beautiful," I said. "He's so beautiful."

I looked at how the baby's eyelashes were so expertly curled and placed at tiny but exact intervals, and at how the little circumference of his nostrils formed such perfect circles. And then I heard Catherine's voice say, "He's not yours, Michael."

It didn't register at first. Then I took in the meaning of what she had just said to me and glanced up at her, struck dumb with total incomprehension. Tears were welling up in her eyes.

"He's not yours," she repeated, and to answer my puzzled confusion she added, "You were never there," and then she started to sob uncontrollably. "You were never there."

I just kept looking at her, searching for some logic.

"But how do you know? I mean, who else did you . . ."

"Klaus."

"Klaus?!"

"I was lonely and we shared a bottle of wine and, well, I don't know."

"What? One thing led to another, I fucking suppose!"

"Don't shout."

"I am not shouting," I shouted. "But you walked out on me for deceiving you, when all the time you were carrying someone else's baby."

Her sobs were louder now; graceless animal snorts that contorted her face.

"Anyway, how do you know it's his? We had unprotected sex, remember?"

"I did that because I knew I was pregnant. To cover myself, so you'd never have to know. When I still thought you were a proper father, but it's too late for that now."

"But he might still be mine," I pleaded hopelessly, glancing into the crib, hoping to spot some distinctive feature that I shared with this baby. There was none. If it was a question of who the baby looked like, then clearly Catherine had had it off with Sir Winston Churchill.

"The dates make it his. I just know. You can do a DNA test if you aren't convinced, but till then you will just have to take my word for it. This is not your child."

She fixed me in her gaze; she looked defiant and almost proud to have been the one to put the final nail into this marriage.

"Does he know? I mean, did you tell him before he went back to Munich?"

"No. This child has no father." And then the weeping started up again, and there was part of me that wanted to say, "All right, stop crying now; it's not that bad," but of course it was that bad; it was very bad indeed.

I really didn't know what to do. It seemed like there was no point in me being there at all. I was visiting a woman who had already said she didn't want to be married to me, and now she'd had a baby by another man. So I stepped out through the curtain, walked back down the corridor and floated out of the ward. A passing nurse gave me a beatific smile, which is the normal way to look at someone in a maternity ward, but I don't think I managed to return it. I don't remember walking through the door from the ward, but I must have done.

All those months that I had watched the bump inside her grow, handing her tissues as she had thrown up in the morning, staring at the little photo of the fetus from the ultrasound machine, going to parenting classes with her, feeling the baby kick inside her, anxiously waiting for news of the birth; all that emotional investment was wiped out in one moment. After she had left me I had dreamed that this baby might be the only thing that could bring us back together. Now it had blown everything completely apart.

I pressed the button for the lift, unsure as to where I might go after I left the hospital, still punch-drunk from the shock. My head was spinning with a hundred confused, angry thoughts. She thought I had done her such a wrong; she had behaved like such an injured party, such a poor victim of my callous deceit, and yet all the time, inside her had been growing this witness to the most fundamental betrayal possible. In my bitter confusion I couldn't help resenting the fact that she'd had sex with our next-door neighbor when she had never seemed to want to have sex with me. It wasn't as if when we'd been together we had made love three times a day and then I'd suddenly disappeared, leaving her insatiable sexual appetite unquenched. Since the children had come along sex had always been something she was too tired for. She told me that when you had the kids pawing at you all day, you didn't want your husband coming home and pawing at you as well. But she hadn't been too tired to have sexual intercourse with the muscular young student from next door. No wonder he'd always been so nice to me. He'd unblocked my sink, reset my fuses, released my stopcock; no job was too much trouble. "Get your wife pregnant? Hey, no problem, Mikey. I'll pop round when you're out."

The lift showed no sign of arriving, so I pressed the button over and over again, even though I knew this never made any difference. Had she thought about Millie and Alfie when she'd cheated on her husband? Had she thought about where that would leave them when I found out about their night of passion? Or maybe it wasn't really just one night, maybe it was lots of nights, maybe this affair had been going on for years. Perhaps he hadn't really gone back to Germany but had set up home somewhere else in London and Catherine and the kids were going to join him with their new child. Yes, when she had found out about my double life it had given her the excuse she'd been waiting for. I mulled over this theory for a while and then decided it had one minor flaw. I had given Klaus a lift to the airport and he had sent me a postcard from Munich to thank me. It seemed like an unnecessarily elaborate cover-up. Anyway, Catherine had told me what had happened; if the truth had been any worse I don't think it would have stopped her relating it.

She'd had sex once with the bloke from next door. Couldn't I forgive her for that? Was that any worse than the extended deception I'd pursued? Hadn't I left her on her own night after lonely night? Hadn't I nearly been sexually unfaithful myself? My resentment was dismantled as quickly as I had built it up. It was as if the lift were deliberately keeping me waiting, forcing me to reflect upon what I was walking away from. I pictured Catherine and me cuddled up with the kids in their pajamas, watching a video together, and I thought about the trust in Millie and Alfie's faces when they looked at me, and then I just started to cry. What had the kids done to deserve this mess? How had we come to this? "Oh, Millie, Alfie, I'm sorry." Everything was in ruins, and my tears gushed forth like a burst water main; all the pressure that had been contained since we split suddenly erupting to the surface. I turned my face to the noticeboard and tried to pull myself together. I looked at the photographs of a reunion of all the babies that had been in intensive care a couple of years beforehand—pictures of tiny premature babies clinging on to life in oxygen tents next to photos of the healthy, thriving toddlers they had now grown into, and that set me off all over again. I was blubbing hopelessly, turning the tap full on, letting it all come out. A couple of lift doors opened and then closed again and, when I'd finally regained my composure, I walked back across and pressed the button once more.

The parting lift doors revealed the skinny frame of an old man in some loose-fitting grubby pajamas. He looked so close to death that I half expected the Grim Reaper to leap into the lift ahead of me, apologizing for being so late. His shaking body was held upright with the aid of a Zimmer frame, and his blotchy skin was stretched taut around his mouth and cheekbones.

"Well, are you coming or going?" he said to me.

In a few years' time my father would look like this, lonely and close to death. One stupid affair in his thirties and then he spent the rest of his life looking for the love he had once had with my mother.

"Well, are you coming or going?" he repeated, adding, "Because I haven't got all day," despite the fact that he clearly did have.

"Sorry!" I said and I turned around and left him there.

I walked up to the closed green curtains around Catherine's bed.

"Yes, he has," I said to her as I stepped through the gap. She looked up, surprised to see me, her eyes still red.

"What?" she said, looking puzzled.

"You said that this little boy hasn't got a father. But he has. I can be his father."

She raised her eyebrows at me, which I took as an invitation to continue.

"This is Millie and Alfie's brother, so why can't I be his dad? This is the child of the woman I love. I wasn't there for my own two, so I'll be there for this one. I promise, Catherine. I'll be there for the hard bits as well as the easy stuff. I know how a child feels when it's abandoned by its father. Let me be this little boy's dad; let me show you I can be a proper dad to Alfie and Millie."

A hospital auxiliary pulled back the curtain to offer a tray of food.

"Excuse me," I said to him, "could you just give us a minute," and I drew the curtain back across again. "Catherine, I'll be there when you're bored and fed up and you just want someone to moan at, someone who's going to offer you sympathy instead of always suggesting solutions. I'll be there when you're worried about him, and even if I don't think it's anything to worry about, I'll sit and listen until we've talked it through. I'll be there just to play endless games with him, pretending that I really enjoy jiggling little plastic Power Ranger figures about on the carpet. And I'll be there when we're not doing anything at all, just passing the hours together, because I didn't understand before that that's what it's all about—just spending time with your family is the end in itself, and you have to timetable in some wasting time together. Now that I understand what I'm supposed to do, I know that I can do it."

Catherine didn't say anything, she just looked at me.

"Have you finished now?" said the hospital auxiliary from the other side of the curtain.

"Yes, thank you," I said, taking the tray from him.

"It's meat curry."

"Meat curry. How lovely. Her favorite sort."

Catherine's expression didn't change. I stood there waiting for some sort of clue as to what she was thinking. "It's not what I want," she said finally. My insides suddenly felt completely empty.

"But, Catherine, you have to give us another chance."

"No. Meat curry is not what I want. Can you see if they've got a salad or something?"

"In a minute. Can we just sort this out first. Are you going to bring this boy up on your own or are we going to do it together?"

"You can forgive me? Just like that?" she said, slowly.

"Well, I was hoping I might be able to do a deal. Is there any little thing that I've done in the past couple of years that you might want to forgive me for, perhaps even just partially?"

It was the first time I'd seen her smile since we had parted. It was only a bleary half smile, but its return was like the sudden faint bleep on a cardiogram; there was life where I'd thought there had been none.

"But you'll always know that this child isn't yours."

"So what? You're right, I was never there. But Klaus won't be there for this one and why should you be left alone again?"

I was thinking so clearly now, speaking with a missionary zeal. I knew it was the only way forward. Catherine had to see that it was right.

"You're really prepared to bring up someone else's child as your own?"

"He will never know he's half German. Now what do you think of the name Karl-Heinz Adams? It has a ring to it, doesn't it?"

And she smiled again, properly this time.

"You have to understand, Michael, that if we were to make another go of it, things could never be like they were. I would never totally trust you like I did before—something has gone forever."

I nodded, nervous as to which way the coin was about to fall.

"You have been selfish and immature and dishonest and blind and callous and self-indulgent."

I tried to pick out an adjective that I felt was being unfairly applied to me, but failed. How was it that she had so many words at her disposal? Why did we always have to argue with words? That way she was always going to win. If we could have argued using musical notes, chords and melody lines I might have stood a better chance.

"But," she continued, "but if you are prepared to forgive me, then maybe we have something to build upon. Can you promise me that from here on, can you promise that you will always be honest, that you will never again let yourself disappear into some stupid solipsistic fantasy."

I paused. "I . . . I don't know."

Her face fell. It was the wrong answer. "Well, if you can't be sure, then I don't see how we can have any future together."

"No, no," I stammered. "I just don't know what "solipsistic" means. I was going to pretend and just say yes, but I'm trying to make myself be honest."

"It means that you have to realize that you are not the only person in the entire bloody universe."

"Well, I do realize that, yes. I just didn't want to promise not to be solipsistic when it sounded like some sort of eating disorder."

"You have to realize that from the moment you have children they become more important to you than yourself."

"They are, Catherine, I promise. All three of them. But you, you're more important still. I love you; I never understood that as clearly as when I'd lost you, and the fact that you ended up in bed with Klaus only confirms to me how abandoned I must have made you feel. Let's start again. Please, Catherine, take me back."

She paused. "On approval only." And then she put out her arms to me and I hugged her long and hard, as if I had just been rescued from drowning.

"Thank you for forgiving me," she said as she held me to her. "I needed to know that you would. If you're really prepared to commit to bringing up Klaus's son as your own then you've got to be worth giving a second chance." She held me close to her, clutching the back of my head tightly as I winced in silent agony, not wanting to mention the tender bruise where I'd crashed into the gas-and-air cylinders after she'd punched me to the ground. But everything was all right. We were together again. We were a family.

"And I forgive you, even if you still have one major flaw that I will never quite get used to."

"What do you mean?" I said anxiously, pulling myself away from her.

She looked me in the eye. "Michael, if you actually believe all that bollocks about me sleeping with Klaus and then having his baby, then you really are an even bigger sucker than I always thought you were."

And a huge burst of canned laughter came from the TV room.

12

The Best a Man Can Get

"I NOW DECLARE YOU husband and wife," said the keen
young vicar and the congregation burst into spontaneous applause. Older women in bizarre hats exchanged approving
smiles and even the vicar joined in the cheers to show that the
church didn't have to be all stuffy and serious. I clapped as
well as any man could considering I was carrying a nine-
month-old baby. The noise excited him and he gave enthusiastic random kicks of his legs and waved his arms about in
giggly approval. Catherine held up Alfie to watch as the bride
and groom kissed slightly more passionately than would generally be considered appropriate. The vicar had added, "You
may now kiss the bride," not, "You may now put your tongue
down the bride's throat and squeeze her right tit."

The invitation to the wedding had been something of a
shock; a message on my mobile phone from someone I hadn't
seen for months. Jim was marrying Kate. The man I had lived
with was marrying the girl I had so nearly slept with. Perhaps I
should have explained this to the ushers in the church when
they'd asked, "Bride or groom?" and let them decide. Once I
had got used to the idea of this union I was delighted for them
both. They were a perfect match: she earned a fortune and
worked very hard and he spent a fortune and didn't work at
all. There is something so hopelessly romantic about white
weddings that you cannot help but think that the couple will
be blissfully happy forever. Even when Henry VIII got married

for the sixth time, the congregation must have all thought, Aaah, true love at last, and he's definitely promised not to chop her head off this time. But as I watched Jim and Kate come down the aisle, I couldn't help but think about how little idea they had of the problems that lay ahead.

My own marriage had been slowly nursed back to health over the previous nine months. We had a little boy that we named Henry—for some reason all our children had names that made them sound like orphans from a Victorian costume drama. He had blue eyes and his hair was blond. Neither Catherine nor I were the slightest bit blond, but following her scam in the maternity ward I decided it probably wouldn't be appropriate to challenge her further about the baby's parentage. Events on the day of his birth were now a rather surreal blur. Elation that this really was my son after all was mixed with a suppressed short-term fury that Catherine could have put me through such an emotional mangle. There was even a secret tiny part of me that was briefly disappointed—that she hadn't been as duplicitous as me, that it wasn't a score draw and I was cast back as the only villain. For years I had watched her trick people and defuse seemingly desperate situations with outrageously bold lies, but nothing had prepared me for the test she set me on the day Henry was born. I asked her what she would have done if I'd not come back and forgiven her and committed to be the father of what I thought was Klaus's baby. She said she would have contacted Millie and Alfie's real father and got back together with him. I laughed long and hard and completely unconvincingly.

Now Henry had grown into a happy little baby who laughed for no apparent reason and who woke us up at night with the most abject tears of sorrow which turned quickly into giggles once he had been picked up by the mother and father that he loved so completely. Babies experience their emotions at full volume, with an extreme intensity that doesn't return until they are grown up and have babies of their own. He behaved perfectly throughout the wedding service, indeed some of the noises he made during the singing of "To Be a Pilgrim" were more in tune than the efforts of the groom's relations standing in front of us. At the wedding reception he fell asleep in the luminous blue nylon backpack that failed to blend in with my rented morning suit. He dribbled on my back, and to all the women at the wedding I became instantly attractive and appealing, and all the other men felt underdressed because they didn't have a baby slobbering on their collars.

We had agreed on the name Henry pretty quickly. It had been my suggestion, and when I told Catherine my reasons she was delighted with the choice. I rang my father and he picked up the phone and said, "Henry Adams speaking." I told him that I was calling from the hospital because Catherine and I were back together and she had just had a little boy that I wanted to name after him. He paused for a moment.

"Ooh, that's a good idea because I've got some old Henry Adams name tags somewhere I could let you have for him."

I wanted to scream, Dad, I've just told you that I have named my son after you. Don't worry about the bloody name tags just yet.

"That'd be great," I said. "Thanks a lot."

Catherine and I actually stayed with my dad for a few weeks until we managed to rent somewhere of our own. She cleared out his larder for him, and claimed that when she shouted, "The war is over!" several packets of powdered egg emerged from where they had been hiding behind the tinned prunes since 1945. Though we were grateful to my dad, in the end we were desperate to move into a place of our own, where the heating wasn't always too hot and the telly wasn't always too loud and where the children weren't encouraged to go out and play on the A347. I'd never have a mortgage again, but many things about our lives would be very different from now on; we both had a lot of adjusting to do. We finally rented a four-bedroom house in Archway, and I set up a studio in a poky room at the top of the house. On our first night there, we looked at the kids all asleep in their new beds and then I said to her, "Three children is enough kids for me, Catherine. I know you always wanted four, but I think we should stop at three."

There was a pause and then she just said, "OK."

Then we went downstairs and I made up the bottle for the night feed, and I realized that as I was measuring out the babymilk powder without leveling it off with a knife Catherine was just sitting at the kitchen table, flicking through a magazine. Now, at last, she felt she could leave me to just get on with it. We'd had one argument after she'd been irritated that I was doing something wrong and I had said to her audaciously, "You can't have it all, Catherine. You can't have a man who does his share at home and yet have everything done the way you want."

The wedding service ended and we took our three children out of the church and into the sunshine, where I half-heartedly suggested that Millie perhaps shouldn't clamber all over the gravestones as if it were an adventure playground. Before me stood my former flatmates, who hadn't known I was a father throughout the time that we'd lived together. They looked at me in amazement, and I felt extraordinarily proud as we approached them. Then I introduced my three kids to the three kids I used to live with. Millie and Alfie both said a cute and polite "hello" and I managed to suppress my astonishment and act as if this was completely normal. Everything about that wedding day seemed perfect. The sun shone, the champagne flowed and none of the other women had the same dress as Catherine. She had been genuinely worried about this, which is an anxiety so completely alien to anything that I could ever begin to understand that I suppose it proves how completely and fundamentally different the two sexes really are. The men were all in morning dress, but I didn't burst into tears when I saw that every other man was wearing exactly the same outfit as me.

I introduced my wife to Jim, Paul and Simon. Jim seemed quietly rather impressed that I had kept this little secret to myself. He was charming with Catherine and paid her compliments and made her laugh and, given that he was the groom and therefore already the center of attention, I was rather concerned at just how much Catherine seemed to be taken by him. Paul was with his boyfriend, who was rather cool toward me, as if I still posed a threat to his new relationship. As for Paul himself, I think he thought that the fact that I had a wife and three children only went to prove the extraordinary lengths to which some repressed gays would go to deny their own sexuality to themselves. But there was something calm about him now; you got the feeling that when the bride cut the wedding cake he was no longer worrying about who was going to wash up the knife. Simon was still single and a virgin. However, in the course of the reception he got chatting to Kate's divorced mother. She had consumed rather a lot of champagne and had a room booked at the hotel and, well, one thing led to another . . .

Kate looked beautiful and, as I approached her to introduce her to my wife, I found myself really hoping that they would like each other. But a terrible thing happened: they got on *too* well. They chatted away for ages and soon Catherine was suggesting dates when they might be free to come over to dinner, while I was trying to catch her eye with subtle shakes of my head. The problem was that I would always fancy Kate. I didn't want to grow into one of those fat old men who kisses his wife's friends goodbye with slightly too much relish at the end of a wine-soaked evening.

"Well, it's been a wonderful wedding," said Catherine. "You make a lovely couple."

"Thank you," said Kate.

"And it's OK, Michael told me all about swimming-pool night."

I had made a decision that it was best to be open and honest about everything. "She's very beautiful," said Catherine later. "I'm amazed that you don't think she's particularly attractive."

Well, honest about virtually everything.

As the reception wore on, I was persuaded to play the beautiful Steinway in the hotel ballroom and I disrespectfully ripped into the polished keyboard and played boogie-woogie piano with careless abandon. The dance floor filled up and Millie and Alfie danced a crazy, excited jitterbug. Each number segued effortlessly into the next and revelers whooped and clapped and cheered, and just when they needed a breather, Millie came and sat on my lap and asked if she could play the tune I had taught her, and the crowd fell still and waited. Then my angelic four-year-old daughter played the opening notes of "Lucy in the Sky with Diamonds" with such perfection, and a natural musician's ear for the tempo and feeling, that everyone just stared openmouthed at her talent, and I looked across at Catherine and saw that she was biting her lip, trying to hold back the tears, and she smiled at me with such love and pride that I wanted to float through the ceiling.

The band came back on and I spun Millie round and round and then she clasped her hands around my neck as tightly as she could and I wanted to keep her that age forever, just dancing with her as she clung on to me, trusting and loving me so completely. We stayed the night in the swanky hotel, all five of us in one room, and in the morning I was woken by the sound of children. They jumped into bed with us and we put on the television and they tucked under the duvet between us as we half dozed, trying not to fall out of either side, and then the Gillette ad came on the telly and I heard the man singing, "The best a man can get," and I laughed to myself and thought, I've got it now, thanks. I told Catherine about the slogan and how I had once made it my own personal maxim. She said that she had never interpreted the phrase in the same way as me. To her it was not "the best a man can get" as in get for himself, grab, acquire, have; it was the best he can be, the best he can grow, *the best a man can become.*

Catherine may have been looking at me, but she was keeping one eye on the television in case the commercial she'd been cast in suddenly came on. That was the other consequence of the day Henry was born. The fact that I had been completely convinced by Catherine's bitter self-defense and defiant tears in the maternity ward reminded me of what a brilliant actor she had always been. With some encouragement from me, she contacted her old agent and started going to auditions again, and soon she got a small part in an appalling sitcom that stretched her acting abilities to the limit when the writer asked her whether she thought the script was funny. The amount she was paid was insulting; it was far more than I ever got.

When she was away working I'd take my turn at looking after the kids. She'd be out from early in the morning till late at night, and sometimes the filming even involved overnights. And so I'd find myself alone with the children for a couple of days at a stretch, being woken up throughout the night and still having to look after them all day. I'd have to put on all their clothes, feed them breakfast, then try to prevent Millie and Alfie from throwing wet Multi-Cheerios at each other while I changed Henry's nappy, get myself dressed while brushing their teeth, then put on their coats and gloves, rush Millie off to nursery for nine o'clock while pushing Alfie and Henry along in the double buggy and always trying to maintain a loving, harmonious atmosphere in the home throughout. Well, nine out of ten's not bad.

Everyone expected me to say that looking after my children all day was the most wonderfully fulfilling thing I'd ever done. Well, it was certainly the hardest thing I'd ever done, but nothing changed my opinion that small children are boring. But now I understood that having kids and raising a family was hard, because anything really worth achieving is hard. It's the difference between one of my jingles and Beethoven's Ninth Symphony.

Catherine's advert never came on, so she consoled herself by disappearing off to use the hotel's sauna and swimming pool while I played with the kids in the hotel grounds. Then she suggested I had some time on my own using the hotel's sports facilities or something, which seemed like a good idea at the time, but I soon discovered you can only play croquet on your own for so long. Now at last we seemed to have established some equilibrium in our marriage, an understanding that we were in this together, for the good of each other as well as for the good of our children. We promised that we would always be straight with one another, that we would always work as a team, and privately I felt rather pleased with myself that after all we'd been through there was now so much honesty and confidence between us.

I paid our hotel bill and the manager said thank you and then, as an apparent afterthought, he shouted after us, "See you again soon, Mrs. Adams." As we walked down the steps I asked her why he'd said that. And then Catherine giggled slightly and told me. None of her acting jobs had involved overnights at all. She'd spent all those nights on her own in luxury hotels like this one.

JOHN O'FARRELL is the author of *Things Can Only Get Better; Eighteen Miserable Years in the Life of a Labour Supporter*. His name has flashed past at the end of such productions as *Spitting Image*, *Have I Got News for You* and, more recently, the film *Chicken Run*. He is a regular guest on Radio 4 for shows such as *The News Quiz* and writes a weekly column for the *Guardian*. He lives in Clapham with his wife and two children, who think that when he is not home he is working.